Rapino/Amato

"You do this thing for us, and you're home free. New identification, new start, a new life with a bonus of cash."

"I have deal. Five more years and I'm out."

"Five more years at Big Sandy, assuming you survive it, and then you're out with a giant target on your back and nothing in your pocket. This deal is different. This deal sets you free. Nothing tying you to your prior life."

Rapino said, "Where you're from?"

"That's not important."

"You bullshit, eh?"

"Not if you decide to help," Han said. "You can get out today if you decide to work for us. Go undercover for us."

"For what?"

"You've had six fights since you're in Big Sandy. Two stabbings. The scars on your back. You think they did you a favor sending you there?"

"What you want?"

"We need you to infiltrate an operation that starts in Mexico and makes its way into California, then back east and north through Yellowstone, Big Sky into Bozeman, Montana. That's where the drugs are scattered to the other bigger cities in Montana and elsewhere. It's dangerous. It's no walk in the park."

"Why you come to me?" Rapino said.

"Your skill," Han said.

"The draw with Stella's books is character development
… It's the verbal back and forth that plants you in your
chair. Clever, brutal, lean, creative, profane, authentic,
hard. Makes you think you're eavesdropping on a reality
that only Stella knows and lays out for the reader…"
—East Coast Don, *Men Reading Books*

"…the dialogue dances while the bodies fall."
—Kevin Burton Smith, *Deadly Pleasures*

"From the highly acclaimed debut, *Eddie's World* in 2001,
through *Joey Piss Pot*, his tenth, the author has raised
the bar so high only window cleaners can reach it.
Charlie Stella now owns the gangster fiction genre."
—Marvin Minkler, Modern First Editions

"Stella is a winner, a true artist." —Ken Bruen

"May just be the best crime writer you've never read."
—*Chicago Sun-Times*

Stella is a kind of obscene *Ring Lardner*, finding a lean,
rancid poetry in his characters' vernacular, and rendering
it with flawless precision and humor."
—*Washington Post Book World*

"Stella writes lean and obscene."
—*The Cleveland Plain Dealer*

"He's a true master."
—Dow Mossman, *The Stones of Summer*

"Stella's capers are populated with criminals who are
more clever than smart and lawmen who get stymied by
clever but eventually prevail with smarts. A delight."
— Wes Lukowsky, *Booklist*

"One of the more underrated writers currently working the vein of crime fiction,"
—Ward Churchill, *Perversions of Justice*

"Stella's characters' voices sound authentic: no macho posturing — just their brutal, hard world."
—Bruce Grossman, *Bookgasm*

"Catches the cadence and daily grind of organized crime grunts."—*Publishers Weekly*

"There's terrifying verisimilitude to his criminals and their dwelling places." —*Barry N. Malzberg*

"There are few writers (except possibly Elmore Leonard and George V. Higgins), who can write mob dialogue as well as Charlie Stella."—Patricia Abbott

"The dialog flows so smooth you'd swear you were over hearing someone's conversation."
—Brian Lindenmuth, *Spinetingler Magazine*

"Charlie Stella is one of the best writers the crime genre currently has to offer."—Craig Clarke, *Somebody Dies*

"Stella cares about his characters and he made me care about them too."—Mike Parker, *Crime Fiction Lover*

"...every time you think you've got a handle on where it's going, Stella throws you a curve ball."
—Michael Scott Cain, *Rambles*

"Fresh, fast, and darkly funny."
—*Kirkus* *Starred* *Reviews*

Charlie Stella Bibliography

Novels:
Eddie's World (December 2001, Carroll & Graf)
Jimmy Bench-Press (December 2002, Carroll & Graf)
Charlie Opera (December 2003, Carroll & Graf)
Cheapskates (March 2005, Carroll & Graf)
Shakedown (June 2006, Pegasus)
Mafiya (January 2008, Pegasus)
Johnny Porno (April 2010, Stark House)
Rough Riders (July 2012, Stark House)
Tommy Red (September 2016, Stark House)
Rapino/Amato (April 2025, Stark House)

Non-Fiction:
Dogfella: How an Abandoned Dog Named Bruno
  Turned This Mobster's Life Around—A Memoir
  (May 2015, Da Capo Lifelong Books)
The Voices in My Head: A Fictional Memoir (2021)

Plays:
Coffee Wagon (1983; Bruno Walter Auditorium)
Mr. Ronnie's Confession, Double or Nothing
  (1984; 45th Street Theatre)

RAPINO/ AMATO

CHARLIE STELLA

Stark House Press • Eureka California

RAPINO/AMATO

Published by Stark House Press
1315 H Street
Eureka, CA 95501
griffinskye3@sbcglobal.net
www.starkhousepress.com

RAPINO/AMATO
Copyright © 2025 by Charlie Stella.

ISBN: 979-8-88601-133-3

Cover and text design by Mark Shepard, shepgraphics.com
Proofreading by Bill Kelly

First Stark House Press Edition: April 2025

RAPINO/AMATO
CHARLIE STELLA

*This book, the same as every book I'll ever write,
is dedicated to Dave Gresham.*

ACKNOWLEDGEMENTS

Author and editor, Merle Drown, for his dismantling some of the messes I make. The usual eyes: My Principessa, Ann Marie and my Bolshevik daughter, Nicole Hope Caliendo. Thanks to them for the time they take to decipher draft after draft after draft, and Jim Nyland for his expertise with the guns.

FACTS

"Some of the most notorious of the CIA's operations to kill world leaders were those targeting the late Cuban president, Fidel Castro. Attempts ranged from snipers to imaginative plots worthy of spy movie fantasies, such as the famous exploding cigars and a poison-lined scuba-diving suit.

"But although the CIA attempts proved fruitless in the case of Castro, the US intelligence agency has since 1945 succeeded in deposing or killing a string of leaders elsewhere around the world—either directly or, more often, using sympathetic local military, locally hired criminals or pliant dissidents." – *The Guardian* (2017)

PART 1

ONE

Two years into his 7-year federal prison sentence, Giovanni Rapino was moved from the Special Housing Unit at USP Big Sandy, a high-security United States federal prison in Kentucky, to FPC Yankton, a minimum-security federal prison camp in South Dakota. He was there two days before two correction officers escorted him from a room he shared with four other inmates to an interview room in an administrative office. Rapino sat at an oblong table while one correction officer stood behind him, the other stood at the door.

"What this is?" Rapino said, putting on his Italian accent thicker since being incarcerated at Big Sandy.

Neither correction officer responded.

It took 20 minutes before there was a knock on the door. The CO at the door opened it, then stepped back as an Asian-looking, 40-something man wearing sunglasses and a gray business suit entered the room. He held a brown briefcase in one hand and set it down alongside the chair across the table from Rapino. He identified himself as Agent David Han, then turned to the COs and motioned for them to leave. They stepped outside and closed the door behind them.

Han removed his sunglasses and stared at Rapino. Rapino returned the stare.

"What you are, FBI?" Rapino said.

"Something like that," Han said. He sat in the chair across from Rapino. "Enjoying your stay?"

Rapino sat back and waited for more.

Han frowned. "I'm here with a deal. Why you were pulled from Big Sandy."

Rapino remained silent.

"You can take it or go back to Sandy," Han said. "Up to you."

"What deal?"

"Working for the government."

Rapino's brow furrowed. "The fuck you're talking about?"

"Ever hear the term black ops?"

"No."

Han's cellphone played a country banjo tune. Han held a hand up, glanced at his phone, and then turned it off.

"It means off the radar, like a secret. Mostly it means deniable."

Rapino waited.

"It's your ticket to freedom," Han said. "You do this thing for us, and you're home free. New identification, new start, a new life with a bonus of cash."

"I have deal. Five more years and I'm out."

"Five more years at Big Sandy, assuming you survive it, and then you're out with a giant target on your back and nothing in your pocket. This deal is different. This deal sets you free. Nothing tying you to your prior life."

Rapino said, "Where you're from?"

"Originally?" Han said, "Korea. And you?"

"Don't fuck with me, eh? You're FBI?"

"That's not important."

"You bullshit, eh?"

"Not if you decide to help," Han said. "You can get out today if you decide to work for us. Go undercover for us."

"For what? I don't kill those Chinese in Brooklyn."

"I believe you called them noodles, but yeah, you killed them. Nobody gave a fuck about a pair of gang banger noodles, or you'd be doing life in the Super Max."

"Bull'a shit. I testify already. No Super Max."

"You've had six fights since you're in Big Sandy. Two stabbings. The scars on your back. You think they did you a favor sending you there?"

"What you want?"

"We need you to infiltrate an operation that starts in Mexico and makes its way into California, then back east and north through Yellowstone, Big Sky into Bozeman, Montana. That's where the drugs are scattered to the other bigger cities in Montana and elsewhere. It's dangerous. It's no walk in the park."

"Why you come to me?" Rapino said.

"Your skill," Han said. "Look, the guys working for the cartels are mostly stupid and very violent. The Americans they put to work see a movie like *No Country for Old Men* and think they're in a movie, having fun playing muscle for cartels. Frankly, you take a few of them out, nobody will pay attention. You might as well because they wouldn't hesitate to take you out."

"Old country for what?"

"You're missing the nuance here. It was a movie."

"New what? I don't see this movie."

"Maybe you should. I'll see if I can get a copy."

"No talk shit. What I'm doing? Where?"

"Montana. The Mexican cartels have a distribution center up there. We'd like to bring you there and take a big shot down. More than just him if you have to. It sends a message you take one of their big shots out. You know, election year and all that."

"The fuck you're talking about?"

"A cartel big shot. We want him dead."

"Why you don't kill him?"

"Because we don't kill people."

Rapino smirked. "Sure. Where Montana is?"

"A couple of states to the west. Big Sky country, it's called. Rocky Mountains, Yellowstone Park. Ever hear of Old Faithful?"

"You're talking shit. I don't know these places."

Han smiled. "None of that means anything to you, huh?"

"I don't know this. I'm from New York, eh? Italy, then New York."

"Then Big Sandy in Kentucky."

"Don't fuck with me. What I'm doing?"

"If you survive? You might be taking out a few stupid but dangerous fellow citizens, but the one we're after, he's a Mexican. A big shot in a cartel. We want you to take him out."

"Take out how?"

Han held up his right hand, stuck his index finger out, his thumb up, and curled his other three fingers into his palm.

"I'm to kill?" Rapino said. "You can't do this? You need me."

"Yes, we need you," Han said.

"Bull'a shit."

"No, no bull'a shit. We can't infiltrate for obvious reasons. Maybe you can. Maybe. And it won't be easy, so don't think it's that. You might have to kill more than just the big shot. In fact, you'll probably have to. Consider it proactive self-defense."

"Pro what? What bullshit this is?"

Han frowned.

"Why I do this?" Rapino said.

"Because then you're free. New identity, new life. One hundred thousand dollars."

"Bull'a shit."

"No, I already said. No bull'a shit."

"And I can kill, why?"

"You can defend yourself. Absolutely."

Rapino frowned. "Why I don't believe?"

"Because I'm with the government and governments lie all the time. But you're not in Big Sandy anymore, right?"

"Okay, so?"

Han pulled an iPad from the briefcase on the floor alongside his chair. Rapino sighed.

Han started a video and handed the iPad to Rapino.

"What?" Rapino said.

Han pointed to the iPad. "Watch," he said.

Rapino squinted when he saw a naked man tied to a tree. There was snow on the ground, some of it littered with the man's intestines. He had been disemboweled and his guts had spilled from his stomach to the ground. The man's head hung down, but he was still alive. Rapino could see the condensation from the man's breath.

Rapino's head jerked back when the man looked up. Rapino could see the man's eyes had opened wide. He appeared to be screaming but there was no audio.

A large wolf came into view.

"What the fuck?" Rapino said.

The man in the video appeared to be screaming before the wolf took a bite of the exposed intestines. A second and then third wolf appeared, and Rapino turned away as the man's body was torn apart at the stomach and below. When he looked up at Han, Rapino pushed the iPad away.

Han pushed it back and said, "Watch it," he said.

A few seconds later the wolves scattered as a huge grizzly bear went up on its hind legs to chase them off. When it turned, it appeared as if the man was already dead when the grizzly bit into the man's throat and ripped side to side until Han took the iPod from Rapino and stopped the video.

"That's what you'll be dealing with," he said. "The people you'll be dealing with did that."

Rapino was shaking his head. "Who does this?"

"Cartel people."

Rapino pointed at the iPod. "This is real?"

"You better believe it's real. These fuckers strapped a camera on a tree directly across from the tree they tied that poor bastard to. You didn't see that camera move, did you? They put it there, sliced his stomach left to right so his guts spilled out and then walked away, got into their vehicle, and had this end recorded by the camera."

"What this guy does, they kill him like that?"

Han shook his head. "No idea, but that's what they did to him to set an example. If a bullet to the brain is enough to keep most people in line, think about how they'd feel after hearing about something like that, never mind seeing it."

"Is crazy."

"Not crazy. Evil. Pure evil, but it works. It's how they keep the law frozen in place in Mexico, here and everywhere else from giving them up. Ever hear of necklacing? That's when they put a tire filled with gasoline around a guy's head and shoulders, around his arms so he can't move, and they set it on fire. That shit started in Africa and made its way to Mexico. It's total terrorism. Total intimidation. It's fear that pushes people one way or the other. Either all in or they run for the hills. Mostly, it weeds out the weak, the ones they don't want anyway."

"What I'm doing with these people?"

"Playing dirty," Han said.

Rapino huffed again. He said, "The fuck you—?"

"Talking about?" Han said. "Look, we don't have the time or the patience anymore with these people or the border policies that do nothing to stop them. My guess, what this is really about? The administration is gonna lose in November if they don't show some positive results on border issues, the drugs being smuggled into the states. It's black ops, my friend. We're taking out a Mexican big shot and whoever else we can whenever we can. Our priority is high, but we may have to go low first."

Rapino frowned.

"The President can't order the army into Mexico to wipe these dirtbags out, although that's what needs to be done. He can't so we have to do what we can when we can. Like I said, it's an election year and his numbers suck."

"We, huh?"

"You."

"And then? What happens for me?"

"You're a free man after. New identity, new everything, and a hundred grand."

"After what?"

Han ignored the question. He said, "I'm not joking about the violence, what they'll do if you fuck up. That video with the wolves and the Grizzly? It's real. That was a local undercover cop from Bozeman, and that tree they tied him to was outside Yellowstone Park."

"You say you don't know why they kill him?"

"I lied, but you saw what happened. That wasn't some Hollywood bullshit. That's what they'll do. They're vicious people, the ones running the show. They expect the scumbags they hire to be the same."

"And how I do this?"

"You do it under another name and record. That's what we'll discuss after your release."

"Without lawyer?"

Han shook his head. "This is as dirty as it gets and there won't be a paper or electronic trail. This is the big leagues. This is how governments used to get overthrown back in the day."

Rapino chuckled. "Back in the day, eh?"

"Okay, they still get overthrown this way. More or less."

"You talking bullshit," Rapino said.

"Look, I can come back in the morning, and you can let me know then," Han said. "In the meantime, this conversation never happened. You talk to somebody about this and you're on the next flight back to Kentucky. You'll still have those five years on your tab, plus whatever we can do to extend it."

"This is threat."

"More or less."

"Okay, so I leave here and go where?"

"We'll have a place set up for you here in Yankton and see how it goes. Hopefully you'll make your way west to Montana once you get your feet wet. That might take some time. Depends on you and maybe some luck. We think your skills from your prior life and the size of your balls are a plus."

Rapino yawned long and loud.

"Bored or tired?"

"My skills. You know what I am. Talk English, eh?"

"You do what you did best when you were on the street back in Brooklyn. You kill motherfuckers."

"You want me to kill."

"I didn't say that."

"You just says it, kill motherfuckers."

"You're confused," Han said. "What I said was what you did in Brooklyn. We wouldn't want you to be killed. We'd want you to protect yourself is more the case. Protect yourself with extreme prejudice."

"Prejudice is what?"

"Protecting yourself."

"You say I get apartment. What else? Money?"

"You'll get a trailer," Han said. "Money too, a passport and a car. A gray Honda with GPS attached for you and us. The money won't be enough to flee the country, so get that thought out of your head if it's in there. Plus, we'd fine you in about 10 minutes. I'll be around as your backup and to feed you when you need something. You'll have eyes on you, so don't think you can walk off in the middle of the night. You do that, you'll wind up in the Super Max. You'll be living a modest life right here in Yankton as far as that goes. We'll see what happens from there."

"You stay in touch? You?"

"Yes."

"And women?"

Han smiled. "You're on your own there."

Rapino gave it a moment, and said, "And if I agree now? Then what?"

"I walk you out of this place and we go to your trailer. We already secured it. It's not far from here. It'll take a few days to school you. Might as well do it there."

"This is no bullshit?"

"It's not, but it's no cake walk either. I'm not kidding about the people you'll be looking to infiltrate. You could wind up tied to a tree outside Yellowstone, you're not careful."

"Fuck tree," Rapino said. "Let's go to trailer."

☐ ☐ ☐

Six hours later, they were sitting in Rapino's trailer home, in Northgate Manor, a four-minute drive from FPC Yankton. Once they were comfortable with coffees and donuts Han had picked up on the way, he handed Rapino a porn video.

Rapino looked at the front cover and then the back cover. Both showed women on their knees in front of a wall with a hole in it, their mouths open with the heads of penises blacked out. "What this shit is?" Rapino said.

"Glory hole," Han said.

"The fuck that is?"

Han smiled at Rapino and said, "Are you kidding me?"

"Why I'm kidding you?" Rapino said. "I don't watch this shit."

"Never?"

"Two times, maybe three, when I'm first here in America. Once in Italy with some *cugini*. We were young, eh? I never like. Why it's here?"

"I guess the videos were leftovers from the last guy lived here," Han said. "Throw them out if you don't like them."

"Is shit," Rapino said.

"Fine. Who knew you were a crusader for women's rights?"

"You know what happened to my mother?"

"Sorry," Han said. "Wasn't that the mob over there did that."

Rapino glared at Han.

"Easy, tiger," Han said. "Just pointing out a fact."

Rapino felt his jaw tighten. He relaxed a moment, then said, "When this drug shit starts?"

"Soon enough," Han said, "but first we need to settle on a name change."

"How long I'm here?"

"Until you can get to Montana and take out our target."

"Who is target?"

"We'll let you know when we're close enough. Meantime, make yourself at home. Get yourself a girlfriend. Or learn to like the porn videos and take care of your own business."

"I don't like porn bullshit."

"Fine, then don't watch them, but speaking of your business, I have a letter for you from Italy. How do you pronounce this? Pizza-frato?"

"*Pizzoferrato*," Rapino said. "Letter is from *cugini*."

"Who's that?"

"My cousins. Let me see."

"In a few days. I don't have it on me now."

"You read already?"

"Not yet, but I will. I'll have it translated."

Rapino was thinking about a second cousin he'd briefly fallen in love with back in his hometown. Maria Theresa was a beautiful young woman but too smart to marry a mafioso. She'd rejected his offer to visit America. He hadn't spoken or heard from her since he was arrested more than two years ago.

"Tomorrow we go through name change protocol," Han said.

"I don't understand."

"Grow a beard, for starters. Maybe we'll cut your hair, or let it grow. Different clothes, a hat, whatever, but we have to change your appearance too."

"I don't shave head."

"Fair enough, but you might prefer a flight back to Kentucky if you think you call your own shots here."

"I don't think so."

"Good," Han said.

Rapino had thought about the deal he'd made with the Justice

Department, which was a straightforward agreement to provide testimony for time off his sentence. This new deal was something else, and he didn't understand the difference. He didn't believe he'd be released with a new identity and life, no matter what happened. If black ops meant secretive, then anything was possible. If the government could deny something like murder or murders, why would they protect him?

Or was he being set up?

Still, the chance to live outside the prison hell of Big Sandy made working with Han and whichever government agency he worked for an easy choice. The prison in Yankton was a picnic compared to the Special Housing Unit at Big Sandy, but if there was a chance to live outside of prison altogether and without reporting to a parole officer, Rapino would do what they asked, and he didn't need Han's permission to save his own skin.

Protecting himself had been part of the deal he'd made with Han in FPC Yankton. He wanted it reaffirmed now.

"What happens there's trouble?" he said.

"Like I already told you," Han said. "You have the right to self-defense, my friend. Compliments of the United States government. Just like the Effa-Bee-Eye."

Rapino stared at Han.

Han said, "You didn't see that movie either, huh?"

"The fuck you—"

"Never mind," Han said. Han set a Baretta 9mm on the table, then a fully loaded clip. He set another two fully loaded clips on the table and then winked at Rapino.

"You can pick it up, jam a clip and shoot me, but my people would know it and hunt you down, maybe tie you to a tree too."

"Your people, eh?"

"There's always strength in numbers, my friend."

Rapino frowned.

"Okay?" Han said.

Rapino nodded.

After a few days of intense reprogramming sessions attempting to change Giovanni Rapino to Ruggiero Amato, David Han felt satisfied with their progress. It was how they left off on the fifth day.

On the sixth day, Han returned to the trailer with a small box of donuts, four cups of coffee in a carrier, and an iPad. He let himself inside the trailer and could hear the shower running in the bathroom. He set the coffees, the box of donuts and the iPad on the living room coffee table and removed one of the coffees from the carrier. He sat on the couch, and sipped his coffee.

He heard the toilet flush, sat back, and waited for Rapino. Ten minutes later, freshly shaved, Rapino stepped into the living room while pulling a Minnesota Vikings sweatshirt over his head.

"Good morning, Mr. Amato," Han said.

"You let yourself in?" Rapino, now Amato, said.

Han held up a key.

"And if I come out with gun and shoot you?"

"You'd be lucky to go back to prison."

Amato frowned.

Han pointed to the coffees. "Those two are black," he said. "They're marked."

Amato grabbed one of the coffees with a D on the lid and sat in the single armchair in the room.

"Sleep well?" Han said.

"I sleep," Amato said. "I take Advil PM. Strong. I'm watching television and I'm sleeping. Some nightmare, but I sleep. Where is letter?"

"Later," Hand said. "You slept, that's good. I need to go over a few things today before you go into town."

"You bring letter?" Amato said.

"I did."

"Give me letter."

"Sure, why not?" He handed Amato the letter.

Amato read it to himself at the table.

Caro Giovanni: I hope you are well. I'm writing you again with bad news about our cugini. Both the twins, Alfredo and Rafael, have been arrested for murder. I don't know more than this. They are in the Pescara Remand prison for now. I will let you know more when the news is available. I'm not sure if or where they will be moved. It was a big scandal here in Pescara. Their mother and our families are inconsolable. Please write back when you get the chance. Perhaps a word from you can help them.

Wishing you the best still, Maria Theresa

Han told Amato that he could neither write nor talk to his cousins in Italy.

"Why no?"

"Because you're still in prison," Han said. "Technically. Nobody should know what you're doing."

"Rapino in prison, not Amato."

Amato folded the letter and was about to put it in his pants pocket when Han took it from him. Han said, "Sorry, Ruggiero. I'll call you Reggie for short. Most people will."

"Reggie easier, yes. Okay. Reggie. Reggie Amato."

They spent the next few hours going over the details of his assignment and practicing the fictional name and history.

Han said, "Ruggiero Amato, also known as Reggie Amato, born to Regina Amato in September of 1987 in Pizzoferrato, outside Pescara in Italy. That information needn't be changed. You lived there until the age of 15, when you parents moved to the U.S. They moved to New Orleans first, then to California, in Lancaster, a suburb of Los Angeles. Your parents were killed in a car accident six months after they settled in California. Ruggiero was moved to a foster home, where he didn't do well and wound up in two more foster homes with two more sets of parents before he was arrested for assault and robbery and sent to the county's juvenile camp at age sixteen. There he honed his criminal behavior. Upon his release two years later, he was sent to a foster home where he remained until his twentieth birthday. He was arrested for armed robbery within a few weeks. Amato then served two years at Avenal State Prison. Upon his release, Amato was believed to be engaged in several nefarious activities, including murder, although he was never charged until twenty-fifteen when he pled guilty to a federal manslaughter charge in California. At thirty years of age, Amato was released after serving five years in California's Federal Correctional Institution at Terminal Island, and the last two years in FPC Yankton. His whereabouts were currently unknown."

They went over the details several times, Amato repeating the details in his head over and over: *Ruggiero "Reggie" Amato, born in Italy and moved to the U.S. when he was fifteen . . .*

Amato was reminded to stop shaving and let his beard grow. In the afternoon, they drove around Yankton to familiarize Amato with his new surroundings and the bars where he would find the right drug connections to begin his project.

When they passed a club called the Anycocklldo, Han said, "You'll want to be here before it closes. We know there's at least one of the dancers working for a local dealer. A total skank you ask me, but she has a connection somewhere in Yankton. The bartender too, but it's probably best you work with the woman. She uses herself and users tend to cling to money sources."

"Money you'll give to me, eh?" Amato said.

"Yes, except these women aren't like the ones in New York. They don't require tens and twenties. These women are some low-grade shit compared to what you saw in New York. A five is like a twenty here. You show a roll of fives or tens, you'll stand out from the slobs stuffing dollar bills in G-strings."

After two tours of the same area, they spent the rest of the day shopping for clothes. When they returned to the trailer, Amato's background history was regurgitated two more times.

Han gave Amato a video and still photos of Avenal State Prison in the event he met up with someone who'd served time there and a local map of where he was brought up in Lancaster, the Los Angeles suburb where Amato had spent the last years of his youth.

Although his trailer was Spartan, it provided more than enough room. His refrigerator was half filled with food, bottled water, soda, and a six-pack of a local IPA. There were kitchen utensils, a television in the tiny living area, bedding, sheets, and pillows in a small bedroom. There was also an envelope with $500 and two maps, one of Yankton and another of Montana.

After Han left, Amato unpacked his clothes, turned on the television and watched the local news. When a commercial appeared for a local bar-restaurant called Mother City, he decided it was someplace he should probably frequent in his search for a drug dealer.

TWO

Amato had been around the Yankton streets for two weeks without any luck finding a drug dealer worth pursuing. He'd never liked the strip joints in New York, neither the ones in Brooklyn nor Staten Island, nor the higher class clubs in Manhattan. He had provided street money to the owner of a Queens operation, but he never spent time there gawking at strippers. He'd always been old school when it came to women and didn't like seeing them touched in public. The two strip joints he'd frequented in Yankton reminded him of why he didn't like the atmosphere. Between the women doing the hustling and desperados angling for a feel, it disgusted him.

Today he'd stopped in for a late breakfast at a truck stop diner and had been drinking coffee served by a different waitress than the one working the floor now. He watched the new waitress bounce from table to table and noticed she kept glancing back his way and smiling. When he caught her attention again, he held up his empty cup. She held up a finger and mouthed the words, *"One minute."*

She brought a check to an old man in a booth near the front door and then headed back to Amato's booth.

"You out of FPC Yankton?" Brenda Lee Beauregard said.

"Excuse?" Amato said.

"I asked because you look like you might be," she said. "Least I haven't seen you before."

"What accent that is?" Amato said.

"Huh? Oh, Southern, what's left of it. And yours?"

"Mine?"

Brenda Lee smiled as she slid into the booth to sit across from him. "Your accent," she said. "Where you from?"

"Italia. Italy, but no for a long time."

"That's something new for here, an Italian."

Amato had been eyeing Brenda Lee since her shift started 20 minutes earlier. She was short, with permed, dirty blonde hair, bright blue eyes, and a healthy bust. She wore a short, brown skirt with a lighter brown blouse buttoned short enough to expose her cleavage. She also wore brown cowgirl boots with heels. Amato figured her for late 30's, maybe early 40's.

"We get a lot of guys from the prison because of our proximity to it," she said. "We're the first truck stop nearby."

Amato was staring into her eyes then. She was starting to lose her smile when someone from another table called to her. Brenda Lee rolled her eyes before heading to the customer in need.

When she returned, she slid into his booth again.

"Where is waitress gives me coffee?"

"Donna? Her shift ended. I have her tables now."

"She gets some of tip?"

"Of course. We do that for each other. No reason to be petty about it. You worried I'll steal her end?"

"I don't worry, no. You are honest, I can tell."

She smiled.

"You say truck stop," he said. "What this is?"

"I do like your accent."

Amato waited for an answer to his question.

"It's different," she said.

"Truck stop is what?"

"A place for truckers to stop and eat. That part is open twenty-four-seven."

"Truckers?"

"All the tractor trailers out back?" she said. "Truckers are the guys who drive them. We're a hot spot for guys on the road passing through here."

"You are from here?" he said.

"Me? No, uh-uh. I'm from Louisiana, hon. Baton Rouge, Louisiana. I'm up here the last ten years. Marriage chased me here."

"You are married?"

"No. I probably said it wrong. I was married in Louisiana a bunch of years ago, but my husband was an asshole, so I left him and wound up here. Arkansas first, then here."

"Truckers tip big?"

"Some do. Most really, but not all."

"They touch you?"

"Touch me how?"

"Grab your ass."

She smiled. "Sometimes, sure. Part of the job really."

"And boss? He does this too?"

"Eugene?"

Amato nodded.

"He owns the place, and he likes to take a squeeze or two when he's tight. Makes it easy for my conscience when I rob from him, though, so there's that."

"What you rob from him?"

"You some kind of investigator?"

"Investigator how?"

"Your questions. They're personal."

Amato smiled.

"Well?" she said.

"I want to take you home tonight."

"You do, huh?"

"Maybe grab your ass."

Brenda Lee shot him a wink. "Maybe I'll let you."

"How many days you work?"

"Damn, you have a lot of questions. I work five days. Nights, actually. Some nights from six to midnight, although I never get out of here before one. Eugene is usually drunk by closing and he moves a lot slower come time to close."

"Eugene is boss likes to touch you?"

"Grope me is more like it. He's not shy once he's drunk and he's drunk every night he's here. Always on Friday and Saturday. Sometimes he pays a working girl. Gets his jollies from one of them."

"Midnight is early, no?"

"Excuse me?"

"When you say you close. Is early."

"Maybe, but it's a state law."

"I pick you up here?"

Brenda Lee smiled.

"After work, I come here?" he said.

"Sure. I'll be here."

"Come ti chiami?"

"What?"

"Your name? What you are called?"

"Brenda. Brenda Lee."

He extended his right hand. "I am Ruggiero. Reggie for short."

"I like it the other way, but I probably can't pronounce it."

"Reggie. You can say Reggie?"

"Reggie. Okay, Reggie."

"After work, I come here for Brenda Lee."

"Okay," she said. "We'll see you then, Reggie."

☐ ☐ ☐

"I like the noise you make," he said.

"Huh?" she said.

"When you get excited," Amato said. "No fake noise. I like this. I never like noise before."

"You mean when I hum?"

"Hum?"

She hummed for him.

"Like that, *si*."

"*Si* mean yes?"

"*Si*. Yes. But you don't fake before."

"Uh-uh, sugar. That was the real thing."

He held her face with both hands. "*Bella*," he said.

"Thank you, but I'm not beautiful."

"Sexy beautiful."

"I'll take it."

He lit a cigarette and offered her one. She declined.

"Who sells drugs where you work?" he said.

"That's a conversation change."

"Who?"

"Why you wanna know that?"

"I want to know."

"A few people have pot to sell sometimes," Brenda Lee said. "That what you mean?"

"No pot. Pot is legal now. Drugs."

"Pot ain't legal here yet. Not in South Dakota."

"Okay, maybe pot, but heroin, cocaine, the Fentanyl. The stuff they put with heroin."

"I think they use that on all of them. Heroin, cocaine, oxy and whatnot. That what you went in for, drug dealing?"

"No drugs. Never. Who sells drugs here? You know?"

"I know of a few people. Couple guys come in the bar sell it to truckers. I know a woman sells too. No big shots, though, if that's what you're asking."

"Which guys in bar?"

"I can point them out to you. One guy is Curly. Him and his enforcer, a guy they call Dog, they sell the hard stuff."

"Point them to me."

"I will. They stop in together at least once a week. Usually for a late breakfast. Sometimes lunch. You should stop in for breakfast. Late breakfast or early lunch. They'll show up sooner or later. I can't guarantee when, but they'll be there sooner or later."

"Point out drug dealers, whoever they are."

"Okay. Sure, but what's it about."

"*Bella*, don't ask questions, eh."

"I didn't say I minded it. My last boyfriend was an addict. I've always wound up with a badass. I guess I'm attracted to them, but the others always turned out to be fake tough guys. You know what I mean. Tough with women, not men."

"We call them jerkoffs, *Bella*."

Benda Lee smiled. "Jerkoffs? I guess I heard that before but not much around here."

"Man is tough with woman is jerkoff, eh? Fake tough guy."

"Okay."

"Now, no drugs. No addicts. I don't like this."

"But you want me to point out a dealer?"

"*Bella*, no questions, eh?"

"You don't wanna tell me what for. That it?"

Amato held his hands a foot apart in front of his face. "Come, do this again. Sit on my face."

Brenda Lee hummed again. "Mmmmm," she said. "Sure."

Five days later, midway through her shift, Brenda Lee took her break and slid into Amato's booth across from him. She held a finger up and thumbed behind her.

"That's Curly there, the fat bald one," she said just above a whisper. "The guy across from him is his bodyguard, what everybody says anyway. That's Dog."

"Dog?"

"From the Game of Thrones HBO series. People call him Dog because he's got a burn on his cheek. It's the bald spot on his left cheek. The hole in his beard. Those two are the big shots in Yankton."

Amato spotted them, then looked away.

"They dress like hobos," Brenda Lee said. "You'd think they'd dress better with the money they make."

"Is smart they don't," Amato said.

"Then they could take a bath," Brenda Lee said. "They both stink to high heaven."

Amato smiled.

"You want, I can introduce you," she said.

"No, I do this myself," he said. "Not in here. These men touch you?"

"Grab is what Dog does. He isn't shy. Once it's getting late and he's already shit-faced, he likes to reach out and grab a cheek. Sometimes both cheeks. Dog is a pig."

"And your boss lets them do this?"

"My boss couldn't care less. I told you, he's guilty of the same thing a few times a week."

"And you stay here why?"

"I stay here because I make twice as much as I'll make anywhere else. And I told you because I can steal from time to time. I wouldn't do that normally, but that's the price the owner pays for trying shit he should have his hands broken for. I never feel guilty about stealing from him."

"Next week I break his hands."

"What? No, or what do I do for work?"

"I don't tell him why I break his hands."

"But he'll see us together sooner or later."

"You want him to grab your ass?"

"No, but when he does, I feel better about stealing from him."

"Stealing what, pennies? No, I break his hands and then I steal from him."

"I believe you're crazy, Reggie."

"Maybe. Now take order. Burger deluxe, fries and the coleslaw. I like this here, the coleslaw."

Brenda Lee winked at him. "Then I'll give you a bigger helping."

He watched her wiggle away and grew angry as he pictured hands reaching out to grab her ass. Amato couldn't get the image out of his head. He stared at the men Brenda Lee had pointed out. Amato knew to take out the muscle first. He'd do that first chance he had.

As the two men left, Amato considered following them out to the parking lot but was too hungry. He waited the ten minutes more it took for Brenda Lee to bring him his order.

"Your boyfriends left," he said.

"Shit, hon, they're not my boyfriends. Besides, they didn't leave. They're out in the parking lot near one of the semis. Pro'bly making a sale. I saw them when I stopped in the lady's room."

Amato pulled a fifty-dollar bill from his wallet and set it on the table. "Leave food," he said. "I come back in a few minutes."

Dog wasn't ready for it, but Amato hit him anyway. A flush overhand right that dropped the man to the parking lot asphalt and left him groggy.

"What the fuck?" the one called Curly said.

He'd been leaning against a trailer cab, his arms folded across the top of his belly until then. He pushed himself off and stopped when Amato faced him with an obvious challenge.

"I don't want no trouble," Curly said.

"Put me to work," Amato said.

"Work?"

"As muscle."

"What?"

Amato pointed to Dog. "Because he's for shit."

"What the hell are you talkin' about?"

Dog tried to get up but was still groggy and slipped back to the asphalt. Amato feigned kicking him in the face and Dog turned his body to shield his face.

"Put me to work," Amato said again.

The man called Curly remained silent.

"Okay, we talk again," Amato said, then headed back to the diner and disappeared inside.

"Everything okay?" Brenda Lee said when she saw him return.

"Everything fine," Amato said. "I finish eating now, *Bella*."

Amato went to pick Brenda Lee up at 12:20 a.m. and saw Curly was talking to her. He waited until the fat man left in his pickup. Brenda Lee smiled when Amato pulled up to the curb.

"What he wants?" he said as she got in his car.

"He was asking about you," Brenda Lee said. "He said you hurt his friend and now his friend was looking for you."

"What else he says?"

"That I should give him a call once I found out who you were. He said he saw I served you earlier in the diner."

"What he says about this Dog?"

"Just that he was mad and wanted to find you."

"You know where he lives?"

"No."

"Too bad."

"Why are you looking for trouble with them, darlin'? They're not very smart and that makes them dangerous."

Amato winked at her again. "He looks for me," he said. "I find him first."

"What are you getting into, Reggie? You're worrying me. I'd like to fuck now and not worry about you and those idiots."

"Okay, we go home, then I get into your pants, eh?"

Brenda Lee smiled. "You're bad, Reggie," she said. "You're definitely bad."

They were on their way to Amato's trailer when Brenda Lee said she needed something from her place. She lived in a basement apartment on Pine Street, a few blocks from an elementary school where she'd worked as a teacher's aide when she first moved to Yankton. It was a single-family home near East 9th Street.

He pulled up to the curb, and she went into her place. Ten minutes later, she was out with a small duffle bag and a smaller gym bag. She set them on the back seat of his government issued Honda, then sat up front.

"You bring changes?" he said.

"Uh-huh," she said, then winked at him.

"Good."

Back at the RV Park, he helped her with the bags and immediately felt the heft in the small gym bag. Once they were inside the trailer, he held up the heavy gym bag to her.

"What this is?" he said. "You have hammers?"

"Guns," Brenda Lee said.

Amato was surprised. "Guns?" he said, then opened the bag.

"Just in case," she said.

"In case for what?"

"Don't pull my chain, Reggie. I know what I'm dealing with here."

He smiled.

"Now can we fuck?" she said.

□ □ □

Four days after being warned about Dog's intentions, Agent Han was waiting for Amato on Mulberry Street outside a Golf and Country Club. It was early in the morning. Amato had left Brenda Lee asleep back at his RV.

Han wore dungarees, a light blue shirt, black shoes and his sunglasses. Amato wore new clothes—black sweatpants, a black hoodie and black Nike's.

Amato pointed to the street sign. "Is rip-off, no?" he said. "From New York. Little Italy."

"I think every state has one," Han said.

"They have Mott too?"

"No clue."

"So, what's next?"

Han passed him a piece of paper with an address on it.

"Dog?" Amato said.

Han winked at Amato.

"And?" Amato said.

Han pointed to a brown paper bag alongside a trash can.

"I have gun," Amato said. "You give it to me."

Han frowned.

"What, you think I'm wired?" Amato said.

"Be careful," Han said.

Amato watched him drive away before picking up the paper bag and bringing it to his car. He knew it was a gun when Han pointed to it. In the car he looked inside the bag and saw it wasn't his favorite weapon, a Walther PPK. It was a Glock 9mm and a sound suppressor.

"Is no Jimmy fucking Bond gun," Amato said.

He plugged the address on the paper into his GPS and followed its directions onto U.S. Highway 81 across the Discovery Bridge into Nebraska. He turned off U.S. Highway 81 onto Nebraska Highway 12 and was in the town of Crofton a few minutes later, a twenty-minute trip from where he'd started. The GPS led him to the address, a small ranch with no distinguishing features. Amato parked half a block away and screwed the sound suppressor onto the barrel of the Glock. He walked back to the address with the weapon inside his hoodie's front pocket.

When he approached the tiny porch, he could see the front door was ajar. He rang the bell twice before removing the Glock and stepped to one side of the door. He rang the bell another two times a few seconds later.

A male voice yelled, "Hold the fuck on!" Then, as footsteps grew louder. "Who the fuck is—"

Dog had stuck his head out far enough for Amato to shoot him in the left temple. Dog bounced off the doorframe on his way to the floor. Amato pulled Dog's body inside the house and then shot him in the forehead. Then he closed the door behind him on his way out.

He stopped at a Dunkin Donuts on his way back to the RV Park. He made it back in just under an hour. He hid the Glock and sound suppressor under the spare tire in the trunk of his car. He walked into the RV as Brenda Lee was stepping out of the shower, naked except for a towel wrapped around her head.

"*Bella*," he said.

"Where'd you go?" she said.

He held the box of donuts up as he looked her up and down. She smiled and did a slow pirouette for him.

"Hungry?" he said.

"That took you an hour?"

"I rob bank first," he said.

She started for the bedroom. "I almost believe you," she said.

Amato sat at the kitchen table and opened the box of donuts. He grabbed the coffee pot and poured himself a cup. He set the pot and an empty cup on the table for Brenda Lee. When she returned, she was wearing light green bikini panties and a white Raglan t-shirt with blue sleeves, and a Mount Mary University Lancers baseball cap.

"What is Lancers?" Amato said.

"The university here," Brenda Lee said. "One of the girls on the team last year gave me hers after the season. I guess it's softball they play."

"I like this."

Brenda Lee poured herself a cup of coffee and sat across from Amato.

"So, an hour for donuts?" she said.

"You writing book?" he said.

"I guess it's a secret."

"This Curly," Amato said. "He asks about me again and you tell him what I told you."

"Which is? Because you haven't told me much, darlin'."

"I'm Italian but move to California when I'm young. I come out of the prison here and we are, you and me, a couple now."

"Are we?"

"*Bella*, you don't think so?"

"I want to think so."

"Then we are."

"Like we are now, me sleeping here, or just fuck buddies."

"Don't talk trash, *Bella*. Women with dirty mouths . . . *come si dice*? How you say *brutta*. Is ugly."

"Is ugly?" Brenda Lee said, offended then. "You calling me ugly now?"

"I say this? What the fuck, *Bella*? *Bella* is beautiful, no?"

"Sorry. What about if he asks what you went to prison for? I don't know that."

"Manslaughter. Now you know."

"How'd that happen?"

"Not so many questions, eh?"

"Oh, boy. Okay. Fine. No more for now."

"You are clever woman."

Brenda Lee frowned before taking a bite from a chocolate frosted donut.

"You like?" Amato said.

"Yes. These are to die for. Next time get more."

"You like chocolate, but no chocolate man."

"Excuse me?"

Amato winked at Brenda Lee.

"Have I ever had sex with a black man? Is that what you're asking me?"

"I ask if you like with chocolate man."

"Good lord, Reggie, I can see I'm gonna have to work on you."

"*Si* or no, the chocolate man?"

"No, but that doesn't mean I wouldn't if I liked one enough."

Amato waved his hands in front of his face. "No more this talk, please," he said. "I can't hear."

Brenda Lee chuckled. "You are too much, darlin'."

"Let's go inside," Amato said. "I listen to news now."

He brought his coffee into the living room. Brenda Lee followed him with her coffee and the box of donuts. He grabbed the remote, turned the television on, and then sat back and channel surfed. Brenda Lee sat alongside him on the couch, then leaned against him as he continued to run through the channels with the remote.

Suddenly he stopped, "Shit," he said. "I like this movie."

"What movie?"

"*Serpico*."

"I don't think I know it."

Amato leaned forward on the couch. "You have to know this movie. Al

Pacino?"

"I know him. What's it about?"

"A cop arrests dirty cops. Was for real, this guy. In New York. Nineteen-seventies, I think. I see it later in life myself, but I like very much. Serpico is snitch, eh? But he arrest dirty cops. They shoot him in the face."

"The cops shot him?"

"Not the cops, but they let happen. It starts with this, then goes back to when he joins police."

"Oh, okay," she said.

He leaned back, put his right arm around her, and then turned up the volume. They watched the movie straight through with one break for each to use the bathroom.

When it was over, Brenda Lee said, "Pacino looks so young there."

"You see how it work?" Amato said. "Just like January six bull'a shit. The little guys go to jail and bigga' shots *niente*, nothing."

"He really live in Switzerland?"

"Huh?"

"At the end it said Serpico lives in Switzerland."

"Oh, maybe. I don't know. He probably run away from the cops."

"Was it like that in California?"

"California?"

"Where you came from."

He'd forgotten his own fictional history for a moment, then said, "Cops? That everywhere. Lots of cops are *sporco*. Dirty motherfuckers. Not all, some, but everywhere, eh? Good and bad."

"I know they're bullies around here. Not all of them but some."

"They have badge and gun."

"What was all that opera about in the movie? Was Serpico into opera?"

"My uncle listens to this when I grow up."

"Really? What kind of opera?"

"Shit," he said. He realized he'd done it again, forgotten his fictional past.

"What's wrong?" Brenda Lee said.

"Nothing. Do me favor today, eh?"

"Sure. What is it?"

"Buy me opera CD."

"Seriously?"

"I don't make joke. Buy me one from the movie."

"Which?"

"No, buy me two. Tosca and Gianni Schicchi."
"You'll have to write those down. I'd never remember them."
"I write them down."
"You into that too, the opera?"
"No, but maybe is time, eh? Why not?"
Brenda Lee shrugged. "Sure, why not."

THREE

Robert "Red" Dalton stood with Curly at the Riverside Park boat launch. Dalton was a tall man with red hair and a matching beard. At 40 years of age, he'd been in and out of prison three times before the age of 30. Ten years down the road from his last incarceration, he worked for a Mexican cartel connection in Bozeman, Montana. He'd been in both North and South Dakota the last two weeks handling issues between drug dealers on cartel payrolls, collecting cash and distributing drugs. A sidekick driving a white Ford E-Transit van handled deliveries to their drug distributors in both states. Yankton was their last stop before heading back to Montana.

Almost a month had passed since Curly's new muscle was on the job. Curly was still nervous about the murder of his former muscle, mostly from fear of his own life, but over a short two weeks, he'd gotten used to Reggie Amato. The police had visited Curly the day after Dog's body was discovered and he'd played dumb. Today he explained to Dalton what he thought had happened and that he was sure he knew who had killed Dog.

"And what?" Dalton said. "You want us to kill him now?"

"No, no way," Curly said. "I didn't mean that. I told you the guy wanted me to hire him. I did because he was tougher than Dog. He's kept things in order since."

"He a cop?"

"What? No, I don't think so. Not if he murdered Dog."

"Where'd he come from? You bother to find out, or you want us to do it?"

"I got a name, but you have the resources to find out his background."

"So do the police we pay have the resources to find out his background. Did you bother to ask Luther? We pay him enough."

"I didn't. Not yet."

"Then ask him. And then you make the decision about this guy you don't know who he is you think killed your guy. Make sure you get it right because our people don't allow for mistakes."

"I hear you."

"I hope so, Curly. I like you. You're a decent earner, but you're not all that sharp and anybody can see you're no tough guy. Don't fuck up. Don't bring in some ringer cop or everything changes."

"You want to meet the guy?"

"Has he done right with collections?"

"He has. Better than Dog even."

"You have our money? All of it?"

"Tomorrow for sure."

"Tomorrow for sure?"

"Huh? Oh, yeah, yes. Definitely. You want to meet the new guy? He's involved with one of the waitresses at one of the bar-restaurants."

"He there now?"

"I don't know. Want to come take a look-see?"

"No. I don't have time now. What's his name?"

"Reggie Amato."

"Italian, huh?"

"I guess."

"Don't guess, Curly."

"Can you look into him?"

"I said I would, didn't I?"

"Yeah. Sorry."

"Okay, then. Maybe I'll stick around another day. Don't forget our money. All of it."

Curly swallowed hard as they shook hands. Dalton headed to his 2022 Chevrolet Silverado 1500 pickup in the parking lot off Levee Street. Curly watched until Dalton waved at him as he drove out of the parking lot onto Levee Street heading west.

It was early in the afternoon. Curly hadn't eaten lunch yet and was hungry. He gave a call to one of his local distributors, then to a detective on the drug pad, and then headed to the Mother City Bar and Grill.

Curly watched Brenda Lee move from table to table and decided to sit in her section. He noticed the extra energy in her step and wondered if it had to do with her new boyfriend, the man Curly suspected had killed his former partner. He and Dog used to wonder about Brenda Lee and her Southern accent and whether she went down on the drunk who owned the place. They wondered about her in the sack too. Curly had gone home to service himself more than once from wondering about Brenda Lee.

He liked to imagine taking her from behind.

One time when they were drunk and Brenda Lee was picking

something off the floor at the table alongside their booth, Dog leaned over, lifted the back of her skirt, and put his face against her rump. He'd started to breathe in deep before she could scramble away and curse him out.

Dog had said it smelled sweet and that if he had the chance he wouldn't come up for air until his face looked like a glazed donut. Curly still smiled when he thought about that, a glazed donut.

Now she was approaching his booth with a pot of coffee, and he kept his eyes focused on her thighs below the short uniform skirt.

"Curly," she said.

"Police ever look into your boyfriend?" Curly said.

Brenda Lee poured coffee into his cup. She went to pour into the other cup across from Curly when he stopped her by putting a hand over the cup.

"Alone again?" she said.

Brenda Lee already knew about Dog being murdered but played dumb.

"Like you don't know why I'm alone," Curly said.

"What?" she said.

Curly frowned at her.

Brenda Lee opened her hands. "What are you talking about?"

"Dog," Curly said. "He was murdered some weeks back. You don't know about it?"

"I don't pay attention to gossip."

"You don't watch television either? Don't talk to your coworkers? The whole state knows what happened to Dog. It was on the news for a full week, here in South Dakota and in Nebraska where he lived."

She feigned anger. "How'm I supposed to know where Dog lives and why would I care?"

"Fine," Curly said. "Whatever you say."

"Hey, I don't need this first thing," Brenda Lee said. She held her order pad in her left hand and a pen in her right hand. "What you want, Curly?"

"Your boyfriend beat the shit out of him the day before Dog was murdered," Curly said.

"I don't know anything about that," Brenda Lee said.

Curly frowned. "Right," he said. "Tell him I have somebody wants to meet him."

"I'll probably speak to him before I get home," she said. "Where can he reach you?"

Curly said, "Look, I know that you know your boyfriend works for me now, so stop playing dumb, okay? I can't always reach your boyfriend. Sometimes he don't respond when I call him."

"Curly, I told you I don't need this shit right now. Where can Reggie reach you?"

"He knows how to reach me," Curly said. He removed a white business card from his wallet and wrote on the back of it. He handed her the card. "Here's my card anyway. In case he forgot how to dial the numbers."

She read it aloud, "Online Kitchen Supplies?"

"Number's on the back. Tell him to call."

"You got it," Brenda Lee said, annoyed at the task she'd been given. "Now, what are you having today?"

"Bran muffin," Curly said. "I need to clear some of the shit out."

Brenda Lee smiled. "Bran muffin'll do that," she said.

Detective Luther Briggs was 18 months from retirement and eager to get there. One year ago, he'd been diagnosed with Type 2 diabetes and had gained instead of lost weight. At 6'4", 260 pounds, he'd lost some of the muscle he'd spent building most of his life. A former offensive tackle for the University of North Dakota and avid powerlifter, Briggs had taken to a more sedentary lifestyle the last few years. A lover of the outdoors, especially fly fishing and hunting, Briggs often spent his vacations pursuing those interests above all else. Two weeks ago, he spent five days fly fishing both Rapid Creek and Spearfish Creek, sleeping in his RV and eating what he caught for lunch and dinner.

To supplement his retirement, two years ago Briggs began taking dirty money from an out of state drug dealer tied to a Mexican cartel. He'd built a small nest egg with the extra $200 a week he'd been receiving since taking a $10,000 retainer for his services.

Briggs planned on retiring with a healthy stash of unreported cash as well as his police retirement package and Social Security when the time came to collect those. He'd been offered a job as security by the same drug dealing operation more than once, but Briggs had no intention of risking anything once he retired. His goal was to move where the fishing was best, somewhere a lot closer to Yellowstone Park in Montana.

He had less than two years to think about it.

In the meantime, he'd been asked to gather as much information as possible about a newcomer to Yankton from California, one Reggie Amato. He spent more than two hours on his computer before using the police computers to gather what information he could. Briggs had tried several versions of the nickname Reggie before finding Amato's real first name, which was Ruggiero. It was an Italian name and suspicious enough for Briggs to run it through organized crime records.

Nothing showed, although there were a few Ruggiero names on the East Coast in the O.C. records. What Briggs did find was a birth certificate stating he was born overseas, a juvenile and adult history based in California and some time he'd done at the Federal Correctional Institution at Terminal Island, then later at Yankton FPC, which he'd recently been released from.

Briggs met up with Dan Osborn, locally known as Curly, in the parking lot of the Mother City Bar and Grill truck stop. Briggs slid his big frame into Curly's boxy 2022 Ford Bronco Sport.

"Learn anything?" Curly said.

Briggs put his left hand out, palm up.

Curly pulled two fifties from the sun visor and placed them in Brigg's palm. Briggs examined each bill before stuffing them in his coat pocket. He removed the police report he'd printed from his shirt pocket, tore off the top and bottom police logos and address, then handed it to Curly.

"The woman he's fucking says he's from there," Curly said as he looked the paper over.

"Then you should've paid her," Briggs said.

"I had to verify it."

"I know."

"You think I should keep him on? He's doing pretty good with collections."

Briggs said, "I've got trout I caught up to Spearfish defrosting in my sink I have to tend to. This guy coming or what? I got better things to do, Curly."

Briggs was to provide security for his meeting with Reggie Amato and now he was getting bored because the mystery man was late.

"He don't show by eleven take off," Curly said. "Fair enough?"

"Fuck fair," Briggs said. "You said ten-thirty and I'm here twenty-five after."

"And you're getting paid to do nothing for it."

"I'm leaving at ten-fifty-five."

Just then a pair of headlights pulled into the lot. Curly stepped out of his SUV and waved at the Honda Accord. The Honda turned right and pulled into a spot facing the water.

Amato waited at the front of his car for Curly. When they were a few feet apart, Curly said, "You kill Dog? I want to know."

Amato lost some of his extra thick accent. "You hired me already, boss. You want to fire me now?"

"I like knowing you won't kill me someday."

"My word isn't good enough, find someone else. When somebody with balls robs you, tough shit."

"I have a guy I want you to meet?"

"The cop in your Bronco?"

"No, not him. How'd you know he was a cop?"

"Stop the bullshit, eh?"

Curly looked askance at Amato. "Your accent," he said.

Amato put it back on. "Who I'm meeting?"

"Not the cop. Tomorrow, if he has the time, the guy brings us the goods. His name is Dalton, but he goes by Red. He's the guy I hand the money to. He's from Bozeman. I answer to him."

"I'm still hired or no?"

"Okay, okay. You can stay hired. For now."

"Why you being tough guy, Curly? You're no tough guy. You have me for protection." Amato pointed at Curly's Bronco at the other end of the parking lot. "You don't need black cop."

"Shit," Curly said. "He's on the payroll."

"I see him a few times at police station. He goes in and out, in and out."

"Forget him."

"I want another hundred a week, boss."

"I paid Dog five hundred a week."

"Bull'ashit."

"I'll have to get approval for more."

"When I know?"

"Tomorrow."

"We come here? What time?"

"I'll call you. You still have your burner phones."

"*Si*. Yes."

"Good."

"That's it? This the last interview?"

"For now it is."

"You trying to sound hard, boss? You're no tough guy. Why you have protection, eh?"

"You an eye-talian, huh?"

"You know this. *Italia* first, then California."

"You got that accent from Cali?"

"I get it from mother and father, in *Italia.*"

"They from over there?"

"Italy, yes. Same town as Bruno Sammartino. Pizzaferatto in Abruzzi."

Curly smiled. "Bruno who?"

"World Champion wrestler."

"Wrestling's fixed."

"*Si,* but he's *famoso.*"

"And he's from Pizza town?"

"Don't make fun, Curly. I said you're no tough guy."

Curly lost his smile. "Call me tomorrow," he said. "Same number. Red approves, you can stay hired."

"For six hundred, eh?"

"We'll see."

"Okay, boss."

"You're welcome."

Amato winked at him and said, "I know."

□ □ □

It hadn't taken long for Amato to earn Curly's trust. He could tell Curly liked watching him in action with drug runners. He liked having the new muscle. Wanting to know if Amato was the one to kill Dog was an act of caution. Amato couldn't blame Curly for that. What if Amato wanted to move up, something he might need to do? Curly wasn't a genius by any measure, but he wasn't a moron. He had to be concerned about his job.

The runners Curly used to sell the drugs supplied by the cartel people in Bozeman were too young to trust. Reggie Amato proved early on that he knew how to handle his business. He complained about a runner who was always late and broke his nose the second time after being warned. He also made sure Curly was there to witness it.

By the third week, Curly no longer thought about Dog. It wasn't as if they had a special relationship. Dog had been recommended by Luther Briggs, the Yankton cop on the cartel's payroll. Curly was weary of Dog when they first met a year ago, but Dog liked playing a big fish in a small pond, which is what Yankton was. Dog had become obnoxious over time, cracking jokes at Curly's expense, especially in front of women.

Curly's sexual life involved prostitutes and watching porn films. He hadn't had a steady relationship after high school. Dog liked to act like a player, but he was coarse and often embarrassing around women, especially when he'd had a few drinks.

Curly liked to check out a woman's ass as much as any man, but when Dog reached out and touched, assuming nobody would challenge him, his actions put Curly in danger too. The day after Amato had floored Dog, Dog had wanted revenge and had given Curly a lot of shit about it.

"Why didn't you do something?" Dog had said.

"That's your job," Curly told Dog. "Don't blame me the guy japped you."

"You should've grabbed him and held him until I got up."

"You weren't getting up, Dog. He caught you good."

"You better find out who that motherfucker is because I'm gonna take him out. I'll show him how to jap somebody. I'll jap him back with a baseball bat."

As it turned out, although nobody could prove it, and Amato would never admit it, the new guy had put Dog to sleep.

Allowing Amato to be his muscle wasn't much of a choice, but once Luther said there was nothing he could find on the guy, Curly felt confident about Amato meeting with Dalton. If they didn't meet tomorrow, it could be six to eight weeks before Dalton could meet Amato again. Dalton was in town to distribute drugs and collect on money owed. Curly was still a few thousand short and needed Amato to collect it. He didn't like having to remind the Italian because Amato could be a bit snippy himself, but not nearly as bad as Dog. In fact, Curly liked the fact that no matter what he said or did, Amato mostly called him boss.

Curly liked being called boss.

So, he was surprised a week ago when Amato told him he was short because Curly had been sloppy with a couple of his runners. Curly was upset.

"You don't stay on top of them, boss," Amato said. "I tell you this two week ago. You go home watch the porn and jerkoff instead of watch them."

"Isn't that's your job?"

"You don't pay me enough to be surveillance for ten runners. Besides, you have cop for that."

"Not me, I don't have any cops. That's the Bozeman people."

"Whatever. You don't pay me to sit on runners. I do that for free, eh? You don't pay me for that. I tell you two guys are short because you don't stay on top. You pay me to collect. Because I don't let them bulla'shit me, eh? That's why you pay me."

Amato had asked for an extra hundred a week. Curly had denied and stalled him more than once. Amato warned him the two runners were skimming and could be trouble, but Curly had said he'd deal with them himself rather than pay Amato the extra cash until more money was approved. An extra hundred would have to come from Curly's pocket and he wasn't anxious to let it go.

And then, sure enough, the two runners became a problem; trouble he didn't need.

It took Amato less than 30 minutes to find the two runners who'd been sloppy with their collections. When he found them, Alex Larson and Tim Anderson were in a strip joint drinking overpriced beers and feeding single dollar bills into the G-Strings of two dancers on the stage. Amato walked them outside to the parking lot. Larson was tall and thin, Anderson was short and muscular. Both were in their 20's and were a little tipsy from their beers.

"This why you two are short?" Amato said, losing his thicker accent again.

"No way, man, this is our money," Larson said.

Amato slapped Larson in the face, then turned to the muscular one. "You have Curly's money?"

Anderson stepped back. "Some, not all."

"Let me see what you have," Amato said.

"This is mine, man," Anderson said. "I got Curly's back home."

Amato stepped forward and slapped him in the face. Anderson looked about to cry.

"This is fucked up, man," Larson said.

"You think so?"

"We'll get his money. Give us a couple days. We'll have it."

"No," Amato said. "You give me what you have now in your pockets."

"That's our money," Anderson said.

"Bulla'shit, your money. Give me now or I fuck you both up before I kill you."

Both runners emptied their pockets. Amato counted less than $200.

Amato pocketed the cash and said, "Okay, what you do now, you get the fuck out of Yankton tonight. Go have cup of coffee, get in your car and take off. *Capisci?* You understand? You take off and don't come back. Curly has his boss here soon and if you're still here, Curly points to you and that's it, you're both dead."

"We're just a couple hundred short, man," Larson said.

"You're nine hundred short. Don't jerk me off."

"We can get it," Anderson said.

"No, you don't can get it. You're too late. You take off and I'll tell Curly I couldn't find you. You two make sure you stay away, eh? Lost. If Curly's boss finds you, he'll take you someplace to feed the wolves. Get out of Yankton tonight and don't come back."

Then Amato pulled the cash back out of his wallet, gave them each $50.00, and said, putting on his thick accent again, "For gas, eh? And a coffee. Now go, *stronzi.*"

Larson and Anderson slunk away to a pickup, got in and drove away.

The way Agent Han had explained it, there were 12 regions in total that the distributors from Montana visited every two to four weeks. Sometimes the man in charge of distribution for each region showed up on the QT to make sure those distributing the drugs in each region remained on their toes. Other times his distributions were scheduled. The man Curly feared the most, Robert Red Dalton, always drove ahead of the distribution vehicle.

The first four regions were in cities in Montana itself. The next four were in cities in North Dakota. The last four were in cities South Dakota, the last of which was Yankton.

Curly had ten runners for his operation. Each was responsible for a smaller section of the city. Han had told Amato that the careful ones operated from stash houses which they changed from time to time. The reckless runners kept their stashes too close to where they dealt from and sometimes carried some of the stash on their person.

Amato had already met and chased the pair of reckless runners away. It was a risky play, but Amato needed to remove Curly from the game, or at least prove he was sharper than his boss and maybe take his job without having to kill the poor bastard.

Maybe get himself invited to Montana somewhere down the road.

Curly was livid when Amato didn't have the money from the runners Amato had chased. He called Amato and the two met in their usual location to talk, alongside the Riverside Park boat ramp.

"You see Larson yet?" Curly said.

"He avoids me," Amato said.

"And Anderson? He avoid you too?"

Amato yawned. "*Si*," he said. "I spend three hours in front of his place. I spend most of the morning at Larson. No sign. I think they're gone."

"You think they took off together? What, they're gonna start their own operation?"

"It wouldn't be here. Too easy to find, eh? I tell you they are sloppy. You don't listen."

"If they were so sloppy, they would've been picked up by the law. I already spoke with Luther. They're not in jail."

"Maybe Luther is asleep?"

"No, he's our guy on the police force. He earns his money."

Amato smiled. "He's no my guy."

"What's the difference, Reggie?"

"You're right, boss. Sorry."

"Any hint where they might've gone?"

Amato shrugged. "They take off. Where do I look for them? North Dakota, Canada, Nebraska? Where? Which way?"

"Fuck me, Reggie, I don't know. But Dalton is gonna want that money. All of it, he said. I told him we'd have it."

"I tell you those guys are no good."

"Enough with that bullshit. I told you they ain't arrested."

"Unless your friend is bulla' shit you. Maybe they get caught. Maybe they flip. Maybe they give you up."

"I don't see how or why?"

"What I just say? Maybe, boss."

"Shit. They're giving me up, I'm fucked either way."

"Unless you go before Dalton come."

"What? He's already here. Didn't I tell you that? He's not leaving here without his money."

Amato opened his hands. "So, you pay the money they took."

"I don't have it."

"You don't save?"

"That's my money, Reggie. What I have is mine and it ain't much. Not what Dalton is expecting. I never skimmed from Dalton."

"Then you run."

"You have enough to lend me?"

"Where'm I getting it? Don't be stupid, boss."

"Don't call me stupid."

"Sorry, boss."

"The fuck am I gonna do?"

"Can you borrow?"

"From who?"

"No loan shark in town?"

"You mean Shylocks?"

"Same thing, boss. You know any?"

"No, not really."

"Nobody?"

"The fuck am I gonna do, Reggie? Dalton and them, they're cartel people. The shit they do to people is crazy."

"I hear bear story."

"What? What bear story?"

"Somebody inside tells me. They tied one guy to a tree in Yellowstone? The park with the wild animal? They tied him to a tree and leave him for the wolves and *come si dice* . . . grizzly bears?"

Curly stepped back and spewed.

"Jesus, boss, you okay?"

Curly spewed a few more times before experiencing dry heaves. It took a few minutes for him to regain his composure, but he was still upset.

"What you think I should do, Reggie? Seriously?"

"If you don't have money? Get out of Yankton. You have family somewhere?"

"Texas."

"Too close to the border, eh? Any friends east? West Coast has too many Mexicans too."

"Not really. Shit. What do I use for money? I have some but not enough to hold out for long."

"If you need to get out, take it all. Maybe get out of the country. Canada maybe. Don't tell me, though. They tie me to a tree, I talk."

"Fuck."

"How much you have for this Dalton?"

"Little more than half."

"What number is?"

"Seveny-six hundred."

"Ming," Amato said. "How much normal is?"

"Ten thousand. Close to ten."

"You're short before?"

Curly was sweating. He looked about to cry. "Not like this," he said, "but I told him I would have it. Fuck me."

"You have seventy-six, you can go."

"Where?"

"Away from here, boss."

"Maybe I stay where Dog used to live. Near there."

"Sure, why not?" Amato said.

Ten minutes later, Curly was on his way and Amato couldn't believe how much he'd misjudged Curly. If these were the morons the cartels were putting to work, they were doomed the same as the mafia back east. Sooner or later, they'd fall apart too.

When Amato returned to the trailer, Brenda Lee was on her cellphone. He kissed her on the cheek and headed for the bathroom. He could hear her giggling as he did his business, then washed his face and hands. When he returned to the kitchen, she was saying goodbye and then kissed the phone.

He waited for her attention. "Who that is you kiss?"

"Jealous?"

"Who?"

"My cousin in North Dakota. Cecily. I told her about you."

"No, *Bella*, don't say this."

"Why not?"

"Is no good."

"Why?"

"Trust me, *Bella*. Please, no more about me to anyone. Not even cousin."

Amato could tell she was upset. He said, "Someday I tell you everything. I promise."

"When?"

"Soon."

She frowned.

"Can we make love now?" he said.

"Make love or fuck?"

"Don't say this, *Bella*, please. No fuck. Make love. We make love. I love you, *Bella*."

Her eyes filled with tears as he went to her for a kiss.

They made love there in the kitchen. He'd lifted her onto one of the cabinets and they did it there. She was crying as Amato told her again and again that he loved her.

Afterward, they sat in the living room and watched the local news. The temperature was going to dip below freezing overnight as the start of a cold front.

"I don't know I like it's so cold," he said.

"Me neither, but that's the weather around here," she said. "Winters can be brutal."

"I like sometimes, but no all the time."

"I like the beach, but I haven't seen one in ages, and I never used my passport."

"Ah, *spiaggia*. The beach. In Italy, in Pescara near where I am born, is beautiful. *Bella*, like you."

She hugged him tightly. "I thought you weren't going to tell me about you yet."

"Maybe a little, eh?"

She kissed him passionately on the mouth. When they stopped, she said, "Don't tell me anything else yet. I want to picture that place you said."

"Pescara."

"Yeah, Pescara. I wish I could roll my r's like that."

"I teach you, eh?"

"I love you, Reggie Amato."

"I love you, *Bella*."

PART II

FOUR

Charlie Bruno, a soldier in the Cirelli crime family, sat in the front passenger seat of a Buick Encore GX and handed Special Agent Brian Fein two mini-cassette tapes.

"What's with these?" Fein said. "You have a body mic."

"Couldn't trust a receiver," Bruno said with a smile. "You know, I'm in and out of a place. I knew once Grasso said he needed a lift, it meant he was heading to Hoboken to get his rocks. He's in the house and I'm outside in my car. This way I get whatever he says while he's with me. No interference and whatnot."

Fein was waiting for more. Bruno laughed.

"Something funny," Fein said.

"I think so," Bruno said. "Grasso's *cumare's* on there."

"What? Why?"

"Because I caught her giving me the eye."

"What?"

"You'll see."

Fein huffed. "What will I see?" he said. "Come on, Charlie, I have something to do after this."

"Fine, relax," Bruno said. "I picked up Grasso at her place over in Jersey. They've been an item for many years now and I think he thinks she's loyal. I dropped him and picked him up there many times."

"Don't you guys have associates for chauffeurs?"

"I do. Grasso was a skipper and now he's an underboss. He has guys like me. Made guys do his driving. Sometimes I bring one of my associates with me, but Grasso doesn't like it. Prefers his privacy."

"There a point to this?"

"I'll skip the particulars. His *cumare* gave me the eye more than once. This time I went back after dropping Grasso off back in Brooklyn."

"For sloppy seconds. Besides risking your life, what's funny about that?"

"I think the wire picked up her slurping."

Fein looked askance at Bruno.

"I didn't go back for Grasso's sloppy seconds," Bruno said, then pumped a fist alongside his face and pushed his left cheek out with his tongue. "I went back for a blowjob. Grasso bragged about her hummers enough it made me curious."

"You were still risking your ass."

"Only if I got caught."

"You wanna be a pussy hound, Charlie, knock yourself out. Just be careful it doesn't get you in the shit."

"Frankly, I forgot I was wired until she's opening my pants. I got the thing tucked under my balls. Then I thought I'd treat you to something extra and activate it. I had to tell her to keep her hands off my nuts. She went down on me sideways onna couch. Hands free."

Bruno laughed when Fein cringed at what he'd just heard.

"You should see your face right now," Bruno said.

"You're a sick fuck," Fein said. "You get caught with your dick in Grasso's girlfriend you won't be laughing for long. What's on the other tape."

"Some back and forth with Grasso about Rapino. Then me and the kid I proposed, Fred Greco."

"What's Grasso's obsession with Rapino about?"

"Claims he's got a guy inside the prison bureau. Something like that. Claims Rapino was moved."

"Inside the prison bureau? Grasso's guy or yours?"

"I don't have that kind of clout."

Fein frowned.

"I don't," Bruno said. "I'm just another spoke in the wheel, boss."

"You run a big enough gambling operation with players using aliases," Fein said. "Or they'd be playing on the Internet and not with your office. You still have those players. Maybe it's time you turn over their names?"

Bruno said, "You think I care what their names are?"

"Yeah, I do. So do we care. So, off the top of my head ... Boca, Marlboro, Seinfeld, Baby Powder and Orange. Get me the names behind those names."

"You lazy or something? All your resources, you can't find them?"

"Guys calling in their action on burners or having others call for them? Just get the names, Charlie. I want them next time we meet."

"Okay," Bruno said. "I still think you're gonna enjoy that other tape more."

"Listening to you get a blowjob? I don't think so. In fact, I think you're giving me one right now. Those names I just mentioned, all multi-dime bettors seven days of the week with your office. You want us in your corner the time comes, you're gonna have to produce."

"Fine," Bruno said. "And if it turns up a judge or Congressman or some other prominent citizen is one of the names, remember I warned you."

"Please," Fein said. "Save that bullshit for your priest someday. If the Borgata you swore an oath to has somebody inside the Federal Bureau of Prisons, we want to know who it is. That clear enough for you?"

"Okay, but you gotta let me know if you spring a woody once you listen to that broad swallow. It's impressive, man."

"Go fuck yourself, Charlie."

Fred Greco, Paul Winkler and Larry Levy were all 28 years old and had been friends since high school. Two of them, Paul and Larry, had gone to college. Paul quit after two years and worked a few odd jobs before making deliveries for a local pizza parlor and pushing marijuana. Larry graduated from Brooklyn College with a BA in American history, had applied and was accepted to three law schools shortly before a fistfight landed him in prison for 15 months. Fred was living off permanent disability from a fall off a ladder while working construction. It was a bogus claim his mob sponsor had arranged for a fifty-dollar kickback every pay period. Fred also earned off the street with a bookmaking sheet and with small street loans to gamblers and those desperate enough to pay 3% weekly interest on borrowed money. The occasional score from robbing drug dealers or robbing in general was also income Fred never had to claim with the IRS.

Paul and Fred were married, although lately Paul had been having issues at home. He'd become suspicious his wife was having an affair and had been in a generally bad mood since finding a condom in her purse a few days earlier.

Larry had never married and currently worked driving auto parts for one of Fred's salvage yard connections. He lived with his girlfriend in her apartment.

Today they were in Fred's basement having a fast-food lunch with sodas packed in an ice bucket while they watched cable news. Fred was a spoken for associate of the Cirelli crime family and had been given a job that could move him up the mob ladder, what he'd been told by his sponsor, Charlie Bruno, a made man. Although Fred couldn't tell his two friends what the job entailed, he had started to give his friends a disingenuous overview of the job when a news report on the television caught Paul's eye.

Fred was about to turn the television off when Paul waved at him to leave it on. All three watched the news report about the war in Gaza until it was over and an insurance commercial began. Fred used the remote to turn the television off.

"What?" Larry said to Paul before taking a bite of his hamburger.

"What, what?" Paul said. "What do I make of it? Nothing. Those people, they're fucking animals. Israel needs to wipe them out already."

"Oy vey," Larry said.

"Oy vey your ass," Paul said.

Larry rolled his eyes.

Paul pointed at Larry. "Don't start with your liberal bullshit, Larry."

"If you had a clue, Fonzalla you wouldn't be such a dumbski," Larry said with a smile.

"Right, like you know."

Larry had dubbed the nickname Fonzie on Paul because of his last name, the same last name as the actor, Henry Winkler, the guy who portrayed the popular character from the television show that ran from the mid 70's to the mid 80's, *Happy Days*.

The nickname stuck, although neither Paul nor Fred liked it. Larry used it to get under Paul's skin, using several Yiddish variations of it.

Fred was getting tired of the bickering and let them know. "Give it a break already, okay?" he said. "We have business to discuss."

Paul thumbed at Larry, said, "Tell the fucking libtard over there."

"I'm telling you both."

Larry, still smiling, said, "Actually, Fonzalla, they all got along before our people decided Israel should become a Nazi state. So, now they are, and with America's help."

Paul's face distorted as if he were in pain. "The fuck you talkin' about?"

"It's over your head," Larry said, "but you heard me."

"They're savages, those people. Who cares Palestinians get whacked?"

Fred rolled his eyes. He started to say something when Larry interrupted him.

"Whacked? Try and remember you're one of us chosen types. We don't talk like Fred. Leave the whack talk to the Dagos."

Fred chuckled in spite of his frustration. "Hey, fuck you," he said.

"I've been there, boychick," Paul said. "To Israel. Palestinians are fuckin' terrorists. Fuckin' animals."

Larry laughed.

"That's funny, huh?" Paul said.

"You were there, why don't you talk like you were there. Call them tehwowists. It's a big show they put on to get you to move there, that birthright bullshit, but don't kid yourself, my good mensch, Fonzi, I'm telling you it's a mind fuck."

"You know what you are?" Paul said.

"Let me guess," Larry said. He closed his eyes and feigned thinking, then said, "A self-hating Jew?"

Paul said. "Yeah, that's right. That's your problem."

Fred wiped his mouth with a paper towel. "Okay, that's enough already," he said. "We got this job I wanna go over and we have a collection to make over in Queens. None of us here are politicians, okay? Whatever the fuck is going on over there, it's none of our business."

Paul thumbed at Larry, "Thinks he's a hotshot because he finished college."

Larry winked at Fred, then thumbed at Paul and said, "Thinks he's a rabbi because he went to Hebrew school."

"Fuck you," Paul said.

Larry raised his hands in surrender. "Easy does it, boychick. Fonzalla, I mean you know disrespect."

"We're gonna throw down you keep that Fonzalla bullshit up."

Fred lost it. "Jesus fuckin' Christ already! Can you two quit it for now?"

"Yeah," Paul said, "anything but listenin' to this putz."

"Okay?" Fred asked Larry.

"Sure," Larry said, then winked at Fred. "Shoot."

Fred and Maria Greco met 13 years ago in high school. Maria was three years younger than Fred and had been a high school sophomore when he proposed. She had been a cheerleader and a good student. The two fell in love over the Christmas holidays and using a phony driver's license for Maria that Fred had bought from a connection, and against her families' wishes, the young couple eloped and were married in Las Vegas.

At first her parents refused to accept her husband, claiming she'd been tricked and stolen from them, but when Maria was pregnant within the first year, her mother, anxious for a grandchild, came to accept their marriage.

Maria lost the baby in vitro and would suffer two more miscarriages over the next three years before finally giving birth ten months ago.

Named after his father, something Maria insisted on, their son was nicknamed Junior. Although her parents still harbored resentment for her husband, the boy was their only grandchild, and they tolerated their son-in-law once Junior was born.

While Fred sometimes engaged in extramarital affairs, he remained dedicated to his son and was very protective of his wife. When he returned home after doing a collection job in Queens, Maria Greco was cooking their dinner. He watched her stirring the *pasta e piselli* at the stove and said, "Hey."

Maria turned to him with a smile but could tell he wasn't in a good mood. He went straight to their son in a highchair at the kitchen table, kissed his forehead, and then sniffed at something foul.

"Junior smells," he said.

"I'll change him soon as I'm finished here," Maria said. "Unless you want to do it."

"Yeah, right," he said, then headed for the bathroom.

The timer sounded and Maria turned the gas jets off. She used potholders to bring the pot to the sink and pour the Ditalini into the colander. She held the colander up and bounced the pasta a few times before pouring it back into the pot. She turned the gas off under the pot where the onions and peas had been simmering in olive oil, then poured the contents into the pasta and stirred again.

When Fred returned, Maria had already set a bowl of the *pasta e piselli* at his place at the table.

"Cheese," he said.

Maria went to the refrigerator and grabbed a tub of Locatelli Pecorino Romano grated cheese before heading to the silverware drawer for a spoon.

Fred glanced at his wife's perky ass and smiled. She had gained weight after giving birth but had lost most of it. It was the back of her thighs that had retained what was left to lose. He avoided looking at the cellulite that had begun to form there.

He was about to add cheese to his pasta when he sniffed his son's shit.

"I can't eat with him smelling like this," he said.

"I only have two hands," Maria said, then took their son out of the highchair and walked him into the bathroom.

Fred spread the cheese on his pasta, mixed it with his spoon. He began to eat, thinking he'd been too harsh with his wife. When she returned with their son, she sat the child in the highchair before sitting herself. Fred grabbed her hand and pulled her to him for a kiss. He made it a good one and grabbed her ass with his free hand.

"That was nice," Maria said.

"Sorry," he said. "I had a shit day with the guys."

"Larry and Paul?" Maria said.

"Those two, they're like cats and dogs. I know what's bothering Paul, but then Larry eggs him on and it's impossible to keep them focused."

"Maybe you shouldn't take them where you're going."

"I wouldn't if I could handle it alone. I need them now."

Maria said, "Paul still thinks his wife is fooling around?"

"And it's making him crazy and me sick of his mood swings. You'd think he was some broad with a period."

Maria chuckled, saw he was serious, then said, "Sorry."

"And then I gotta deal with Charlie Bruno and all his secrets," Fred said. "I mean, he tells me we gotta do something out of town, but he don't tell me where. He says it's serious, but he can't tell me until we're ready to go. When the fuck that is, who knows?"

"You can always step away from it all. My father said he'd show you the business."

Fred held both hands up. "Let's not go there again, okay? I wanted to be a plumber, I would'a went to plumber's school."

Maria chuckled again.

"What's funny?"

"Daddy didn't go to plumber's school, hon. I'm sure they have them now, but plumbing is something you learn little by little on the job."

"Good to know for my next life. Meantime, I have a job. A few jobs, come to think of it, or we couldn't have afforded this house. Maybe your old man is a little jealous."

Maria rolled her eyes when Fred wasn't looking. She wasn't as nervous as her parents about the people her husband dealt with, but she was concerned about their future should anything go wrong. She knew he was involved with the mob and she feared him being killed, but the chance he'd go to prison someday was also on her mind. Her father had warned her several times about winding up a single parent without a source of income if Fred did wind up in jail someday.

Fred said, "Anyway, Charlie has me running in circles and I think he's fucking me with money again."

"What he do now?"

Maria waited, but Fred went silent while he ate two more spoons of pasta. She stirred the *pasta e piselli* into a small bowl for her son, then sprinkled cheese on top, then stirred it with her spoon.

She was about to feed Junior when Fred said, "He's paying us with the money I gave him from another job."

"I don't understand," Maria said.

"He's jerking me off."

Maria frowned. It was her husband's way of explaining half of what was bothering him whenever he was upset with the mobster he reported to. She knew he didn't want her to know his business, but sometimes he'd say what was on his mind, whether she understood what he was talking about or not. She also knew when not to push him.

"Should I change the subject?" she said.

"Don't be cute, Maria."

"I'm just saying."

"Don't say it. I have to eat it for now, at least until I get made, but he'll probably be a skipper when that happens. If it happens."

Then she pushed it anyway. "How do you know—"

"The money he gave me for this next job, I recognized one of the bills. Same cash we made off the last job. He's a fuckin' thief, Charlie Bruno is."

Maria huffed.

"What?" Fred said.

"I hate to see you so frustrated. You could walk away, hon. You could do something else."

"Like what? I'm too far down the road now to walk away. Our income is dependent on it now. There's no making bigger money without being made. Until then I have to eat his shit and smile while I'm doing it."

They went through the rest of their dinner in silence. Maria was washing the dishes when the baby began to cry. Fred took him out of the high chair and walked him into the living room. Fifteen minutes later, Maria joined them after she finished in the kitchen. Fred was on the couch cradling Junior in his arms.

Maria rushed back to the kitchen to retrieve her cellphone. She returned to the living room and snapped a few pictures of her husband and son.

Fred said, "This one isn't getting involved."

Maria said, "I hope not."

"He's not. I'll break his legs first."

"Maybe let him finish school and figure it out for himself instead?"

Fred smiled.

"I love how close you are to him," she said.

"He's my son," Fred said.

Larry Levy was checking what he'd packed into a suitcase when his girlfriend returned from work and stepped inside their bedroom.

"You're leaving tonight?" Maryanne Kelly said.

"Tomorrow night," he said. "Fred'll be picking up Paul, then me."

"Isn't Paul a little out of his way? Why him first?"

"Please, thank God he's picking up Paul first. I get the backseat to myself."

Maryanne stretched her arms out to her sides and yawned. "I wish you weren't going," she said.

"It's money, Maryanne. I can't turn it down right now."

"Yeah, but you're going with two knuckleheads that can get you in trouble," she said, then moved to the end of the bed alongside the suitcase.

She wasn't a fan of Fred or Paul. She didn't like Fred because he'd once hit on her while Larry wasn't home. She felt bad for his wife. She didn't like Paul because she thought he was too macho, too stupid, and too sure of himself. She also knew that Larry felt the same way about Paul, but couldn't let go of the fact they'd been friends since they were young.

What she wanted was to get married already. She and Larry met at the law office where she worked as a legal secretary. Larry was there for a consultation with one of the criminal attorneys at the firm. That day the attorney was busy, and Larry had spent nearly an hour sitting across from Maryanne's desk waiting. The two began to chat and then flirted and she gave him her number on his way out after his consultation. That was a few months after Larry had been released from prison. They moved in together a few months later.

Now that she'd been promoted to executive secretary and was working for one of the big shots at the firm, a partner specializing in white collar crime, she made good money and had excellent benefits. All Larry needed to do was marry her and he'd be covered medically.

Maryanne knew that the longer he worked for or with his two friends, the better the chance he would return to prison. She also knew when he was bullshitting her about some of the things he did with his friends.

"And don't think for a second that I believe it's to deliver something to somebody," she said. "There are way too many ways to do something like that without requiring three guys and seven days to do it. I'm not like your friends' wives, Larry. I know when something smells."

"Not if what we're delivering is valuable."

"Yeah, like cocaine or gold bars somebody robbed from a bank or some shit? You get stopped along the way, you're back in prison. Delivery like that?"

"I promise you we're not delivering stolen money."

"Then drugs? Is it drugs you'll be driving wherever you're going?"

"No."

"But you can't tell me."

"No, I can't. And that's for your protection."

"Please."

They had been together for almost two years, during which Larry had worked at several different jobs, mostly off the books, until Fred hooked him up driving, delivering and picking up car parts for a connected mob car lot. He'd been without insurance for several years. A year ago, when one of his teeth had abscessed, Larry had Fred Greco pull it with pliers. The infection that ensued cost him more than $800 he didn't have. Maryanne had paid the bill.

"I'm tired of being broke," he said. "My record keeps me from getting legitimate work with benefits. The hell am I supposed to do?"

"Am I complaining about it?" Maryanne said. "You make what you can. I don't care. We're not rich, but we're not starving either. I don't mind and I hate that you feel you have to be the breadwinner. I make enough for us."

"I don't have to be the breadwinner, but I can't be a deadbeat either."

"If we get married, I can put you on my insurance, damn it. You know this, but you don't want to get married. That's crazy."

"Not yet I don't, no. I don't want charity."

Maryanne stood up off the bed. "Jesus Christ, Larry! Listen to yourself. You're going to risk going back to prison because you have to play macho man? Those two, Fred and Paul, they're nothing more than another arrest waiting to happen."

Larry rubbed his face with both hands.

"Well?" Maryanne said.

Larry held his arms out to his sides. "What, Maryanne? What do you want me to do? You wanna get married so I have insurance coverage? Fine. Soon as I'm back from this, which pays a few grand, we'll get married. Okay? At least then I can pay for our wedding dinner, the two of us, not some dumbass reception."

"I'd rather we get married now and you don't go wherever those idiots are taking you."

"They're my friends, Maryanne. Lifelong friends, and Fred's connections have been allowing me to contribute here. I can pay for my own gas when I have to drive somewhere. I don't have to ask you for a ten or twenty. Until there's something better, I do shit with Fred so I can contribute to our lives, yours and mine. You don't get to ignore that."

Maryanne put both hands up. "Fine," she said. "But only if we get married when you get back. Make that a promise, Larry. I mean it."

They continued staring at one another, neither yielding until Maryanne frowned and left their bedroom.

"Where the fuck were you?" Paul Winkler asked his wife.

He was packing a duffle bag with the clothes he'd need for the trip he was taking with Fred Greco and Larry Levy the next night. Lately Sharon had been late home from work, sometimes several hours late. Tonight was like that. It was nearly nine o'clock and she'd just come home.

She knew her husband would be packing to leave for a few days, maybe longer, he'd said, and she wasn't around to help. When Paul saw she was high, he lost his temper.

"The fuck is with you?" he said. "Getting high is so important now? I thought you were working?"

"Relax," she said with a look of disgust. "We smoked on the way home."

"We? Who the fuck is we?"

"Me and Liz. She's a friend from the office. We're working on the same project."

"Project, huh?"

"That's what they're called, Paul. It's intense work, very stressful, so we get high on the way home to relax."

"I find out you're fucking around, Sharon, I'll kill you and whoever it is you're fucking."

"Oh, Jesus, stop it already. You're not killing anybody. There's nobody to kill. I wish you'd get over yourself already. I'm not fucking around on you."

"You fucking better not be."

Sharon retreated to the kitchen for a soda. She needed to get into the shower before he tried to strip search her again. He'd done it twice so far, but both times after she'd showered at a motel before heading home. Today, after work, she'd gone with her boss into a storage closet and fucked there. Now she knew she was leaking. She had made the same mistake 10 days ago when she fucked in a car and had to go home with semen-stained panties. That time she'd tried to bury the panties in the hamper, but Paul had taken the laundry out searching for a favorite T-shirt of his and when he spilled the hamper's contents on the bathroom floor, there they were, her semen-stained panties.

When he confronted her, Sharon told him it was from a medicine she was using for vaginal discharge, a lie she'd learned on a public Internet website. Paul didn't have a clue what she was talking about until she showed him her container of AZO pills.

Paul went to open the container and realized it had never been open before. He thought her having the vaginal medicine was a preemptive excuse. When Sharon told him it was a new supply she'd bought, he still didn't believe her and shoved a threatening finger in her face. "I'll shoot you in the fucking face," he'd told her. "I swear it."

It had scared her enough to not answer. Most times she fought him tooth and nail, but Paul had scared her that day. Now she knew the best way to calm him down was with a blowjob, but he'd become so paranoid and repulsive lately, she couldn't do it.

"I was working late," she said instead. "I'm sorry you don't believe me, but it's true."

She'd come home wearing a short rabbit jacket over a white turtleneck, a short skirt, and thigh-high black leather boots. Now she was changing into her pajamas. Paul picked up her short skirt and held it out to her.

"This makes you look like a hooker."

"Oh, stop it."

"Stop what? You dress like you're looking to get laid."

"Don't be stupid."

Paul pointed his finger in her face again. "Don't call me stupid!"

Sharon ducked his finger and backed away. "What's the big deal. I'm here now."

"I swear to God, Sharon, I find out you're fucking around on me, I'll kill you myself when I get back."

Sharon changed the subject and said, "Did you make a checklist to pack?"

"What?"

"A checklist. Are you sure you packed everything you need?"

"I think so. I didn't make a list."

"Then let me ask. Socks?"

"Yeah. I got'em."

"Underwear?"

"Check."

"T-shirts?"

"Check."

"Pants and shirts?"

"Check."

"Jacket?"

"I'll wear one."

"Bathroom stuff?"

"I'll take those last."

"You have money?"

"Yeah."

"Can you leave me some?"

"Why, so you can get high?"

"No, so I can buy groceries to eat and pay the rent. It's due in three days."

"Shit, I forgot. Yeah, I'll leave you enough."

"Can you leave extra, just in case you're late getting back?"

"Extra. Sure. Can you give me a goodbye blowjob?"

"I'm tired, Paul."

"Come on, I'm gonna miss you."

"Sure you are."

"The hell does that mean?"

"You like to accuse me, but how do I know what you and your two friends are gonna do? I don't even know where you're going? You're gonna tell me you won't stop at some strip joint, maybe call a couple escorts? Don't deny it because I won't believe it."

Paul frowned.

"Well?" she said.

"Well what?" he said, then, "Come on, Sharon. I got blue balls already."

"How much extra can you leave me?"

"Are you serious?"

"You said I looked like a hooker. How about you pay me?"

Paul thumbed toward the kitchen. "Why don't you get the fuck out of here now and let me finish packing? You can blow me later."

"I will," she said as she left him in the bedroom. "If you leave me an extra hundred in case you get lost coming home."

Paul stared at her ass until he noticed she raised her right arm over her head and was giving him the finger.

FIVE

Charlie Bruno had pointed at the stacks of cash on the card table and said, "That's ten thousand there, kid. Understand that's unheard of, what I'm doin' here, paying up front. Our people want it done. It's a new administration and it needs to show it has stones."

"That's not a problem," Fred Greco said. "You point and I shoot."

That was a few days ago. Charlie Bruno was 50 years old and seeking a bump-up to captain within the Cirelli crime family. He was also a criminal informant for the FBI's Organized Crime Task Force. On word from one of the gamblers placing bets through his office, Bruno learned the whereabouts of a former Cirelli soldier who'd testified against higher-ups in the same crime family. Since there was a new boss of the crime family, strict enforcement of traditional mob rules had returned. Bruno was hoping to capitalize on taking out Giovanni Rapino, the soldier whose testimony had sealed the fate of two captains, an underboss, the former boss, and a host of other soldiers and associates.

Because he needed the credit within the organization, Bruno had shared the information with his former skipper, now the underboss of the family, Umberto Grasso. Although he had no delusions about the potential of the government pulling the plug on his informant status, Bruno also knew they were anxious to have somebody atop a mob ladder, someone they could use to take down the leaders of the other four crime families. Other higher-ups in the mob had done it before, getting protection while earning and knowing they would have an out when push came to shove and the federal prosecutors were ready to make their cases. The key was dragging it out and putting away as much coin as possible in the process.

Also getting laid. Charlie Bruno liked the ladies and was a well-known pussy-hound.

He'd smiled at one of a few protégé associates under his control, when Fred Greco said he'd kill for Bruno.

"That's cute," Bruno had said. "I point, you shoot. That's very cute. You wanna sound like a tough guy. I can understand that, but don't kid yourself with this, Freddy, my boy. It's an opportunity. A good one, but this guy, Rapino? He's nobody's fool. Whatever name they gave him now, the feds, they'll also do something with his appearance. We know he's the same build from our people in the system, which is lean and muscular, but maybe he grew a beard, shaved his head, whatever. The verification is on you, kid. No fuckups. You get this done, it's a step up. You fuck it up, you might as well stay out there in South Dakota, wherever the fuck he is."

"I understand," Fred said, then turned to the money still on the table and frowned.

Two weeks ago, after a score that his cousin, a dirty cop, tipped him off to, Fred and his friends robbed a pair of drug dealers of exactly $22,000. He'd counted the stash twice himself. He could see the hundred-dollar bill on the top of one of the stacks on the table was one he recognized from a torn corner and ink stain. He'd given Bruno $10,000 as tribute and lied about the total take being only $20,000.

He saw he was being paid with some of the money he'd stolen from the drug dealers. It was another lesson about the life of crime he'd chosen. It was a back-and-forth endless cycle of scams within a nest of vipers.

"What?" Bruno said when he saw Fred's frown. "What's wrong?"

Fred gave it less than a few seconds of thought before lying again and saying, "It's more than enough. I got two guys I'm gonna bring with me, but we're gonna drive to make the money stretch."

"Which two?"

"Paul Winkler and Larry Levy. You've met them."

"The kid you call the Fonz? That one?"

"That's Paul. People call him that, the Fonz, because of his last name. Same as the actor who played Fonzi, Henry Winkler."

"He's the one you say has the blowjob wife, no? Lives on Flatlands Avenue?"

"Flatbush Avenue, yeah. Near King's Plaza. Sharon. She's good. Really good. She's the best head I ever had and I heard the same thing from another guy was with her. She's like a vacuum cleaner."

"Careful your friend doesn't find out."

"I'm careful. So's she. Paul is a cheap fuck with her, so I drop her a few bucks after she blows me, or we fuck."

"That's smart, but you know the rules, right? Not just the ones about fucking somebody else's wife."

"No, I know, but Paul and Larry are Jewish. Associates is all they can ever be."

"I'm talking about another rule," Bruno said. "An unwritten rule. Always best to do something on your own, especially a hit. You bring help, they become a risk. What they do with you is something they can trade with the feds if or when they get pinched for something else."

Fred waited for more.

"Understand what I'm saying here?"

"Yeah," Fred said.

"Okay, then, you were told. I assume you're paying them, Fonzi and Larry."

Fred had pointed to the money. "From that, sure."

"I hope you can trust them."

"I do. We're friends forever, since we're kids."

"You know how many guys claim the same thing until one of their friends for life gets pinched and decides to rat? They're involved in this, a hit, you better be sure they'll hold their water. Honestly, I don't know I'd tell them until we were there. You tell them beforehand, they may not wanna go along, but then they'll have it on you either way."

Fred remained silent.

"Divide it however you want," Bruno said, "but if you change your mind and think one of them can't hold his water if he gets pinched for something else, he needs to bargain, consider leaving him or the both of them out West. It's the safe way to handle this kind of business, kid."

Fred swallowed hard. What Bruno said was something Fred couldn't imagine but was coming to understand was the world he'd chosen.

"You gonna drive, you better get going," Bruno said. "Our people said he was transferred out of Kentucky a couple, three months ago. They tracked him to this other place in South Dakota, but they can move him again. Our guy inside the Federal Bureau of Prisons loses track and you guys can't find him, it's over and I want that money back."

"We're gonna leave in a couple days. We all have things to take care of before we go."

"You might miss him."

"Airfare out west is too expensive. All three of us drive, so we'll take turns and make it in a day, day and a half."

Bruno hesitated before nodding. Then he took a moment while he looked at his cellphone and said, "He's in South Dakota. Yankton, South Dakota. They call it a camp. Federal prison camp. It's where they serve soft time, rats like Rapino. This one's in Yankton, South Dakota."

That conversation had taken place two days before he'd met with Larry Levy and Paul Winkler about the trip they had to make. It still burned Fred about being paid with money he'd already turned over in tribute. Charlie Bruno was exactly what Fred was learning about most wiseguys. They were greedy fucks and there was no way to trust them.

As much as he didn't want to believe Bruno about his friends being potential rats against him, Fred understood why he couldn't mention anything to Larry or Paul until the last minute. He hadn't told Larry or Paul what they were heading west to do, just that it was an important trip for important people, and that they'd have to stay sharp. He'd let them know about the hit when it was time, not a minute before.

Now he felt guilty about passing off information about Paul's wife's ability to swallow a load, but he knew it was one way to put a smile on Charlie Bruno's face. It wasn't a secret about Bruno and the loose snatch he chased. Word on the street was he was hung like a horse and took great pride in fucking as much strange as he could if they met his standards, which weren't very high when he was drunk or in the mood. There was a story about him being so cockeyed drunk one night, he'd given a 68-year-old, toothless barfly a fifty for a blowjob in his car. It was one of those rumors joked about behind his back.

As far as Paul's marital problems, both Fred and Larry had often discussed their friend's obsession with the woman he'd married. Both knew that Sharon Winkler wasn't the right woman for their friend. She had a reputation going back to high school, which included a rumored blowbang involving several players on their high school basketball team. What Sharon saw in Paul had to do with him being a handsome kid who could handle himself and had developed street cred as a tough guy. The girls Sharon hung out with were envious of her choice of badass. Paul's reputation in their neighborhood had been building and the nickname he'd been tagged with from the old television series, *Happy Days*, was attractive to the woman he eventually married.

According to Paul, he and Sharon dated a couple of times before she gave it up, at which time Paul fell in love with her. Whether she had tricked him into believing she was a virgin, or he was embarrassed to admit she wasn't, once they were married, he'd become overly possessive. Sharon was a street-smart girl and was experienced in the ways of male manipulation. She certainly knew how to handle guys like her husband. She knew when to let Paul vent, when to let him rant, and how to calm his ass back down, leaving him more desperate to keep her with him every time.

Larry didn't know that Fred had been with Sharon Winkler himself. That started four months ago when the couple, their wives and Larry's girlfriend included, went to Riis Park for a seafood barbecue on the beach. Somebody had told Fred one of his tires was flat and Sharon Winkler waited long enough for no one to notice how she made her way to the parking lot where Fred was changing the tire. When he saw her standing there while he removed the jack from the trunk, he said, "Come to help?"

"Get in the back seat," she said.

"What?"

"You want a blowjob or not?"

They had been meeting whenever it was convenient without raising suspicion ever since, usually when Fred had sent Paul on a job far enough away to stop at their apartment or a motel for a quickie. The last time was a week ago at a motel in Sheepshead Bay.

Telling Charlie Bruno about Sharon Winkler probably wasn't a good idea. Bruno might take a shot at Sharon while her husband was away, and if Paul ever found out, there wasn't much his friend could do about it, except to his wife.

Fred was supposed to see her before picking up Paul for their trip to South Dakota. He became excited thinking about her, but when Sharon called to verify their tryst, she said she had to go straight home because Paul was acting like the gestapo lately.

"You think he suspects us?" Fred had said.

"No, I don't think so," Sharon said. "Not us, but his radar is up and it's not worth he doesn't go with you guys and stays home to torture me."

"Okay," Fred had told her. "I'll see you when we get back."

"Bye," she said, sounding slightly upbeat again.

Now he was on his way to picking up her husband, his friend since they were kids. Fred closed his eyes and imagined her thick lips around his cock and became excited all over again.

"You don't look happy," Fred Greco said.

Paul Winkler frowned.

"What?" Fred said. "Don't let him get you crazy, Paulie. Larry likes to break balls. You two shouldn't talk politics anyway. The fuck good is ever gonna come from it?"

"Fuck Larry," Paul said. "It's my wife. Fucking cunt is making me nuts."

"Time of the month?"

"I wish. I think she's steppin' out on me."

"Sharon? No way. No fuckin' way. Where the hell do you get this shit from?"

"I don't know. It's a feeling. I know something's up."

"Hey, you need to get that shit out of your head, Paulie. This job we're on is no joke. I need you a hundred percent. You can't be thinking crazy shit about your wife now."

Paul nodded.

Fred frowned, said, "Okay?"

"Yeah, okay."

"Good."

Talking about Sharon with her husband was the last thing Fred needed. If Paul had finally figured out his wife was screwing around, Fred had to be extra careful once they were back home. In the meantime, Fred needed Paul to forget about his wife. Their business in South Dakota was too important to Fred's future with the mob.

"If I didn't love her so much, I'd dump her tomorrow," Paul said.

"She loves you too, you dumb shit," Fred said. "You're making something out of nothing."

"Maybe."

"Not maybe. Definitely."

Paul sighed.

"Just don't let Larry break your balls about politics again," Fred said. "We all need to be focused on this job. No fucking around. We all step up if we pull this off."

"Me and Larry are Jewish," Paul said. "How do we step up?"

"With me, you dumb fuck. We're a crew, no? You two are the lucky ones. You two get spared the organized crime squads. Once I get made, we're on the fast track to major coin and don't forget it."

Neither spoke until they stopped to pick up Larry Levy. Once he was in the car and they were on their way, the conversation turned to sports and the last few weeks before the NFL playoffs. Fred was relieved until Paul asked Larry if he'd bet on any of the games.

"Bills-Jets," Larry said.

"The Bills are choking dogs," Paul said. "When are you gonna learn?"

"They're at home and it's the friggin' Jets, Paulie."

"The Jets are immune to the cold."

"Josh Allen versus Zach Wilson? Are you serious?"

"Wilson already beat him the first game of the season. Josh Allen is a turnover machine."

"That was a fluke. Please."

Paul turned on his seat and grabbed his crotch. "Please this."

Larry chuckled. "You taking the Jets?" he said.

"You bet your ass I am."

"Then let's make the bet between us and save the loser's ten percent."

"Sure," Fred said, "cut my end out."

"Or we can bet something else," Larry said.

"I'm taking the Jets. We're' gonna sweep those choking dogs," Paul said.

"End of the season? Without Rogers?"

Paul turned to Fred. "Rogers went down after the fourth play of the game in September, and we still beat them," he said, then turned to Larry. "Your boy Allen threw how many picks that game? Three, in case you forgot."

Fred said, "Why don't you two make a gentleman's bet and leave money out of it?"

"We could do that," Larry said.

"Fuck that," Paul said. "Hundred bucks, but the Bills have to cover that stupid spread."

"They will. Done. Hundred bucks. No vig."

"Done," Paul said.

"Morons," Fred said.

Larry laughed. Paul shot him a dirty look, then turned to Fred again and said, "How long is this trip gonna take?"

"A week maybe," Fred said. "I'll drive through Pennsylvania, but one of you has to take over after. Might as well catch a nap if you can."

Larry said, "Let Paulie explain how Israel isn't committing genocide. That'll put me to sleep."

"Fuck you," Paul said.

Fred looked at Larry in the rearview mirror. "Jesus Christ," he said. "Do you have to start that shit now?"

"Sorry," Larry said, then smiled as he lay down on the back seat.

They had left Brooklyn close to midnight. Paul started calling his wife halfway through Pennsylvania. It was nearly six o'clock in the morning when he began complaining that his wife wasn't answering her phone. Both Fred and Larry tried to explain how it was too early in the morning and that maybe she had turned her phone off when she went to bed.

Paul wasn't hearing it. He tried every 30 minutes, then every 20 minutes until they were close to Ohio, when Fred pulled into a rest stop for gas and to switch drivers. Paul walked away from the gas pumps and tried calling his wife again. He was pacing the area with his cellphone to his right ear.

"He's out of control," Larry said.

"You think?" Fred said.

When they turned and looked for their friend again, Paul was out of their view.

"Go see where this nut went," Fred told Larry. "I can't take much more of his bullshit."

The entire time Paul was whining about his wife, Fred was both angry and excited. Sharon Winkler wasn't the type you married. That was Paul's problem. All Fred knew was that she was the best thing he'd ever had in bed, and he looked forward to seeing her again.

Now her crazy husband was making them lose time they couldn't afford to lose because he couldn't reach his wife on her cellphone, probably because she had kept her phone off while she was getting fucked by somebody else. Sharon Winkler was a looker and Fred thought maybe a sex addict too. He'd never been near a woman who craved sex as much as Sharon.

He looked out and saw Larry pulling Paul by the back of his shirt. As they approached the car, Paul twisted away from Larry and yelled, "Enough! Keep your hands off, fuck-face."

Paul sat in the back of the car and Larry sat up front this time. A long moment of silence passed.

Fred said, "Okay now? Can we get out of here?"

Larry thumbed back at Paul.

"What?" Fred said.

"He's hot about something," Larry said. "He almost got into it with some guy back there."

"The guy was a jerk-off," Paul said. "Jumped the line to take a piss. I saw it and stopped him."

"And then Paul was ready to take a swing."

"Guy deserved it."

Fred looked at Paul and said, "This what I think it's about? Still?"

"Yeah," Paul said. "I called her half a dozen times. She won't answer."

"Jesus Christ," Larry said.

"Hey, fuck you, Larry," Paul said. "She's my wife."

"Yeah, we know," Fred said.

"Fuck both of you."

"Down boy," Larry said. "We're just a little shocked here."

"Is this a private talk we're having here?" Fred said. "Because I don't care to hear the particulars and we got a fuckin' job to do another eight to ten hours from where we are now."

"I don't care anymore," Paul said. "Soon's we're back, I'm throwing her ass out."

Fred said, "Paul, not now, okay? I told you I need you sharp for this. Sharon isn't cheating on you. That's all in your head."

"Fuck it," Paul said, then opened his door, stepped out and walked across the parking lot again.

"Goddamn it!" Fred yelled.

He started to open his door when Larry grabbed his arm. "Let him go."

"What?"

"Give him ten minutes. Let him blow some steam."

"We have a job, Larry."

"Give him ten minutes, and we'll both go get him."

"And if he starts another fight and gets locked up?"

"Then we go on our own."

Fred huffed.

"What's this about anyway?" Larry said. "He figured out she's steppin' out? Took him long enough."

"Who fuckin' knows," Fred said. "You know the way he is. He loves her like crazy, but he's got his ways. I didn't think they'd last this long."

"She still loose or what?"

"The hell do I know? I knew a couple guys she's been with before Paul, but I wasn't telling him that. Maybe I should've."

"I don't know her well enough anymore," Larry said, "but back in the day . . . well, you know."

"What do I know?" Fred said a bit too defensively.

"Nothin', calm down," Larry said. "If Fonzi's mind is fucked because of her now, it won't do us any good later. Maybe we put him on a bus and send him back."

"Sure, waste another hour. And quit calling him Fonzi. He's Paul. Let the douchebags call him Fonzi."

"Fine."

Fred was watching Paul hold his cellphone to his ear again. "Maybe she answered," he said. "He isn't gonna help his case he starts cursing her out."

"Paulie can't help himself," Larry said. "He's too insecure to handle most things, never mind his wife."

Ten minutes later, Paul was still fuming when they approached him. He slipped his cellphone into his jacket pocket and said, "I'm going back."

"The fuck, Paulie," Fred said.

"She hung up on me, so I'm going back. I catch her in bed with somebody, I'll kill them both."

"And spend the rest of your life in jail?" Larry said.

"Fuck you. It's not your wife."

"You're serious?" Fred said.

"I'm going back," Paul said.

Larry said, "Let him, he wants to go."

"And how you gonna do that, Paulie?" Fred said. "How you getting home?"

"Just get me to the other side of the Interstate. Drop me there and I'll get back on my own."

"Jesus Christ," Fred said.

"Please, Fred," Paul said. "I can't think straight until I know what's going on."

"Fuck me."

"Please!"

Fred waved toward the car. "Then let's go and get it over with," he said.

"Thanks," Paul said.

"Shut up," Fred said.

Larry stayed up front with Paul in the back. They drove west another 30 minutes before they could turn around and head back.

When Fred pulled into the rest stop, he said, "You have enough money?"

"I got a couple hundred," Paul said.

"Motherfucker," Fred said. He pulled out his wallet and took two hundred dollar bills out. He handed them to Paul and said, "You owe me."

"No problem."

"No problem, except now I gotta add another two hours to our drive."

"I'm sorry, Fred. Really, I am."

"Get the fuck out. Get your shit out of the trunk."

Paul removed his suitcase and slammed the trunk. Fred burned rubber pulling away. He could see Paul waving at him in the rearview mirror. Fred held up a middle finger.

☐ ☐ ☐

Charlie Bruno had already made sure his recorder was working before he arrived at the social club on 18th Avenue in Brooklyn. The recorder was inside the lining of his winter coat. He also wore a gray sports jacket, a light blue shirt, black slacks, and black shoes. He exchanged a few cheek kisses with fellow wiseguys as he made his way to the back room where Umberto Grasso, the new underboss of the family, held court.

Bruno removed his heavy coat and draped it over the back of his chair before walking around the table to exchange a cheek kiss with Grasso.

"New?" Grasso said.

"Getting things in order," Bruno said.

"It's important you do. Our new regime is starting where the old one left off. It's going hardcore on the rules."

"Can't do it any other way anymore. My people know."

"Good," Grasso said before picking up his espresso cup. "Coffee?"

Bruno held up a hand. "I'm over caffeinated as it is. Thanks, no."

"You speak with our guy?"

"The gambler?"

"I did," Grasso said.

"And I talked with my guy," Bruno said. "He took a couple guys with him. Left last night, I think."

"This the kid you're sponsoring?"

"Freddy Greco, yeah."

"He don't know about our guy, I hope."

"No way."

"Because your guy in the office said the dumb fuck is dropping money left and right," Grasso said. "He comes in under different names and all, but he's getting sloppy. Bets everything. Baskets, hockey, college, the NFL. I told the dumb fuck, I said, slow the fuck down before you fuck yourself.'"

"He seemed cocky when we spoke."

"Tell me it was over a burner and not that fucking computer. Jerkoff sent something to the kid working the phones in a personal email, you can believe it. Just sports talk, which game he liked and whatnot, but still."

"That's crazy. Guy in his position? Which kid in the office?"

"Teddy. He's okay, the kid. Told me right away. I told him delete it and never open another one, the jerk does it again."

"Stupid fuck," Bruno said. "Any word on a location?"

Grasso sipped his coffee, then said, "There's no paperwork yet?"

Bruno frowned. "Not yet."

"Any idea when?"

"He says he's working on it. Gotta be a name change by now. I told them. Probably a beard, shaved head, something. They were told."

"I don't know I like it your guy is taking people with him."

"He's been warned."

"It's the safe move he goes it alone, no? I assume your guy knows the other two have to go."

"He's been told. Besides, I think he's banging one of their wives."

Grasso squinted. "You serious? Jesus."

"Supposed to be a hole, but one with a magic mouth."

"That's a strike against him right there, fuckin' a friend's wife. It's not a good selling point."

"The guy with the wife is Jewish, so he's not breaking any rules, but I warned him about that too. Besides, he can't handle what we gave him, it's not an issue."

"Well, you're my guy, Charlie. It's a bump up these kids pull it off."

"Still a long shot," Bruno said. "But there's nothing to lose."

"They fuck it up and get pinched there is."

"The kid, Greco, he's street smart. He knows the consequences."

"Long as you know it's on you."

"Absolutely. Trust me, I sniff something with the kid, I'll handle it myself."

Grasso winked at Bruno. "Then you can console his wife."

"Not, Greco's wife," Bruno said. "She's a good-looking broad too, but she gave birth a year ago or so. Not for me. Like I said, her husband, Fred, likes his friend's wife too much to bring her husband back. Jewish broad. She's a hot piece of ass."

"You test-drive her already?"

Bruno said, "Not yet, but somebody's gotta do it."

"Just be careful. Jealous husbands and all that."

"I know. I figure she must be out of her husband's league, the Jew broad. Even if they don't pull it off in South Dakota, dollars to donuts Fred comes back alone. At least not with the husband. Fonz they call him, Fred's friend with the wife. Fred told me she's the best blowjob he's ever had. I've had my share of world class BJs, believe me, but somebody has to verify things like that, the best ever stuff, right? Can't get into the Guinness Book of World Records without somebody verifies it."

"Or it's not an official magic mouth," Grasso said. "Sure."

"She gets my ten inches down her pipes without choking, she's in the book."

Grasso squinted as he thought a moment, then said, "Wasn't that Deep Throat broad a Jew?"

"Uh-uh," Bruno said. "Good little Catholic girl got herself knocked up before the porn stuff. The computer said her mother tricked her and had the baby adopted."

"What do you study this shit?"

"I'm an aficionado."

"Figures," Grasso said. "Jewish broads, at least back in my day, they did their practicing on gentiles to keep their cherries for the Jew doctors and lawyers. Giving head instead of getting laid before it pays."

"Yeah, it was the dumb Catholic girls got themselves knocked up with first timers. That said, today, the way things are, you'd be accused of being anti-Semitic for saying that about Jew girls."

"The fuck do I care, anti-Semitic. Best blowjob I ever had was from my Cuban broad over in Hoboken. Still the best. I suppose I've been with a Jewish broad or two over the years, none of them were anything special, nothing close to my Cuban. She can suck the chrome of a trailer hitch."

Bruno pointed at Grasso and said, "The Dice man."

"Guy had me on the floor back when he did those routines. Now he's almost respectable. Doin' movies, no less."

"Crazy, right?"

"What's he do for a living, the magic mouth's husband?"

"Fred takes care of him from time to time with shit I give Fred. His steady gig is delivering pizza, believe it or not."

"Jesus Christ, no wonder she's blowing everybody."

SIX

After they dropped off Paul, Larry drove into Iowa before he was too hungry to continue. He woke Fred up when he stopped at a gas station rest stop. Fred was still upset about Paul bailing on them.

"It's probably for the best," Larry said. "Whatever he's going through with his wife, his head isn't in the game. Paulie's never been very rational about anything."

Fred decided he had to tell Larry why they were going to South Dakota. He'd never told Larry or Paul the trip had to do with a hit. Killing Giovanni Rapino would put Fred in the on-deck circle for those waiting to be made. He'd lied for the sake of having the extra muscle he assumed was necessary.

He wasn't sure how Larry would handle it, especially now without Paul along. Larry was the only one of them to do time, and even though it was a trumped-up charge by cops too embarrassed to admit what had really happened in a bar years ago, Fred knew his friend wanted nothing to do with going back to prison.

"We have to take somebody out," Fred said. "That's what this trip is about."

"Excuse me?" Larry said. "Take somebody out?"

"Yeah, so if you're not willing to, let me know now. I'll drop you off at an airport."

"Freddy, what the fuck are you talking about? Take somebody out? This what they expect you to do, kill somebody? Is this to make your bones?"

"Something like that."

"And you trust it? You trust Charlie Bruno?"

"Do I have a choice?"

"Duh, yeah. What makes you think if we get this done, Bruno doesn't tie up loose ends?"

"What?"

"You and I will know, right? We'll know what went down. That's leverage in that fucked-up world of yours and you know it. You don't think Bruno hasn't thought that far ahead? If you haven't, you better. That's like, I don't know, at least ten steps ahead of where you are."

Fred gave it a moment, then shook his head. "Charlie wouldn't do that," he said.

"You sure about that?"

"I have to be."

"What happens if we can't find this guy and we return without evidence he's dead?"

"I have to pay back the expense money is all. For the record, hits aren't paid in advance or at all to guys looking to step up. That's an assumption you'll do what you're told."

"But you had to pay us to come along, and they had to know that."

"No, Charlie didn't know that until I told him. He was paying me up front for expenses."

Larry squinted at Fred, incredulous at how anxious his friend was to get his button. "And when nothing happens," he said. "If you don't find the guy?"

"I'll have to wait a little longer to get my button."

"And I'll be making this trip for nothing?"

"You're still getting paid, so don't shit yourself."

"You just said you have to pay him back. With what, buttons?"

"I didn't say you have to pay it back. I said I do."

"I think we both need to rethink this."

"Rethink what?"

"Three grand to kill someone?"

"I'll give you half Paulie's share."

"Half Paulie makes it forty-five hundred. To kill someone? Not that I'd kill someone for half a million, but forty-five hundred, Fred? Is that how desperate you think I am?"

"You won't have to do anything but back me up. I'll take care of the guy."

"With what?"

"Jesus Christ, Larry, you gonna back out too now?"

"Fred, had you told me, told us, me and Paulie, what the fuck this was about instead of all the mystery, I never would've agreed to this. Meet somebody and get instructions to do something once we're there is what you said, but you never said we'd be involved in a murder. Not for three grand and not for three hundred grand. So, yeah, come to think of it, I want out too."

"You're serious?" Fred said.

"I'm not killing anybody, Fred. No fucking way."

"And you won't back me up?"

"To murder? No. That's your thing, getting a button. That doesn't do shit for me."

"There are some Jews and Irish who are like made guys, Larry. You know that. They do pretty good for being around somebody."

"The ones that are doing twenty years for being associated with a murder? Don't try and sell me some mob bullshit. For fuck sake, I'm not that stupid."

Fred was grinding his teeth. His worst nightmare had come to pass. Charlie Bruno was right about not taking someone. Now that Larry knew what it was about, how could he be trusted?

Larry said, "I'm sorry, Fred, but this is not for me. No way."

"Fine," Fred said through clenched teeth. "I'll drop you at an airport. Look for one on the map but make it close enough I don't lose more time than I already have."

Larry grabbed the map from the glove box and opened it. "There's one in Cedar Rapids," he said. "It's on the way, so you won't lose much time. I don't know if there are direct flights back to New York, but I can deal with that. Maybe to Chicago first, then New York."

"Yeah, well, I wouldn't want to inconvenience you, right?" Fred said. "And thanks a lot, Larry. Thanks for nothing."

▢ ▢ ▢

Fred Greco had to pull over twice to catch naps before moving on to South Dakota. After dropping Larry Levy off at the airport in Cedar Rapids, Iowa, Fred took Interstate 80 West to Des Moines, where he napped for nearly two hours, then stayed on Interstate 80 to Missouri Valley, where he exited to grab a meal at a diner before continuing.

Thinking about the job ahead was unpleasant. There was strength in numbers and now he had none. Going head-to-head against a known hit man wasn't something to look forward to. He dreamed about it during his last nap and saw himself walking along a street in Yankton searching in a paranoid state of mind for Giovanni Rapino until he heard footsteps behind him, turned and saw himself staring at a dark figure holding a handgun with a sound suppressor. Fred couldn't sleep after his dream and now he was exhausted again. He'd wanted a cup of coffee, but never got out of the car. He napped again instead.

Half an hour passed, and then someone tapped on his passenger side window. Fred looked up and saw it was an Iowa State Trooper.

"You okay?" the trooper said.

Fred yawned.

The trooper signaled for Fred to roll down his window.

Fred did so. "Sorry, officer," he said. "It's been a long drive."

"Where you headed?"

"Yankton," Fred said, and instantly regretted it.

"That's another couple of hours from here. Plate says you started from New York. How long you on the road? That's more than twelve hundred miles from here."

"Where are we?"

The trooper smiled. "Missouri Valley, Iowa. Almost in Nebraska."

"Oh, I left two days ago. Visiting family."

"It's good you're taking naps, but I suggest moving your car around back so as not to take up space where people might think you died."

"Yeah, sorry. I was going to go in for coffee, but I guess I closed my eyes."

"Just shoot around back where the truckers park and you'll be fine. Take a good long nap. Don't drive again until you're feeling fully awake."

"I will. Thank you, officer."

"Have a good one."

He waited until the trooper went inside the restaurant, then backed out of the space and drove around to where the truckers parked. He saw a woman climb out one of the cabs and wondered if she was a hooker, then decided he was too tired for that too. He took a deep breath, yawned again, then closed his eyes.

Paul Winkler bribed a trucker heading east for a ride into New Jersey for fifty dollars. It took them just under 15 hours with two short stops along the way. The driver was a big man in his 50s from Arkansas named Hank Tillerson. He wore a red Razorbacks hat and chewed tobacco. His constant spitting into a coffee can was distracting to Paul.

Paul said, "Why do you chew that shit? I heard it'll give you cancer of the mouth."

"Shit, son," Tillerson said, "we're all gonna die from something or other. I'm stuck in this rig six days of the week, sometimes seven. I can listen to the radio and fall asleep at the wheel or chew snuff and try to stay awake."

"How's it taste?"

"Like shit. So, I won't give you any if you never tried it before because it'll make you dizzy and then sick before you know it and I don't need you puking up in my cab."

"Fair enough."

"Now can I ask you a question?"

"Shoot."

"The hell are you hitching a ride for? You don't look like no bum."

"I'm paying for this ride, ain't I?"

"All the more reason. You can toss a fifty my way you can probably rent a car or am I poking my nose where it don't belong?"

Paul bit his lower lip. Part of him was ashamed to tell the guy why he was heading back to New York and part of him wanted to talk about it. Worrying about his wife cheating on him had consumed Paul. After a few minutes of silence, he opened up and said, "I was on a trip with some friends and turned back. Why I'm heading back to New York. I think my wife is cheating on me."

Tillerson turned to Paul. "Jesus, son, sorry to hear it. Are you sure?"

"Positive. She thinks I'm gone for the week, but I intend to watch her. You know, not let her know I'm back."

"That could be dangerous."

"Not for me."

"Oh, hold on a second. It sure can be dangerous for you. I have some years on you so take some advice here. Find out what you need to find out but don't get yourself in trouble with the law over it."

"I find her with somebody in my bed, in my apartment, I'll kill the two of them."

Tillerson turned to look at Paul and found his passenger was looking back at him. "You don't want to do that, son," Tillerson said. "You don't want to throw your life away."

"The hell do I have to live for if my wife is making a cuck out of me?"

Tillerson sighed. "Boy, let me tell you something. There's not a woman on the planet worth spending the rest of your life in jail for. Not a one. You need to get that shit straight out of your head and think long and hard about what you're doing."

"I appreciate the advice, but you don't understand."

"I understand better than you think, kid. I have a truck driver friend doing time for catching his wife foolin' around. Good man, but he lost it one day after searching their place and finding a used condom didn't flush. These long hauls we have to drive keep us away from home, so who knows why she found herself somebody, but the bottom line was she did. She comes home and he starts accusing her, gets all worked up and then she gets worked up and tells him she's been fucking some guy where she worked, and he shoves the condom into her mouth, started choking her and wound up killing her. He's doing fifteen years now. Fifteen. I only made it up to where he's at once but let me tell you that guy wishes he never saw his wife after the shit he's putting up with inside. Trust me on this, you don't want to kill anybody."

Paul's face turned red. He had already found stained panties in their hamper and his wife had tried to bullshit him about the stains being some kind of medicine, but he knew she was lying.

"Hey, you okay?" Tillerson said.

"You married?" Paul said.

"Not anymore. Wasn't a cheating situation, she told me she couldn't hack the lifestyle and we came to an agreement. We divorced, but then saw each other for a few years when I was around. The sex was good enough for both of us, I guess, but then came the time she couldn't wait me out and told me she met someone. I couldn't blame her. I've stayed single since. Can't blame a woman for avoiding truckers. Gets old fast for a woman married to one of us."

"My wife works for a bank in the city."

"Think it's an office thing?"

"I don't know. All I do know is sometimes I swear I want to punch her in the face."

Tillerson frowned. He saw Paul yawn and said, "Why don't you take a nap for now. We still got a ways to go. Crawl into the back and rest yourself. Might keep you calm later you're not sleep deprived."

When he finally made it to Yankton, Fred Greco stopped at a bar and grill and ordered a breakfast of scrambled eggs, sausage, bacon, home fries, toast, and a short stack of pancakes. That plus tomato juice and several cups of coffee left him on the toilet for nearly 20 minutes. He picked up a local Yankton map before gassing up again.

He planned on taking a hotel room near the center of the city, but when he saw signs for Federal Prison Camp Yankton, he decided to make a pass around the grounds. He wound up on Douglas Avenue, where he made a series of left turns, starting with East 10th Street, then Pine Street and then East 12th Street.

Fred was surprised at how the prison looked. He knew it was minimum-security, but the buildings didn't have the look of a prison at all. It looked more like a junior college than a federal prison. A couple of buildings were old, but not ancient. Other buildings looked modern.

He never asked why the man he was looking for was transferred to a minimum-security prison camp, except it was public knowledge that Giovanni Rapino had turned federal witness against his former crime family a few years ago. Charlie Bruno had implied that Rapino wouldn't be at FPC Yankton for long, just that he was being released. Whether Rapino had stayed in Yankton or moved somewhere else was the information Bruno had yet to provide.

Fred wondered if Rapino was still under witness protection. If he was still in Yankton, Rapino probably was, which meant federal agents would continue to keep him protected. Fred needed Charlie Bruno to get him the information he needed and soon.

He found a Best Western in the southeast part of Yankton and booked a room for just under $100 a night. He was cash rich from being abandoned and could pocket at least an extra six grand if he finished the job. He'd owe his mob sponsor, Charlie Bruno, the money back if nothing came from his trip, but for the time being, he had enough cash to last a week or more.

Before heading out to call Bruno for updates on Giovanni Rapino, Fred looked over the few pictures he'd been given of the snitch. He doubted the guy would look the same, but there was always a chance he might be recognizable.

He brought two pictures with him and set them under the driver's side sun visor. He parked in a gas station lot and used a burner phone. Charlie Bruno answered after two rings.

"Hey," he said.

"Okay to talk?"

"No. Everything okay? Yes or no?"

Fred hesitated as he swallowed hard. Then he lied and said, "Yeah."

"Okay, I'll call you tomorrow. Text me a number."

"Will do."

Bruno ended the call.

"Shit," Fred said. "Now what the fuck do I do?"

Charlie Bruno handed Special Agent Brian Fein two new microcassettes as he sipped hot coffee from a container. The two had met up in the Plum Beach parking lot off the Belt Parkway in Brooklyn. Both were wearing heavy jackets over their clothes. Both were smoking cigarettes. The butts burned in the ashtray.

"I already told you about the cassettes, yes or no?" Fein said.

Bruno held a hand up as he took a call from Fred Greco. The call didn't last long.

After Bruno killed the connection, Fein said, "That was short and sweet."

"Gotta keep up appearances, no?"

Fein held up the microcassettes.

"I told you, the body mics are no good when I'm separated from a guy."

"And if they frisk you one day, just for the hell of it, you're a dead man."

"Let me worry about that," Bruno said. "Meantime, you got what you want on those."

Fein pocketed the microcassettes. "You got any names yet?" he said.

"No, not yet."

"Why not?"

"It's complicated."

Fein said, "It is, huh? Try and explain it."

"First of all, it's under Grasso's control, my office. He sees who bets and how much they bet. He knows more'n me."

"That's the complication? You fuck around with his *cumare*, which is a death sentence, but you're worried about giving up names on a bookmaking sheet?"

"Think about it," Bruno said. "What business is it of mine to know who those guys are? You don't think Grasso would be suspicious if I asked?"

"I think you already know, is what I think."

"Hey, you have Grasso on tape, thanks to me."

"Maybe you need some more coffee, Charlie. We have inferences. We don't have him giving an order. We have you giving an order."

"I think you mean offer," Bruno said. "I didn't give an order. I made suggestions. Offered guidance."

"Right, of course. What am I thinking?"

"Well?"

"Well what?" Fein said. "We don't have the underboss giving an order. That means we have shit."

"You do realize I have to tread lightly around Grasso. He's no dummy."

"Whatever. The bottom line is if this kid and his friends you sent pull off this miracle hit on Rapino, they'll all three be dead the day they get back."

"I don't know that."

"Yeah, you do. So does Grasso. That's a link none of you can afford."

"I still don't get why you guys can't figure it out on your own."

"First off, we didn't pull Rapino out of Yankton, which means another agency with more pull did. If that's the case, if it's another agency, nobody'll know why until whatever they're doing is done. We don't have a name. Whoever pulled him out had a reason and we don't know it. If anything, he's being protected."

"Now you tell me something like that?"

"Better now than never. My advice, give your guys out there a few days of dicking around and then call them back. Your guy, he's married, right?"

"He is," Bruno said.

"Save his wife some grief."

"I'll look stupid I call him back. Grasso will want to know why."

"Don't worry about Grasso, Charlie."

"What?"

"Let it go."

"He on your payroll too?"

"I say that?"

"No, but maybe you don't have to."

Fein frowned.

"What?" Bruno said, annoyed then.

"Give the kids a few days and then call them back. They snoop around in the wrong places they could get themselves killed."

"Jesus Christ, you guys kill me. How do I know it's not one of you guys gave us Rapino's move out of Big Sandy? You think I trust you because you're FBI? That's a fuckin' laugh. That's a good fuckin' laugh."

"We don't kill people, Charlie."

"Right. Sure."

Fein pushed the start button. He let the car idle.

"That it?" Fein said. "I can go fuck myself now?"

"I tell you I don't know, it's complicated and you give me shit for it. So, yeah, I guess you can go fuck yourself now."

Fein burned rubber leaving the parking spot and headed for the exit back onto the Belt Parkway.

"Unbelievable," Bruno said. "Now you're pissed off at me."

□ □ □

Hank Tillerson let Paul Winkler call ahead for a Perth Amboy car service to pick him up on the New Jersey side of the Outerbridge Crossing. The cab was waiting for Paul on Pfeiffer Boulevard and took him across the Outerbridge, through Staten Island, and across the Verrazzano Narrows Bridge into Brooklyn. Paul arrived at his mother's house less than an hour after getting inside the cab. He ate some of her leftover pasta, drank two beers, and yawned over and over. He didn't explain his situation to his mother but asked if she could wake him in a few hours.

When he woke, he showered, made a sandwich to take with him, kissed his mother, and thanked her for letting him borrow her car. Paul drove to the house where he and his wife rented a second floor two-bedroom apartment in Bath Beach. It was a weekday with alternate side of the street parking, and many of the parking spaces were filled. He found a spot ten houses from his address. He put on a pair of sunglasses and his Yankees baseball cap. He'd already tried calling his wife twice since he woke up. He avoided leaving a voicemail so she wouldn't know he was back.

Either she had turned her phone off and left it off or she was using a burner phone for her own personal calls. Paul was determined to catch her going or coming from their apartment and had no intention of letting her see him first.

When his wife finally came out of the house it was after ten o'clock in the morning and Sharon was dressed for the gym. Paul had waited nearly an hour for her to leave. Since it was a workday, either she'd called out sick or used one of her personal days. He grew angry as she sat in their car, made a phone call, and then drove away.

He waited until she was gone, then went into the apartment as quickly as possible. He wasn't sure if their landlord knew he was supposed to be gone, but they usually didn't interact except for the days they were late paying rent.

He used the bathroom first, then headed inside their bedroom. The bed was unmade. He went through his wife's night table but didn't find anything incriminating. He found marijuana roaches in her ashtray, six in total. Sharon liked getting high and was probably smoking more since he left.

He went to the kitchen and frowned at the mess in the sink. Dirty dishes and glasses were piled in dirty water. Normally, he'd wash them. Paul was a bit of a neat freak and hated seeing dirty dishes in the sink. Normally, he'd clean the dishes, wipe the cabinets and mop the floor, but he couldn't do that now without tipping off his wife that he was home. What he did was make a fresh pot of coffee.

He sat in the kitchen and noted the time, 11:15 a.m. If Sharon had gone to the gym, she would likely be home soon. He drank a second cup of coffee and wondered if maybe he'd been wrong.

Paul headed into the bathroom and emptied their hamper. A few minutes later, he had all the evidence he needed. The semen stains on his wife's panties were thick and disgusting. Two different pairs were stained, one of them with the stain still wet. He didn't know who her lover might be, nor did he care. She'd made a fool of him for the last time.

He stood at the front door watching the street and waiting for her car. Another hour passed before he spotted it. She parked across the street and then stood alongside the car and seemed to be waiting. Then another car pulled up alongside hers, and Paul could see his wife smiling. She pointed further up the street and the car moved away. Still, she waited until a man who looked familiar met up with her and the two crossed the street holding hands.

Paul could see that Sharon wasn't worried about their neighbors.

He headed into the bedroom and grabbed his .380 from on top of a shelf on his side of their closet. He opened one of the closet's sliding doors and moved the clothes on the rack to one side. He closed the closet door most of the way, leaving it open a crack. He heard the front door open and then Sharon was giggling.

"I'm gonna use your bathroom," the man said, and then Paul knew who it was.

"Motherfucker," he whispered to himself.

The bathroom was the first door on the left outside of the bedroom. Paul thought about waiting for Charlie Bruno to step out of the bathroom before shooting him, but he wanted Sharon to see what he did. Paul heard the toilet flush and waited.

"Coffee?" his wife said.

"I don't really have time," Bruno said.

"No, I mean I don't think I made this pot," Sharon said. "Maybe I left it plugged in?"

"Happens all the time."

"It's still weird I don't remember. How about a soda or something?"

"Water's good. You got bottled?"

"Sure."

Paul heard the refrigerator door open and then close.

"Your ass is something else in those tights," Bruno said.

"I'm just a size two, but it is perky, right? I work on it enough at the gym."

"It's an apple ass, honey. A perfect little apple ass."

Paul's jaw was clenched.

"Com'ere," Bruno said.

Paul had stepped out of the closet and was waiting just inside the bedroom door, which was half open then. He listened to sounds he could see in his mind's eye. A minute passed before he could hear Charlie Bruno say something Paul couldn't make out. Then Paul heard his wife's interspersed humming, a sound she made when she was blowing him. He bent at the waist from a sudden pain. Then he removed his shoes and opened the door. He still couldn't see them, but he could clearly hear the sounds they were making.

"Freddy wasn't kidding," Bruno said.

"I still can't believe he told you," Sharon said.

"It's what men do, hon. They talk. Christ, that's good. All the way down, that's it. Jesus Christ."

Paul had thought they'd come to the bedroom, but they were doing something in the kitchen, and he couldn't take it any longer. He slowly and quietly stepped into the hall where he could see Charlie Bruno sitting on one of the kitchen chairs, his head tilted back as he moaned. Paul leaned out a little further and could see Sharon's head bobbing in Bruno's lap. Then he heard Sharon humming again, and it was too much.

He was on them fast and shot Bruno in the left temple. Sharon fell back onto her ass at the explosion from the .380. Then Paul stood over his wife as she held both hands up to block her face.

"Look at me!" Paul yelled.

Sharon pulled her hands away enough to see the rage on Paul's face. A moment later, the first bullet passed between the fingers of her right hand and entered her right eye. Her head banged against the refrigerator door and Paul fired again. The second bullet entered her forehead, and her body curled onto the floor, her back against the refrigerator. Paul used his right foot to push her onto her back, then fired one more time. The bullet entered her chest between both her breasts.

He stood there looking at her a long time before sliding down the wall. He continued looking at her and began to sob hysterically a full minute before putting the barrel of the .380 into his mouth and blowing his brain out the back of his head.

PART III

SEVEN

A few weeks ago, Brenda Lee was halfway through her shift when the murder of Curtis Lawrence, also known as Dog, was confirmed. It was the same day Reggie claimed he went for donuts. At work she heard two customers talking about a murder in Nebraska but never thought about Dog until one of the Yankton police officers, Billy Wilson, asked Brenda Lee if she'd heard about it.

"That thing in Nebraska?" Brenda Lee said. "That was Dog?"

"Yeah," Officer Wilson said. "Somebody walked up to his house and popped him. That's the rumor."

"What about Curly?"

"Nothing yet. He was questioned but had nothing to say. You know, the criminal code where they don't talk. At least until they're arrested."

"I wonder who did it."

Wilson shrugged.

When she had her break, Brenda Lee called Amato's cellphone. He answered the call with a question.

"*Bella*, can you bring home liver?"

"Huh? Oh, sure. There's a policeman here talking about Dog."

"Old news, eh?"

"Reggie, I'm worried."

"Don't worry, *Bella*."

"And Dog?"

"Somebody shoots him," Amato said.

Brenda Lee swallowed hard. She thought about asking him directly but stopped herself.

"Hello?" Amato said. "Where you went?"

"Sorry, I'm here. I'll bring you liver for dinner."

"Liver with the onions and French fries."

"Got it."

"Maybe we watch a movie tonight. We watch together, eh?"

"Okay."

"I see you later."

"Later."

As soon as the call ended, Brenda Lee felt certain that it was Amato who'd killed Dog, and then wondered if she'd made another mistake with a man she'd fallen for and allowed into her life.

That was a few weeks ago. Lately she wasn't sure if she cared if Reggie was a murderer.

Maryanne Esposito was watching television on the couch when Larry Levy let himself into the apartment. At first, she was frightened when she heard someone at the door, but then she jumped up off the couch and ran to him. The two hugged and kissed and then moved further inside the apartment to the kitchen.

"Why didn't you call?" Maryanne said. "I could've met you."

"I wanted to surprise you," Larry said. "Can I get a beer?"

Maryanne took a can of beer from the refrigerator, popped the top and handed it to him. "You okay? I've been scared shit since you called."

He'd called from the airport in Cedar Rapids, Iowa. He didn't go into details but said he was coming home. When she asked why a second time, he told her he'd tell her when he was home.

He drank deep from the can of beer and then told her everything that had happened and why he was done working for Fred Greco. Maryanne restrained herself from encouraging him while he spoke. When he was finished, she moved to his lap and kissed him passionately.

"And we can get married now," he said. "I'm done with that shit."

"I love you so much, Larry Levy," Maryanne said.

"And I love you," Larry said.

She led him to the bedroom where they had sex, satisfying one another for the next half hour. Afterward, Maryanne was wiping tears from her face. Levy held her head with both hands and told her he was going back to school and would work shit jobs until he graduated with a master's degree in history.

"That would make me so happy," he said.

"I'll need the refresher before trying law school."

She clung to him again, crying openly. When she relaxed again, Larry wondered aloud about Paul Winkler.

"Is his wife really having an affair?" Maryanne said.

"Who knows?" Larry said. "He never should've married Sharon anyway. She was out of his league. Way smarter and way more treacherous. Tell you the truth, I think she saw a sucker and got married. He was nuts when they first married. Always running around for her, always canceling time with us to be with her. I think he smothered her, and I never thought she felt about him the way he felt about her. She might've seen some security with him early on, but he's like an anchor now. For everybody, not just her."

"She did seem a little slutty the few times I met her. The stringy tight halters and short skirts. She seemed to enjoy the attention. I always thought it was a bit much."

"It's not a big leap being sharper than Paulie, but she was way sharper. She did have a reputation in high school, so there was that too. Paul couldn't see it. Fred felt the same way as me."

"Fred, the lifelong friend who wanted to get you both involved in murder. Who cares what he thinks?"

"Please, that's over now. Let's not discuss Fred. This is about Paul. He's got a temper and if he catches her screwing around who knows what'll happen. The other thing about Fred and what he's doing now, we can't ever discuss it. You can't, not with anybody. It's serious shit. Nobody can know what he's doing."

"Including the friends he tried to hoodwink."

"Let it go, Maryanne. There's no point in being angry about it now. It's over."

"Fine. Okay, but I assume you didn't take any money from him. Tell me you didn't."

"None, and I doubt Fred ever talks to me again. Like I told you from the airport. Paulie left first. Then Fred told me the deal and I wanted out. He's pretty pissed off at both of us, but me more, I'm sure."

"Good," Maryanne said. "You don't need that asshole. Who tries to be a mobster today? Morons, that's who. They're all full of shit and they all snitch on each other."

"Maybe not all, but enough of them. Anyway, I'm done. I'll call and tell them at the junkyards tomorrow. I'm out of work now. Officially."

"We'll find something else. Something legitimate."

"We'll try."

"No, we'll find something. I'm sure of it."

Larry forced a smile.

The woman Fred Greco picked up at the strip club the night before called herself Jade. She was a petite Asian woman somewhere in her thirties with a scar from a three-year-old C-section. Fred was able to lure her back to his motel with $200. Once they were there, they had sex twice, and then he offered her another $100 to spend the night, promising her breakfast and a ride home.

During their short conversation the night before, Fred didn't notice an accent and asked her where she was born.

"Kansas," Jade said.

"Your parents from here too?"

"My father. My mother was born in South Korea. They met there. Married there."

"How long you dancing?"

"Stripping or hooking? Two years for both."

"Any problems? Arrests, I mean?"

"No."

"Kids?"

"One. My mother watches him when I work."

In the morning, Fred gave her another $50 for her kid, he told her. Then he drove her to a nearby diner where they had breakfast. She asked for an extra breakfast for her mother and Fred was fine with it.

"You tell her you were staying with me last night?" he asked while they waited for an extra order of scrambled eggs, bacon, home fries and white toast.

"Of course," Jade said. "Or she worries."

Fred was supposed to call his wife but couldn't while Jade was with him. He'd do it after dropping her off.

"You working again tonight?" he said.

"No, not tonight," Jade said. "Tomorrow night."

"I should still be here."

"Okay, you come to club."

"Absolutely."

She gave him a quick smile, then glanced at her watch. "I have to go home soon," she said.

"Soon as the order is ready," he said. "You live near here?"

"Not far."

He dropped her off 20 minutes later, then took his time driving around Yankton again. He had no idea how to look for Giovanni Rapino and had already wasted two days. What was he supposed to do without the information Charlie Bruno was supposed to provide? When he called Charlie the day before, it was a 20 second call that provided nothing new. Charlie was supposed to call back but hadn't yet. Fred still didn't have the information he needed.

So, what was he supposed to do, knock on doors?

He remembered he needed to call his wife and pulled alongside the curb on Railroad Street.

Maria answered his call in a panic.

"Jesus, Fred, where are you?" she gasped.

"Yankton," he said. "What's wrong?"

"Your friend, Paul. He killed his wife and Charlie. He killed himself too."

Fred was taken aback. "What!"

"Paul killed himself after he killed his wife and Charlie Bruno. It's all over the news here."

"Jesus fuck!" Fred said. "He killed Charlie Bruno?"

"Yes! He killed his wife too. He killed Sharon, then he killed himself."

"Fuck. It'll take me a couple days to drive home. I should've taken a flight."

"Why was Paul home?"

"Because of Sharon. He said she was cheating on him. Larry took off too."

"You're out there alone?"

"Yeah, I'm fucked now. I have to drive home with no help."

"Any way for you to leave the car?"

"How do I do that? No. I'll get started in a little while. I'll call you again when I'm on the road."

"Okay, but be careful, please. If you're tired, pull over somewhere. There's nothing you can do now anyway."

"Okay, let me get going."

"I love you."

"I love you too."

Larry Levy and his wife spent the morning in bed without watching television. They talked mostly, making plans for their future, and planning their wedding. Larry preferred going to a Justice of the Peace. When he said he wanted to take a ride to talk to Paul Winkler, Maryanne wasn't happy about it.

He'd called Paul Winkler the night before but there was no answer. He'd ended the call without leaving a message. Now he called again, this time leaving a message when Paul didn't pick up.

"Hey, Fonzala, you okay? I came home too. I'm at my apartment if you want to stop by. Or we can grab lunch if you want. I'll pick you up. Give me a call when you get this."

Maryanne heard the last of the message and waited for Larry to end the call.

"You sure that was a good idea?" she said.

"What are you talking about?"

"Getting involved with Paul again now."

"I know the guy since we're kids, Maryanne. He was in a bad way over his wife. I'm just checking up on him."

"I was hoping when you said you were done with Freddy you meant Paul too."

"Paul basically can't stand me, but in that crazy friendship way. He's wrapped a little too tight and he's not the smartest guy in the world, but he's got a good heart."

Maryanne frowned. "Right," she said. "You and Paul working for Freddy the wannabe gangster. You're all good guys."

"Excuse me?"

"I know you're not like Freddy, and you're a thousand times smarter than Paul, which is why you need to break clean of both of them. They'll only take you down. So, either way, you make the break for real, babe. Those two are knuckleheads and you know it."

"Their wives probably think the same about me."

"So do I when you're with them."

"Thanks."

Maryanne smiled. "You're welcome."

Half an hour after Maryanne left the apartment to go shopping. Larry decided to go see Paul at his apartment. It was a 15-minute drive, but Larry stopped to pick up Paul's favorite, an Entenmann's crumb cake on the way. When he turned onto the block where Paul lived, he slammed his foot on the brake. There were several police cars and at least one EMS truck parked in front of the house where Paul lived on the second floor. Eyes down the block had turned from the squeal of his breaks. Cop eyes. He was afraid if he tried to back out onto the avenue, they'd follow him for sure.

Then one of the cops headed straight for him.

"Fuck me," he said to himself.

Once he was home again, Maryanne was putting groceries away. Larry said, "I think I just fucked myself."

"What are you talking about?"

"Check the news."

"Why?"

"Paulie killed his wife and Charlie Bruno, then himself."

Sharon gasped. "Oh, my God! Oh, my God."

"Must've happened before when I first came home or something. I was right there on his block. I turned the corner and saw the cop cars and panicked. I hit the break hard. Cops turned in my direction. One came right to me and pointed to a spot alongside a fire hydrant. There were cops going house to house, asking questions probably. The one cop came to me and took my driver's license. He has my name. I played dumb but that'll last until they figure it out, how we're friends and whatnot. Plus, I called his number before I went and left a message. They'll trace that in two seconds."

"Jesus, what did you say to the police?"

"I lied when they asked me what I was doing there, why I had turned onto Paul's block. I said I was on my way home and was surprised to see all the police cars. I saw I couldn't get through and panicked."

"That's okay, no?"

"No, I said he took my name. I had to give him my driver's license. They run that and listen to my voicemail, they see I'm a felon, they'll be back to ask more questions. I don't know what happened, except for what they're saying on the news. I heard it on the radio on the way home. I can't believe he killed Bruno. He's a wiseguy. That'll bring all kinds of attention. They'll want to talk to everybody around that guy, including Freddy. They already have my name now. I should've backed out of that street and took my chances. Fuck!"

"If you left a voicemail they wouldn't ignore it. What happens now? Shouldn't you have a lawyer?"

"From your firm? What do they get an hour? One, two grand?"

Maryanne tried to rub his shoulders, but Larry couldn't stay still. He stood up from the table and began to pace.

"Can you call Fred?" Maryanne said. "Does he know?"

"I don't know. He's not talking to me anyway. Jesus Christ, what a fuckin' mess."

His cellphone rang a few minutes later. Larry answered without looking to see who was calling.

"Yeah?"

"It's Fred. I heard what happened. You home?"

"Yeah, it's fucked up. I was on my way to his place when I saw all the cops."

"He killed Bruno."

"I know."

"He should've killed himself first."

"Tell me about it."

"I don't know what to expect when I get back."

"You're coming back? Good."

"I don't have a choice."

"The cops questioned me."

"How?"

Larry explained, and Fred said, "Jesus Christ, can it get any worse."

"Bruno should get you off the hook, no?"

"No. Grasso was involved too. I don't know what the fuck is gonna happen now."

"Where are you?"

"Almost home. Still in Pennsylvania but close to Jersey. If it wasn't for those things on the side of the road, whatever they're called, I'd be dead myself. I fell asleep twice already."

"Then stop and get some rest.

"I wish it was that easy."

"You okay?"

"I'm gonna have to be. Talk to you later."

"Okay."

The call ended and Larry turned to Maryanne.

"What?" she said.

"I have no idea what happens now."

Special Agents, Brian Fein and William Ryan, met with their boss, Special Agent in Charge, Thomas Wells, in a diner at Union Square East, off 14th Street. Fein and Ryan sat on one side of a booth facing the street. Wells sat across from them. All three sipped at their coffees while they looked over their menus.

"So?" Fein said, after setting his menu down.

"Interesting few days, eh?" Wells said.

Ryan thumbed at Fein and said, "Only if it was your guy bought it."

"Jealous?" Fein said.

"Extremely," Ryan said. "It's been fifteen months since my last vacation, a real one, and my wife is breaking them with gusto over her niece's wedding in South Carolina next month. She doesn't want to go alone, and I don't want to go, except I figured I'd take a couple weeks and do some fishing while I was down there."

Wells said, "I think we have bigger problems."

"Such as?" Ryan said, "because my wife can be pretty intimidating when she's pissed off at me. Not to mention her turning off any chance at my ever getting laid again."

"We don't know who pulled Rapino out of Big Sandy," Wells said. "We know he was pulled, but not by who."

"Which means?" Fein said.

"CIA is our best guess. Those motherfuckers, whomever pulls their strings, NSA, DOJ, DOS, the President, they'll never tell us or anybody else."

"The fuck would the CIA want with Rapino?"

"They wouldn't say even if we had somebody in the bureau with the stones to ask them."

"They never say," Ryan said.

"Just remember, the shit they pull around the globe, assassinations, kidnappings, whatever, they'll always have plausible deniability," Wells said. "Even that Nord Stream thing, the pipeline. The CIA was supposed to know about that. A team of Ukrainian special operations forces and the Russia-to-Germany natural gas thing."

"Or the beard and his cigars," Ryan joked.

"Or the beard and his cigars," Wells repeated.

Fein said, "What's the point of those assholes anyway? If we're not all working for the same cause, it's kind of dumb already."

"They're national security or something," Ryan said.

"It's a big umbrella of clandestine ops," Wells said. "And there is a border crisis involving drugs and it is an election year."

"And there you have it," Ryan said. "What they might want with Rapino is anyone's guess, but the best guess is a hit."

"Has to be to whack somebody," Fein said. "That was his deal with the Cirelli crew. He was a hitman. He mentioned traveling to North Dakota to pick off some lawyer, I remember right. Part of his proffer."

Ryan said, "The old bastard dying of cancer they wound up whacking inside anyway."

"Carmine Montalvo," Wells said.

"Rapino didn't do him," Ryan said. "Montalvo was inside on a bid. The federal joint in North Carolina, I think. The medical one."

"Butner," Wells said.

Fein said, "If that's the case, it's the CIA, there's no way they're leaving Rapino around to talk about it, never mind sell the story to some magazine publisher."

"Doesn't make a difference if we don't know and they won't tell us," Wells said. "We need a push on that."

"Don't look at me," Fein said. "My guy is dead. If it was Charlie Bruno had a guy inside, unless Grasso knew, that ship has sailed."

"Grasso'll hold onto that until he needs it," Ryan said.

"We already know Grasso knew something about it," Wells said. "It's on at least one recording."

"I'll press him, but I doubt he'll give it up until he has to."

"Meaning if Falzone knows and he needs to give him up."

Ryan frowned and said, "Something tells me I'm gonna miss that wedding, huh?"

"Tag you're it," Wells said.

"What you need is a Mrs. Winkler," Fein said. "You're not getting any at home, make friends with some sword swallower. Someone with skills like the ones we heard about on a dozen different tapes."

Ryan said, "Tell the truth, Fein, you got off listening to those tapes."

"A time or two, sure."

"Can I hear a couple? Like I said, my wife is turning off the spigot on me getting laid again I don't go to that wedding."

Fein thumbed at Wells. "Ask him. I turned them over soon as my balls went dry."

Fein and Ryan laughed. Wells didn't.

"We're just having some fun," Fein said to Wells.

"We're back to cracking jokes and none of this is very funny," Wells said, visibly angry then. "The thing of it is those tapes are now wasted on our federal prosecutor. Guy's a swish."

"Can we laugh at that?" Ryan said.

Wells frowned.

"Shouldn't matter," Fein said. "He might pick up a thing or two. Mrs. Winkler, according to her husband's friend, Freddy Greco, was hands free—tip number one. And she swallowed without coming up for air to pump a second load according to another tape."

"Now I'm hard," Ryan said.

"And there's your angle with Mr. Greco," Wells said to Fein. "Now that you're free from Charlie Bruno, you can go after the Greco kid with tapes I'm sure he'll never want his wife to hear."

Ryan said, "See, that's how you climb to the top. You become as heartless as Special Agent in Charge, Thomas C. Wells. It's like a rocket to the top you can squeeze someone like that without skipping a heartbeat."

Wells rolled his eyes.

"It's cruel is what it is," Ryan said.

Fein said, "You got a point."

"Who has?" Ryan said.

Fein pointed at Wells. "Him."

"Okay, I said enough with the jokes," Wells said. "What about the gambling angle? Anything?"

Fein shook his head. "Bruno was being a first-class prick with that. Holding on for dear life. I guess to use as a trump card once we shitcan his cooperation."

Ryan said, "Can't we do a deep dive on the names we have?"

"Not without the manpower to sit on them, once we find them," Fein said.

"If we find them," Well said. "Some of those guys have beards call in their bets. It would take manpower and lots of it."

"I have a suggestion," Ryan said.

"Uh-oh," Fein said.

Ryan winked at Wells. "Since Fein is off the hook, maybe he can spend a little more time snooping on those gamblers."

"Good idea," Wells said.

Fein said, "Hey, don't forget I have that Greco kid to extort information from now."

"What'll that take you, twenty minutes?" Wells said.

"Fuck me," Fein said.

"My heart bleeds," Ryan said.

Fein shot him the bird.

Wells said, "Start digging."

EIGHT

When Dalton couldn't find Curly earlier in the day, he called Amato to arrange their lunch in the Mother City Bar and Grill. Now they were sitting in a booth facing one another and were almost finished with their meals. Dalton took a last bite from his Bison burger and said, "I think the fat fucker took a powder."

Amato said, "I try him all afternoon yesterday, mister Dalton. Went to his place this morning and he's no there."

"Then he's gone," Dalton said. "By the way, call me Red."

"Okay," Amato said. "Red." He used his fork to stab a chunk of pickle.

"You told Curly about those two kids he was working with being fuckups?" Dalton said.

"I tell Curly to watch them."

"And he expected you to watch them?"

"Maybe Dog does this for him."

"But you wouldn't."

"Not without more money. I talk to them when I meet them. Curly tells me they don't always have what they should have. I tell them to be careful. I warn them. They don't fear Curly, eh? They . . . *come si dice* . . . lock horns? They take off. Curly was cheap not to pay me."

"That accent. Italian, right?"

"*Si.*"

"Like Spanish a little."

"I'm told."

"What was he paying you?"

"Curly? Five hundred. He says he needed approval for more but is bullshit."

"He paid Dog six."

"He lies to me. He was stupid, eh?"

"And he didn't see it coming, getting ripped off, because he was stupid."

"Curly was a *mameluke*, eh? A fool, except for what you tell me, but he's no tough and no smart. Dog did his work."

"And Dog is dead. He liked you for that, just so you know."

"Because I beat shit out of Dog."

"Why was that? Curly never said why. He just said you did it."

"Whatever Curly says, I don't know, but Dog put one of his hands under Brenda Lee's skirt and grabbed a handful of her ass. That's why

I hit him."

"She the waitress works here?"

"*Si.*"

"You gonna marry her?"

"What?" Amato said, acting surprised and chuckling. "No. No marriage for me."

"What about her? She wanna marry?"

"I didn't ask. Why?"

"We tend to stay away from people are married."

"I'm not marry anybody."

"Good."

"Back to Curly. Why you think he took off?"

"Some bear story he heard."

"Bear story?"

"A man tied to a tree and left for wolves and bear. He gets sick when he told me about it."

"And when was that?"

"A while ago. I think he was trying to scare me."

Dalton huffed. "Fucking Curly."

"Look," Amato said, "Curly no could even fake being tough guy. It was matter of time before somebody steals from him."

"And now he's gone with whatever he did collect."

"What I give him. What I collected."

"That means this spot is a goose egg."

Amato shrugged.

"Then we'll leave it that way. I'll get two others to cover a piece each and that'll be that."

"And Curly?"

"If he has half a brain, he'll never come back. If he does, he'll wish he didn't."

"I can take over for him. I'm careful."

"You, if you want, I'm sending to Bozeman."

"Bozeman?"

"Montana. You're too smart and too tough to waste here. You okay with that?"

"Sure," Amato said. "Is okay with me."

"When can you leave?"

"When you says."

"How's tomorrow?"

"I go tomorrow."

"You taking the waitress?"

"That no good?"

"It's fine, but why? Montana has women too."

"Not like Brenda Lee. How they say? She has skills. Is good woman."

Dalton smiled again. "You're fresh out of Yankton FPC," he said. "I'd think any woman would make it seem that way."

"Maybe. So, tomorrow?"

"Just so you know, the guy you'll be seeing. They call him Peaky. He prefers to be called that. He's a girlfriend fucker, another nickname he has."

"Girlfriend fucker? What this is? I never hear before."

"He fucks other guys' girlfriends. Gets off on it, I think. He's got this skank he lives with I think does his dirty work. Drugs other women so they can party. Just so you know."

"They let him?"

"He takes care of business, so people look the other way. The day he goes after the wrong woman, gets himself fucked up or killed, nobody is going to much care. Look, I'll get you an address to go to in the morning. It's a little more than eight hundred miles from here. About a dozen hours driving with meals and bathroom breaks. Take two days and enjoy the ride."

"And it pay how much?"

"You'll start at a grand a week. First month is rent free. Five hundred a month after if you wanna stay in our building. You prefer your own place, rents on you. There's a hotel there rents apartments. Utility apartments, I guess they're called. Small one-bedroom apartments. Whatever they charge, first month is free. Salary goes up depending on what you do, but it's a grand a week to start. More with more responsibility. Never less money as long as you hold up your end."

"Sounds good to me," Amato said.

Dalton extended his hand. Amato took it.

"Now," Dalton said, "how's the dessert in this joint?"

Amato almost felt bad for Curly. As baby-faced and weak and pathetic as the fat man was, Amato sometimes enjoyed his company. He liked breaking balls like the old days in New York and missed the camaraderie of the crew he had been involved with before getting his button. Once he became a made man, his former associates were sure to be more careful about joking around him. It was the price of becoming somebody within the mafia, and he didn't like it. It was one of the things that upset him most when he was still on the streets in New York. The fact that many of his fellow made men had neither earned nor deserved the respect they received through a childish ceremony that no longer meant a thing. The nobody crowd, all his former associates and everybody else who wasn't or couldn't become made men, were forced to walk on eggshells around the so-called somebody crowd—the made men.

It was late when Amato met with Special Agent Han outside the Sacred Heart cemetery on Douglas Avenue. The two men stood among a clump of trees out of the moonlight.

"You getting a feel for it?" Han said.

"Is done," Amato said. "Curly is go. I think Dalton, this Red knows this. Curly is big kid. Stupid kid. I think Dog was boss. Curly learns to curse, that's all."

"And your meeting with Dalton?"

"I'm going to Bozeman."

Han was impressed. "When?"

"Tomorrow," Amato said.

"Shit, this is great news. The sooner the better. It might take some time in Bozeman before one of their big shots show up, but you'll be in position a lot sooner than we anticipated."

"Who is we?"

"Wouldn't you like to know."

"Don't fuck with me."

"Fine. Now, how'd you do it? How'd you get rid of Curly, or do I already know?"

"Curly is hick. Stupid hick. Was easy."

Han nodded. "Good, but how?"

"I scare his runners. They steal from him. I steal from them. What you care how?"

"Okay, fair enough. Dalton is a direct line to one of the cartel's people."

"What this means?"

"He's like a made guy in your old world. Dalton is like a captain. A capo. He reports to what might be an underboss. We need to grab somebody from Mexico. If we grab somebody above Dalton, we could hit them with life. That's when the boys are separated from the men, and most of them revert to boyhood real fast and give up whomever they can."

"Life and then he talks?"

"Usually."

"When they don't?"

"If they give a fuck about their families, they tend to hold their water. If not, the cartels will kill everyone in their family. Some rather kill themselves than live with who they go after. Two we know of killed themselves rather than talk. On the other hand, some of these guys are the worst forms of human scum. Pure dirtbags. They won't care if their grandchildren are set on fire. There's no guarantee about what you'll run into there. I told you about the guy they tied to a tree."

"For the bears. I tell that to Curly, he throws up."

"I'll bet," Han said. "And don't forget the wolves. It's a horrible way to die, but that's what they do. No bullet to the head unless they're in a big rush."

Amato said, "And if I have to kill bigshot from Mexico?"

"You mean in self-defense?"

"Then you have no one to talk," Amato said. "Nobody to snitch."

"Maybe we already have one we're trying to impress."

"You fucking guys."

"I'll take that as a compliment," Han said. "Either way, it sends a message."

Amato smirked. "CIA, eh?"

"How you doing with the waitress?"

"I like her."

"She in love?"

Amato sneered at Han. "How I know this?" he said. "Love? We fuck. We kiss, we sleep together. We eat together. All free time together. I like her. She like me, but she don't like when I went with Curly. She don't like Curly."

"Like a wife," Han said.

"*Si*, like wife," he said.

"It's best you don't marry her."

"For me or for her?"

"For both of you."

"And if I want to take her with me?"

"Why would you want to do that?"

"Yes or no?"

Han gave it a moment. "I wouldn't advise it, but if she wants to go, if she'll keep you happy, sure. Knock yourself out."

"I don't know she wants to go. I ask. I don't force."

"She has family in North Dakota."

"You look into her, eh?"

"We look into everybody."

"CIA, eh?" Amato said.

"Okay, then," he said. "Good luck."

Maryanne Esposito was about to leave for work when she opened the front door and was facing two NYPD detectives. When they presented their badges and asked for Larry Levy, she told them he was asleep and asked them to wait outside while she woke him.

She wanted to stick around, but Larry insisted she go to work. He let the detectives inside the apartment where they spoke in the kitchen. He knew what they were there for but played dumb until he couldn't without looking more suspicious than was necessary. He denied knowing anything about what had happened at the Winkler apartment, stating the truth about him being on his way to see Paul and maybe going to lunch together.

They knew about his phone call to Winkler's cellphone. Larry could tell that both detectives were eye fucking him to make him nervous, but he held his water and continued to deny knowing anything at all about what or why Paul killed his wife, or about the wiseguy with the Cirelli crime family Paul had killed.

Halfway through their questioning, a cellphone buzzed. One detective took the call in the living room while the other made small talk about how warm the weather was of late. The detective started to talk sports when the other detective returned and ended the interview. He didn't look happy about it and said someone else would be coming to talk to Larry.

Larry was confused. He had no idea why the police had suddenly left without giving him more of an interrogation or explanation. He didn't know what they meant about someone else speaking with him until ten minutes later when there was another knock on the front door. Larry answered it wondering if it was the FBI.

"Special Agent, Brian Fein," the man said, holding his FBI identification out for Larry to see.

Larry frowned. There was nothing to wonder about anymore. He felt a hollow feeling in his stomach and stared back at the Special Agent.

"May I come in?" Fein said.

Larry waited a moment, then stepped back to let the Special Agent inside the apartment. They went to the kitchen where Larry offered the agent a cup of coffee.

"No thanks," Fein said. "I'll assume you know what this is about."

Larry waited.

"The cops that were just here?" Fine said. "We called them off. They were homicide. I'm with a task force."

"Organized crime?" Larry said.

"That task force, yes," Fein said.

"I hope you know I'm Jewish."

"I do."

"So, I'm not a wiseguy. I can't be one. And I don't know why Paulie did what he did."

"We already know it had to do with his wife."

Larry tried shrugging again.

"And we know why you and Paul and Fred Greco went to South Dakota."

"I left after Paul did. I didn't go to South Dakota."

"Why didn't you go to South Dakota?"

"I missed my girlfriend."

Fein smiled, then said, "You and Paul were friends, correct?"

Larry nodded.

"You're also a felon. Correct?"

Larry nodded again.

"And you were both heading to South Dakota with a known associate of the Cirelli crime family. Correct?"

"I think this is when I should talk to a lawyer."

"You're prerogative, but I do know the answers to most of the questions I'm asking."

"I think I should talk to my lawyer anyway."

"Fine. Now let me tell you something rather than ask."

Larry waited.

Fein said, "Your friend Fred was directly under Charlie Bruno, the guy Paul killed, probably for whatever Bruno was doing with Paul's wife, the other person he killed. Do you wanna guess how Charlie Bruno knew to visit Winkler's wife?"

"Huh?" Larry said.

"Charlie Bruno learned about Sharon Winkler from your friend Fred Greco, who has also spent some of his carnal spare time with Sharon Winkler. I guess he's the lucky one in this so far, Fred is. Could've been him Paul Winkler shot in the head."

Larry was stunned. Fred and Sharon? He gave it a moment, then wondered if it was bullshit. He knew that cops did that sometimes, make up shit to foster betrayal between friends. It was one way to get what they wanted confirmed.

Then he remembered asking Fred directly while they were on the road about Sharon and whether he thought she cheated.

"Fuck," he said.

Fein said, "What's that?"

Larry shook his head.

"Okay, so how long you think it'll take before Fred fesses up to the trip you guys were making? And trust me, we know what you were expected to do in South Dakota."

Larry swallowed hard. "I'm going to have to speak to my attorney," he said.

"Okay, but if you actually have one and he's any good, he's gonna advise you get yourself into our offices sooner rather than later. That rumor about the guy who cooperates first gets the best deal? It's true, unless you're a wiseguy and you can take down somebody higher up. Like you said, you're Jewish, so I don't think you're gonna have that option."

Larry swallowed hard again.

Then Fein left his card on the kitchen table and headed for the front door. He stopped before exiting the apartment to say, "Have a good long talk with your girlfriend, Mr. Levy."

Larry remained silent.

"Fuck me," Larry said once the door closed. "Motherfuck me."

Maria Greco's morning began with a phone call from Larry Levy asking for Fred. Larry sounded anxious and said he needed Fred to give him a call. He told Maria that the FBI had questioned him, and Larry thought he should get a lawyer. He also said he thought Fred should do the same thing and that they needed to work with the FBI.

Maria had just fed her son and was too nervous to eat herself when the doorbell rang. She was holding her son when she went to the door. She went up on her toes to look through the small window at the top of the door and saw a man in a business suit holding something in his hand. She took a moment to compose herself, then opened the door and the man introduced himself.

"I'm Special Agent Fein with the FBI," he said. "Is your husband home?"

She had to swallow before she could answer. "I'm sorry," she said, "he's not right now."

"Are you expecting him anytime soon?"

Maria shook her head, afraid to say anything.

"It's okay," Fein said. "We know he was out of town. Is he on his way back?"

Maria swallowed harder this time. She said, "I'm not sure when he'll be back."

Fein produced a business card and handed it to her. "If you could have him give me a call when he's back," he said, "I'd appreciate it."

Maria felt her mouth twitch. Fein smiled at her before turning and heading toward the stoop.

"Oh, God," Maria said behind the door. She suddenly felt dizzy and quickly set her son on the floor before she fainted.

It was six o'clock in the morning when Fred Greco made it back to Brooklyn. He'd taken several hits of NoDoz caffeine pills washed down with Coca Colas and several cups of coffee to make the trip on his own. He'd stopped for bathroom breaks and gas only. He wasn't far from home when exhaustion took over, and he fell asleep in a rest stop parking lot in Pennsylvania for more than five hours. The trip from Yankton to Brooklyn took him just under 30 hours, eight to ten more than if Paul or Larry hadn't abandoned him.

His system was going through a nervous withdrawal when he arrived home. His wife insisted he eat something before trying to sleep. He had spoken to Maria a few times to update her on his progress heading home until his exhaustion won out at the last rest stop in Pennsylvania. He knew that an FBI agent had gone to their home and that Larry Levy had called asking for him.

"I think Larry is going to cooperate with the FBI," Maria said. "He sounded very nervous."

Fred knew there would be no escaping his own direct connection. "I'll call him when I know more of what's going on," he said. "He left me alone, the prick. I don't care if he's nervous. I'm the one who has to worry now."

Maria was glad he was home, but nervous about her husband's mob connections. She knew who Charlie Bruno was and what he was and the faith her husband had in the gangster. She remembered the day Bruno sponsored Fred in front of a mob meeting of some kind and how proud her husband had been the next day.

Now she was fearful of the possible consequences for her husband. Television and radio news had already reported that Charlie Bruno had been a cooperating witness. And then an FBI agent showed up at her door.

When Fred finished eating, he was too tired to shower and crawled into their bed to sleep. He slept soundly for five hours before he woke up again. Fearful he might pass out, Maria stood in the bathroom while he took a quick cold shower. When he got out of the shower and dried and moved to the kitchen, Fred struggled to focus. He was overwhelmed by all that had happened since he left for South Dakota.

Maria stayed by his side afraid he might suffer a heart attack.

"You okay?" she said.

"Paul killed Charlie Bruno," Fred said. "You tell me."

"I know, honey, but is there anything they can arrest you for? Did Charlie ask you to do things they might know about?"

"Not murder, if that's what you're asking. But other shit? Yeah, of course."

"Then maybe it's time to walk away."

"Where'm I walkin', Maria? This shit has been my life, for nine, ten years now. If I walk, I have to walk from everything. Besides, now that the FBI or the police, whichever one did it, let the world know Bruno was cooperating, then he has me on tape with Bruno and I'm fucked anyway. I'll have to confess to crimes I was involved in, that's how those deals work."

"Then you need a lawyer. Or do what Larry said and the both of you go meet with that agent."

"Right, sure. That's all I need to do now. After Bruno was wearing a wire? First, I gotta know what that piece of shit gave them on me."

"How can you do that?"

Fred huffed, then looked at the highchair and said, "Where's Junior?"

"Taking his nap. Tell me, Fred. What happens to us now? What did you do?"

"Beatings, robberies, shakedowns, bookmaking, loansharking. Enough."

"With Larry and Paul?"

"Most of it, yeah, except Paul is off the hook now, isn't he? The prick."

"Was his wife really cheating?"

Fred couldn't look at her then. "Who knows," he said. "Maybe. Probably, if he killed her and Bruno, that rat bastard."

"Who can you talk to now?"

"I don't know. I tried calling Grasso from the car, but they wouldn't take my call at the social club. That wasn't a good sign."

"Grasso is someone important?"

"He's the underboss, so yeah."

"Do they suspect you of cooperation?"

"I don't know, Maria. Please. No more questions. I'm going out of my mind trying to figure this shit out."

Maria gave it a moment, then said, "You need to get a lawyer and go see that agent. You and Larry both. Go talk to him. What do you have to lose?"

Amato was in a good mood when he picked up Brenda Lee from work. He noticed a tear in her blouse and that one of the nails on her left hand was covered with a band aid. She avoided kissing him hello and he turned the engine off.

"What happened?" he said.

Brenda Lee turned away from him. "Nothing," she said. "Let's go."

"Oh!" Amato yelled, then grabbed her left hand. "The fuck is this?"

"Eugene."

"Eugene what?"

"He's drunk. It's no big deal. I took an extra hundred from the register when he used the bathroom."

"And your finger? Your shirt?"

"It's nothing, Reggie. Let's go home."

"Fuck home," he said, then opened his door and stepped out of the car.

"Don't!" Brenda Lee yelled, but it was too late.

Eugene had just stepped out of the employee's door and was locking it. When he turned around, Amato punched him in the stomach with a quick uppercut. Eugene dropped to his knees and spewed, some of it landing on Amato's construction boots.

"Motherfucker," Amato said.

He wiped the tops of his boots on Eugene's shirt, then kicked him in the face and had to wipe the blood off, again on Eugene's shirt. When he returned to the car and sat behind the wheel, he could see Eugene was spewing again.

"He's gonna fire me now," Brenda Lee said.

"He no fire you," Amato said. "We going away tomorrow."

"What? Where?"

"Montana."

"Why?"

"New job for me. You coming with me?"

"Jesus, Reggie, what's going on?"

"I tell you when we get home, *Bella*," he said, then leaned across the console and kissed her forehead.

Then he started the engine, backed out of the parking lot, and headed to the trailer.

Back in the RV, Brenda Lee showered while Amato watched the local news. A rash of violent crimes had ranked Yankton, per capita, one of the worst smaller cities. Armed robberies, aggravated assaults and rape were on the rise. There was a vague mention of drug related crimes until fentanyl was mentioned. Three people had died from overdoses within the last two weeks.

Amato wondered if Brenda Lee's boss would report what had happened earlier. It wouldn't make a difference if she went with him to Montana.

When she came out of the shower, Brenda Lee was wearing a robe. She went to the kitchen for a glass of milk, then returned to the living area and sat on the couch a few feet from Amato.

"What's wrong?" he said.

"You," she said. "You're scaring me. What's this about Montana?"

"The fuck you talking about? How I scare you?"

"I don't think you're being honest with me. I don't know why. I love you, Reggie. At least I think I do. But what if I'm wrong and you want to kill me too?"

"Kill you?" Amato said, forcing a smile.

"I know you killed Dog."

"How you know this?"

"I just do."

"And if I did?"

"I'd ask you why, but you wouldn't tell me. That or you'd have to kill me."

Amato laughed.

"It's not funny, Reggie."

"It's very funny. I never kill you, *Bella*. And if I tell you what I'm doing, you have to make decision maybe you don't want, but I don't kill you either way."

"Tell me."

"You're sure?"

"Tell me, please."

Amato told her everything, from where he was born in Italy to his mother bringing him to New York to live with her brother and his sons, to her return to Italy where his father died from his cancer to his mother being raped and murdered, his stint as a member of the New York mafia, and so on to his last days in the Yankton Prison Camp and the deal he'd made with the FBI or CIA, he wasn't sure which, to infiltrate the Mexican cartels operating in Montana, and why he'd killed the man they called Dog.

When he was through telling her his story, Brenda Lee was in tears.

"Now you know I am killer, that I've killed, you want to run away," Amato said. "I'm sorry for that."

She clung to him then. "No," she said. "Not at all. I told you, I love you."

"No, *Bella,* you say you think you do."

"And you? Do you have feelings for me? Real feelings?"

He took her face in his hands and kissed her forehead again. "*Bella,* I love you or I'm not here, eh? This is over, we get married. Now, you coming with me or no?"

Brenda Lee was crying then. "I'll go anywhere with you."

"Then we go to Montana."

"I don't like it about the cartels. That's dangerous."

"You come or still scared I kill you?"

"Stop it. I said I'm sorry."

"You come?"

"Of course."

NINE

"Still practicing your answers?" Special Agent Fein asked Larry Levy.

Larry was blocking the front doorway with both arms extended up and out, his hands grasping the doorframe. Two minutes ago, he heard the doorbell ring and peaked through the living room blinds and saw it was the FBI agent again. He went to the door and was surprised when the agent presented his badge.

"We already met," Larry said.

"I tried calling last night," Fein said. "You must've been too busy to answer the phone."

Yesterday Larry had ignored half a dozen phone calls to his cellphone, all from the same number.

"I haven't hired an attorney yet," Larry said. "I can't answer your questions without speaking with one first."

Fein said, "Care to go inside to talk or do I freeze my balls out here?"

"I'm fine right here," Larry said. "Besides, I already told you, Paul thought his wife was fooling around on him. Turns out it was true."

"She was probably banging half of Brooklyn," Fein said. "That's not why I'm back. The reason you returned. It might help you down the road, because nobody is gonna buy that bullshit about you missing your girlfriend."

"It's the truth."

"Sure it is. And Fonzalla, that how you say it? He learn about why you were going to South Dakota or what?"

"That's fucked up," Larry said. "He was a friend of mine. A longtime friend."

"You get in on his wife's action?"

"Fuck you."

"Sorry, but I have to ask. Since your buddy Freddy Greco has been with Paul's wife, we saw it as a possibility. Apparently, a few guys, but Freddy and Charlie Bruno were the ones named on tape."

"You should talk to my attorney."

"You don't even have one yet and I can't imagine what the hell you're waiting for," Fein said, "but since Charlie Bruno was a cooperating witness and was wired for sound and we picked that much up in a conversation with another wiseguy, there's very little we don't know about, including, like I said yesterday, your trip to South Dakota."

"That's enough," Larry said. "No more questions."

Larry started to close the door when Fein said, "When did you know what you were going to South Dakota for? Freddy Greco explain it before you left or while you were on your way?"

Larry paused a long moment, then shut the door.

☐ ☐ ☐

The agents met at a Brooklyn diner this time. Special Agent Ryan had been talking with an NYPD Detective on the organized crime task force. Special Agent in Charge, Thomas Wells, was there for the agents' report and a briefing.

"Larry Levy is ready to fold," Fein said, "but he wants to talk to an attorney he certainly can't afford. His girlfriend is a legal secretary, so the attorney they use will probably come from her firm. I give him another day or two, maybe after he talks to Greco."

"The longer he sits on it, the more nervous he'll get," Ryan said. "Good play."

"What've you got," Wells said to Ryan.

"NYPD task force isn't holding anything back," Ryan said. "They're as clueless as we are about the sudden disappearance of Giovanni Rapino from Big Sandy. They didn't even know about his move to Yankton."

"Charlie Bruno was wired when they found him?" Wells said. "But unless it was one of us, somebody released he was a cooperating witness."

"NYPD," Ryan said. "They won't admit to it but who else?"

"One of ours," Wells said. "It's not like we're above suspicion."

Fein said, "If he was wearing a wire while he was getting a blowjob or whatever, it was NYPD released it. They're the ones found the bodies after some neighbor called in the gunshots."

Ryan chuckled. "We need to see the coroner's report," he said. "I gotta know if the woman had a mouthful or not."

Wells chuckled. "I gotta admit, that was something else," he said. "A wiseguy gets whacked by a jealous husband."

"Probably not the first time," Fein said.

"A guy kills a wiseguy, then his wife, and then himself," Ryan said. "Nice and tidy for the NYPD."

"And a nightmare for us since," Wells said. "You know about this woman?"

"Not really," Fein said. "She was mentioned on the last tape with

Grasso."

"True that," Ryan said. "Apparently, the late Mrs. Winkler was skilled at giving head. That's how she was mentioned on the tape."

Fein said, "Freddy Greco was getting a piece of her too. He mentioned it to Bruno."

Wells set his menu down. "What about the other guy, the shooter. Winkler? Anything from Grasso on him?"

"No," Ryan said. "Grasso only mentioned Greco a time or two, and only while talking to Bruno."

"Paul," Fein said, "the husband, he's Jewish like Levy. They nicknamed him Fonzi or some shit. He was on his way to South Dakota with Greco and Levy when he turned around and came back. Never made it to South Dakota. Levy neither. Those were the two heading west with Greco."

A server stopped at their table. Both men ordered toasted bran muffins.

Wells said, "Both guys turned back. Let's accept Winkler's reason. Why'd Levy take off?"

"He gave me some bullshit about missing his girlfriend, but that's not the reason," Fein said. "Either Greco told him at the last minute what they were doing, or he shit his pants after Winkler headed back."

"Could be he didn't know why he was going and found out once Winkler split," Ryan said. "That rings true. He doesn't seem the type to pull off a hit."

"He's the one did time, though, right?" Wells said.

"Small bid over an assault," Fein said. "Hit a cop in a bar and the cop had witnesses probably were home sleeping. Some cops have very fragile egos, especially when a civilian kicks one of their asses. Still doesn't make him a killer, not from what I sensed. I think he's nervous now. Probably waiting for Greco. I'm hoping they both come in."

Wells sipped his coffee. "You think Greco can be flipped?"

"Anybody can be flipped," Ryan said. "He's got a wife and young kid, he's the perfect candidate."

"Where using his situation with Winkler's wife doesn't work," Fein said. "I thought about it. The wife might opt to walk away from him she learns he's been sticking it to his friend's wife. Would Greco still talk after something like that?"

"It's still a powerful option," Wells said. "Don't ignore it."

"I think I'm going to have to. Levy knows Greco was involved with Winkler's wife now."

"You had to tell Levy. Give him reason not to think so highly of his friend."

Ryan said, "You two are too cruel for me."

"Yeah, right," Fein said.

All three chuckled.

"We don't have an insider on South Dakota yet," Wells said. "Every now and again I have a nightmare about how things sometimes get fucked up. And three letters pop into my head. C, I and A, and if that's the case it won't make a difference if they fess up about going after Rapino."

"That's a hole we needed to be plugged a few weeks ago," Fein said before sipping his coffee. "If it's not CIA, then who? No record of a change in appearance. No record of location. That's not us."

"The hell would the CIA want with Rapino?" Ryan said.

"All I know is Bruno wasn't about to ruin his proffer giving us that kind of information," Fein said. "That was leverage for what it was worth. Dopey bastard got himself killed for what?"

"We sure it's Bruno's connection with the prison bureau?" Wells said. "Maybe it was Grasso."

Ryan said, "Grasso's one tight-lipped SOB. He deflects on that at every turn."

"Another trump card maybe?" Fein said.

"Maybe," Ryan said.

"And we have this mess all because Charlie Bruno couldn't resist a blowjob," Wells said.

"Not just any blowjob," Ryan said. "Apparently she had a magic mouth, according to the last Bruno-Grasso tape. That always intrigued me when I heard shit like that on some tape. I try and picture it, you know?"

"Because you're a sick Irishman," Fein said.

"Where'd he get magic mouth from?" Wells said with a smile.

"No idea," Fein said. "It's what he said."

"Think it's possible Greco never made it to South Dakota?"

"I already went to his apartment. His wife answered. Claimed he wasn't home. Pro'bly he heard about Charlie Bruno getting whacked from his wife."

"Maybe," Ryan said, "But it's standard operating procedure they school their wives how to answer questions about their husbands."

Fein said, "Maybe he is home and sweating it out about Bruno wearing a wire. I'll let him stew for now."

The server appeared with their muffins and all three agents thanked her, and then proceeded to eat.

The morning they left for Montana, when Brenda Lee woke up, she began packing her things and was smiling when she thought about the only other man to kiss her forehead the way Reggie had. When she was a young girl, her father used to kiss her forehead whenever he told her how much he loved her. None of the other men in her life had ever done the same thing until Reggie. She was sure she was in love with him yet fearful of his mafia past.

When Amato awoke, she told him they had to stop at her place to get the rest of her things. Amato told her to make sure she took her guns.

Brenda Lee said, "Why?"

"No questions now, *Bella*. Bring guns."

Brenda Lee also wanted to leave the next month's rent for her landlord before taking off. Amato didn't understand leaving the money but agreed to do the right thing before they headed west to Montana.

"We have two days," he told her. "We can stop wherever you want on the way. Is a twelve-hour drive, Dalton says."

"Can we visit Yellowstone?"

"Sure. Where this is?"

Brenda Lee was smiling. "Montana," she said, "but we might have to go through Wyoming to get there."

"Then we go there. Sure, why not?"

"I always wanted to go. Thank you!"

She jumped his bones again, but when he went to pull her panties down, she told him she was too sore. When she went to give him head, Amato stopped her. "No, *Bella*," he said. "Only when we do together."

Brenda Lee couldn't remember a man ever turning down a blowjob because he wanted to satisfy her too.

During the drive to her apartment, she remembered her car and said, "I need to do something about the car."

"What we can do?"

"We don't have time to sell it, but I have a cousin up in North Dakota I can give it to."

"We have time to drive there? Where in North Dakota?"

"Pretty far north. Minot is where she lives. It's near an Air Force base. Maybe I can let her know about it and she can come get it. I can leave the key in the ashtray or something."

"Sell to her?"

"No, not Cecily," Brenda Lee said. "She's my girl. My cousin. She's gay and the only one in my entire family I can talk to. She's like me, a black sheep, I guess."

Amato was confused. "How she's black?"

"Not black, silly. Black sheep. She's the bad one in her family, what they think because she's gay. Our family is super conservative. Very constipated."

"You make me dizzy, *Bella*."

She kissed him long and hard.

"I like this, but make call to your *cugina*, okay? We have to go now."

"*Cugina*, what's that?"

"Cousin. *Cugina* for girl. *Cugino* for boy. *Cugini* for more than one cousin. Now, make call."

Brenda Lee called her cousin in North Dakota, telling her where the car would be and that she should pick it up as soon as possible since there were only two weeks left on her lease for her apartment. It would be in the street waiting. Brenda Lee didn't get into details, except to say she'd met someone, and they were moving to Bozeman, Montana, and that she'd contact her again once they were settled.

When she was off the phone, she had tears in her eyes.

Amato said, "Why you cry, *Bella*?"

Brenda Lee shook her head. "I miss her," she said.

Amato drew her in with his right arm as he leaned toward her and kissed her cheek. A few minutes later he parked in front of the house where Brenda Lee lived in a basement apartment. They both went inside and packed more of her things, then left an envelope with money for her landlord. Amato moved the stuff she wanted to take from the apartment to his car, filling the trunk and the back seat. When they finally took off again, it was a little after eleven o'clock in the morning.

Five hours later, after one stop to use the bathrooms and pick up coffee, they were in Rapid City, close to the Black Hills National Forest. They had lunch at a Pub and Grill before stopping at a motel for a round of sex that led to sleep and a five-hour delay before heading out again.

Brenda Lee was feeling good about Amato and their relationship because at the least it had taken her away from the stagnation of life of Yankton. Until she met Amato, her life there had become a boring routine that involved an occasional fling with someone from out of town, usually a trucker she'd met at the restaurant passing through on his way across the country. She didn't trust the local crowd. From prior relationships, she felt a local relationship was more dangerous, at least as regards being stuck in something difficult to leave.

Amato was different. Far different from anyone she'd ever met. She was immediately attracted to him and hadn't been scared off by his immediate past, neither FPC Yankton nor his admission of being a killer for the mafia.

She was no longer concerned about how long they'd remain a couple. Amato had been loyal to her thus far. There might be younger competition where they were going, but she could always do her crying over a lost relationship on a flight to her cousin in North Dakota. Cecily would never turn her down.

There were a few ways to get to Bozeman once they left Rapid City, but Brenda Lee had said she wanted to visit Yellowstone National Park. Amato knew they had enough time and took US-14 through Wyoming to the East Yellowstone entrance to the park. It would be a 7-hour drive and both would be hungry. They stopped after 6 hours in Cody, Wyoming to eat. Rather than drive through Yellowstone while tired, they opted to nap in the car instead.

Neither was in the mood for sex. They napped for three hours before heading through the East Yellowstone entrance. Amato paid the fee that was good for several days. There were on U.S. Highway 14 and quickly found Yellowstone Lake. It was enormous. Amato stopped at one of the roadside pullouts to view the Lake. Brenda Lee wanted to get out and walk down to the water until Amato pointed to a sign that read: *"Bears can run up to 35 MPH. Can you?"*

Brenda Lee remained in the vehicle.

They drove slowly around the lake until they hooked up with U.S. Highway 20, which also ran along the lake, then hooked up with U.S. Highway 191, which would take them through a larger portion of the park, then Big Sky and into Bozeman.

Brenda Lee was excited by the views, especially when they passed the occasional bison or elk. When she saw the sign for Old Faithful, she wanted to stop and wait for it to erupt. Amato parked in one of the lots. They walked into the Old Faithful Lodge and saw a clock inside that suggested the geyser would blow again in 30 minutes.

Amato saw there was a big line for the restaurant and thought they should grab snacks and sodas inside the gift shop instead. By the time they brought them outside to a sitting area around the geyser, a large crowd had already gathered. They decided to stand rather than sit.

Ten minutes later than the clock suggested, the geyser sent a stream of boiling water more than 150 feet high. Brenda Lee was excited as she clung to Amato's right arm. He smiled at her as she jumped up and down.

When they were on the road again, they passed through a half a dozen springs, stopping at one where a crowd of people were walking along a boardwalk around the geysers. She stopped at several of the signs along the walkway. When they reached the starting point, they walked the length of the parking lot to use the bathrooms.

Back in the RV, Amato said, "Pew, what a stink in those things."

Brenda Lee said, "Right? I had to squat over the toilet and hold my breath."

They shared a laugh before Amato headed out of the parking lot back onto 191. They drove along the Firehole River and spotted a big herd of bison close to the highway, then a herd of elk resting in the grass about half a mile from the road.

"Think we'll see bears or wolves?" Brenda Lee said.

"I hope so," Amato said. "But I don't want to see them kill anything. I don't like to watch animals kill each other."

"Just people?" Brenda Lee said with a smile.

"Some people, *Bella*, they deserve it," Amato said.

"Uh-oh."

"Never mind, uh-oh. Look for bears, *Bella*."

Fred Greco waited in his car until Larry Levy's girlfriend left the apartment for work. Once she was out of sight, Fred headed up the stoop and knocked on the apartment door. Larry was both surprised and eager to see him. He let Fred inside the apartment and looked both ways at the street below before closing and locking the door.

They went to the kitchen where Larry poured a cup of coffee for Fred.

"Thanks," Fred said.

"You okay?" Larry said.

"Either one of us okay?" Fred said. "Let me know now if you cut a deal because I can't talk to you if you already did."

Larry shook his head. "I was waiting for you," he said. "I don't even have a lawyer yet."

"Thinking I would have one?"

"No, just wanting to know what you're going to do and if I should do the same thing."

"I don't think it's you who has to worry, Larry. I'm the one they have on tape. Bruno, that piece of shit, was wired. I'm the one spoke directly with him. You guys were no doubt mentioned, but I'm the one with the hammer over my head now."

"What do they have you on?"

"Every fucking job Bruno gave me directly. At least that much."

"We were in on some of those, Fred. Me and Paulie."

"Fuck Paulie. He's got nothing to worry about now."

An uncomfortable moment passed. Fred sipped his coffee. Larry poured a cup for himself.

Larry said, "You get any sleep?"

"Sleep?" Fred said. "A little, but this has been on my mind since my wife told me about it. Fuckin' Fonzi. I used to get upset when people called him that and now he's turned my life upside down."

"The agent that came by left his card. Fein, his name was. Said he knew about us going to Yankton and some other shit."

"What other shit?"

"Said he knew you were talkin' about Sharon to somebody. He said you'd been with her too."

"And you believe that shit?"

"I don't know who to believe, Fred, but that's what he said was on some tape."

"You hear it, this tape?"

"No."

"Ever think maybe it's bullshit? Fuckin' agents lie all the time."

"Like I said, I don't know. But how the fuck would he know about Yankton."

"You tell him why we were going there?"

"I didn't have to, Fred. That's what I'm sayin' here. He knew. Charlie Bruno was wired. That's what he said. Bruno was a cooperating witness. Sounds to me like that's how he knew about Yankton."

Fred clenched his teeth.

"Sounded like it's true," Larry said. "Wiseguys flip all the time now. They must've had something on him, and he decided to make a deal. All I know is you should probably talk to this agent, maybe we both should. Maybe they'll let us both hear those tapes."

"Fuck that," Fred said. "I'm no rat."

"It's not about being a rat now, Fred. If Charlie Bruno was a rat, the fuck do you care what anybody else thinks? He was gonna sell you out along with everybody else."

"This is fucking crazy."

"Yeah, I know it is, and I don't wanna get clipped because of Charlie fuckin' Bruno."

"Clipped how? Who would wanna clip you?"

"For fuck sake, Fred, I don't know and I don't wanna know. All I do know is they already caught me in a lie. What I told the street cop. I didn't mention I knew Paulie. I didn't mention shit, yet this agent shows up knowing everything."

"Charlie being wired puts me in the shitter, not you. He's the guy sponsored me, remember?"

"Then why'd the guy question me?"

"To scare you, and apparently it worked."

"We need to see that agent, Fred."

"Fuck you."

"We need to go."

"You go."

"I intend to."

The drive through the rest of the park took a few hours. Amato asked Brenda where she wanted to live someday.

"With you," Brenda Lee said.

"No, *Bella*, where? Where you want to live?"

"I don't know. Someplace where it's hot, warm at least. Someplace with beaches too."

"Puerto Rico? I go there once. I like it."

Brenda Lee shrugged. "Sure."

"Or Dominican Republic," he said. "Nice beaches. I like there too. American money is very good there. *Come si dice*, exchange rate?"

"Exchange rate," she said, giggling. "Mexico too for that matter. The dollar goes far wherever there's poverty."

"So maybe there. Puerto Rico or Dominican Republic, eh?"

"Sure. Sounds good to me."

There was an accident on one of the roads with a very steep drop. Two cars had managed to collide head-on. All traffic in both directions was halted for more than an hour. Brenda Lee napped while Amato listened to news from a local radio station. There was nothing of interest until a drug arrest was mentioned, but he didn't recognize the town.

Once the traffic was cleared, they drove through the park without spotting any bears or wolves. Outside the park, they stopped in the town of West Yellowstone to use the bathroom and grab coffees to go before heading through Big Sky and further north to Bozeman. Five miles outside the town on State Highway 191, Brenda Lee yelled, "Bear!"

"Huh," Amato said, his head turning left to right and back searching for whatever she'd seen.

"Bear! Stop, Reggie! Stop and turn around! It's back there."

Amato did what she said and was surprised to see a big grizzly bear walking along some brush about 70 yards from the highway. He opened his window and whistled, but the bear continued lumbering south.

Amato leaned on the horn before putting the RV in park. He stood outside near the edge of the highway and waved his arms.

"Hey!" he yelled.

The bear turned and went up on its hind legs.

"Madonna mia!" Amato said.

"Get back in!" Brenda Lee yelled.

"One minute," Amato said, then yelled at the bear again.

Suddenly the bar charged. Amato rushed back inside the RV and shifted the transmission into drive. He raced away. When he looked back, the bear was close to the highway and up on its hind legs again.

"That was crazy!" Brenda Lee said.

"Big fuckin' bear," Amato said.

"It sure was."

"That thing kill me."

"And then eat you."

"Fuck that. I never do again."

Brenda Lee was giggling then.

"What?" Amato said.

"You should've seen your face," she said. "You were scared shitless."

"Hey, I'm no fight a bear," Amato said.

They talked about the bear another few minutes before Brenda Lee said she was hungry again. Amato turned off State Highway 191 and took Lone Mountain Trail. He stopped at the Big Sky Town Center and pulled into a parking lot. Brenda Lee went inside a pizza parlor while Amato took the time to call Special Agent Han.

"Still in Yellowstone?" Han answered.

"It's a big place," Amato said, "but no, we're out of there. I see sign for

Big Sky Town Center. We're there now. She gets a pizza."

"Enjoy it. Listen, when you get to Bozeman, you might be tested."

"Tested how?"

"A mock execution, except it might not be a mock execution if you didn't sell whatever you told Dalton."

"Maybe a murder. Maybe not. I understand."

"Before or after, like in prison, someone will test your stones. I'm not sure which will come first."

"We go there after sleep."

"There's an RV park you can stay until you're ready. It's a hot springs campground. You can take her to the hot springs and enjoy the hot water."

"We see geyser in the park. Old Faithful. Big deal."

"Yeah, but this is like a health resort. They got pools with different temperatures. All from natural springs."

"Okay, maybe."

"We'll talk."

"Okay."

"Watch out for bears anyway. They're all over that part of Montana."

Amato killed the call. A few seconds later, Brenda Lee stepped out of the pizza parlor with a pizza box. They ate in the RV. Amato made a face after taking a bite of the pizza slice.

"What's wrong?" Brenda Lee said.

"This no pizza, *Bella*. This is shit. Someday I take you to New York for real pizza."

"Sounds good to me."

"You like this shit?"

"I'm hungry, darlin'."

"Okay, finish eating shit, we go."

Brenda Lee finished a second slice, then tossed the rest with their garbage in a trash can. She kissed him when she was back inside the car. Then Amato headed out of the parking lot back to State Highway 191 north.

Half an hour after Fred Greco left his apartment, Larry Levy went to the FBI Manhattan offices. "You couldn't get Greco to call, huh?" Special Agent Brian Fein said.

Larry had bought a cup of coffee from a vendor outside the building and set it on the conference table where Fein sat across from him. A tape recorder microphone was facing Fein. Another microphone faced Larry.

"We have coffee here," Fein said. "It's pretty good too."

"I didn't know," Larry said.

"You didn't bring a lawyer."

"Can't afford one."

"If you're going to mention crimes you were involved in, you'll want a lawyer."

"Don't I have to be arrested first?"

"No. If you want to make a proffer, you need a lawyer. Depends on what you have to say, Larry."

"I don't want to go back to jail."

"Did you speak to Greco?"

"Yes," Larry said.

"And?" Fein said.

"He was pissed off. I think more so because I mentioned you claimed he'd been with Paul's wife. He said it was bullshit. He said you guys make up bullshit all the time to keep us guessing or against each other. Maybe if he heard the tape?"

"He can't hear them if he doesn't come in."

"Can I hear them?"

"Not without a lawyer."

"Mr. Fein, I'm not kidding. I really can't afford one."

"We have nothing to charge you with yet, Larry. I mean, if you were aware that your trip to South Dakota was to kill Giovanni Rapino, that's something we can work with. Conspiracy to commit murder is a serious charge. Last time I asked you this, you said you needed a lawyer. You thought you needed a lawyer. Look, if you worried about turning on your friend, try and remember Charlie Bruno had already done that. And make no mistake about the situation should Fred Greco be charged. He'll do what they all do when it's them or somebody else."

Larry said, "But I'll still need a lawyer, right?"

"Did you know what you were going there for? Nod if you don't want to say it. Then get yourself a lawyer and come back and we'll see if your proffer is worth anything."

"What if I turned back when I learned what the trip was about?"

"Doesn't mean anything until you have a lawyer and corroboration. If it's your word against Fred's word, you'd probably get the nod since it was him who brought you the job."

Larry frowned, then said, "I don't want to have to testify against Fred."

Fein said, "I'll tell you this much, whether you learned while on your way or not, Fred Greco knew what it was about, and we can corroborate that already. Your testimony would be another nail in his coffin regarding that."

"You mean the tapes."

"The tapes," Fein said with a nod.

"I can't go back to jail."

"You get caught up in this mess, you sure can go back to jail. Talk to somebody who can lend you the money and find a lawyer. Doesn't have to be some high profile, thousand an hour attorney. Just somebody competent enough to advise you in a proffer."

"You keep saying that word, proffer."

"It's a chance for you to tell us something we can use against others while admitting to crimes you committed. It helps you down the road if you're charged. Most proffers are offered by guilty parties seeking immunity or a reduction in their sentence. There've been plenty of wiseguys who've gone that route, but proffers can also work against you, especially when you tell half-truths. You can't lie to protect yourself or anybody else."

"Thousand an hour? I can't afford fifty an hour."

"Talk to somebody who can help you, Larry. That's the only advice I can give you. This has been recorded in the event you do proffer, which is why I'm insisting you have a lawyer. If I ask you to talk to me without one, it can ruin our case."

"I can borrow from my girlfriend, but I hate doing that."

"You talk to her yet?"

"She knows."

"If she's willing to help you, it seems silly to not let her."

Larry swallowed hard and thanked Fein.

"Just give me a call first," Fein said. "I won't meet with you again unless you have a lawyer."

He removed a card from his wallet and handed it across the table. "My number is on my card in case you lost the first one."

TEN

Amato and Brenda Lee took a room at a hotel that rented utility apartments by the week or month. They showered, had sex, and then fell asleep. A phone call from the lobby half an hour later woke Amato.

He answered it after a yawn. "Hello?"

"I'm Dalton's guy," the voice said. "Meet me downstairs in fifteen."

"Right," Amato said.

"What's going on?" Brenda Lee said.

"Go back to sleep, *Bella*," Amato said. "I meet someone. Stay here."

Amato used the bathroom, then dressed and was out the door within ten minutes. He took the elevator down to the lobby and spotted a man wearing a cowboy hat near the coffee machine. Amato went to him and nodded once.

"Reggie?" the man said.

"*Si*," Amato said.

"Dalton said you was Italian," the man said. "I'm Eddie Warren. Call me Peaky."

"Peaky?"

"They claim I look like the guy on that show Peaky Blinders."

Amato was confused.

"You don't know it?" Peaky said.

"I was inside the prison. No show."

"Right. Anyway, let's go for breakfast and I'll fill you in."

The Last Cowboy Diner was less than ten minutes from the hotel. Peaky was silent until they were stopped at a red light, then he asked how Amato's trip through Yellowstone went.

"See any bears?" he said.

"*Si*, on our way out," Amato said. "Big thing. I tease it and it stands up like a man. When it come to me, I run back inside the RV and took off."

"You don't wanna play with those things," Peaky said. "They're vicious."

"Don't worry. I don't again."

Peaky pulled into the diner lot and both men stepped out of the car. Amato followed Peaky's lead inside the diner to a booth facing the Street.

"Your woman going to work?" Peaky said after a waitress poured two cups of coffee.

"Eventually, sure."

"We can help with that, depending on what she can do."

"She was waitress in Yankton."

"We can definitely help her with that."

"I tell her. Thank you."

Peaky nodded at the waitress as she took their orders. When she left, Peaky said, "Okay, so whatever you've been told about this operation, forget it. I'll tell you once you're ready to know. I'll make that determination. All I can tell you now is common knowledge. The law and everybody else know it. We don't use Mexicans in our day-to-day operations. They're too obvious. That doesn't mean there aren't a few around. Vicious bastards. We use good old Joe and Jane Americans to move the product. Some have legitimate cover-up jobs, some don't. You see that Clint Eastwood movie, *The Mule*?"

"No."

"It don't matter. Most of the people we do use, it's only for a few trips each. Later you'll meet a couple we use. They do the California and back route. It'll make you complicit in drug trafficking if you're caught with them or they roll on you. You already have a record and far as we can tell, you're a standup guy, but you haven't faced twenty-to-life. Those kinds of numbers can make people rethink their honor."

Amato knew to wait for more.

"Dalton claims you're the one probably killed one of Curly's guys to get the job."

Amato remained silent.

"How you feel about Curly?" Dalton added.

"He's *gibroni*," Amato said. "Stupid, eh? Accident waiting to happen."

"He'll be here tomorrow," Peaky said.

Amato was surprised. "Curly?"

"And he's gotta go."

Amato said, "He no have money?"

"Dalton has whatever Curly had when they caught him."

"Stupid guy."

"Yeah, he was. And he'll be your first real job."

Amato chuckled. "So, no mock execution?"

Peaky smiled. "Not that bullshit again. Trust me on this, they don't waste their time on mock anything."

"Who they are?"

"Mexicans, the cartel people. There's always one around. When they want somebody killed, it happens. They don't play mock murders.

Wherever you heard that shit, it's a fantasy."

"Inside is where I hear it."

"Figures," Peaky said. "Inside is loaded with bullshit. Anyway, he'll be in town tomorrow and that'll determine whether you stay with us or not."

"I'll be here."

"Good. There'll likely be a snowstorm in a couple days. You'll get a real taste of Montana weather. It snows here, it's no coating. Shit gets deep. Two, three feet sometimes."

"*Merda*," Amato said. He couldn't imagine trying to navigate in snow that deep.

"Shit?"

"*Si*, crap. Means bad."

"Yeah, it is, but you'll get used to it," Peaky said.

After breakfast, Peaky took Amato up State Highway 191 South toward Big Sky. "Beautiful, ain't it?" Peaky said.

"*Bella.*"

"It's like that television show," Peaky said. "Nothing more beautiful than the Rockies covered in snow."

Amato spotted a few men fly fishing on the banks of the Gallatin River. "Those guys don't worry about bears?" he said.

"I don't know, but they should," Peaky said. "Then again, once it's close to winter, the bears aren't around as much. Torpor."

"What this is?"

"Something like hibernation but not the same thing. They go into deep sleeps but can be woken."

"I don't turn my back to woods like fisherman."

Peaky chuckled. "Me neither."

The drive became a climb through the mountains with sharp curves and steep drop-offs.

Amato said, "I get dizzy looking."

"Don't look down," Peaky said, then pointed up at the mountains they were driving through. They were spotted with patches of snow.

They wound up in a Big Sky condominium complex overlooking a small lake. Peaky explained it was a timeshare operation the cartels had taken through American couples in California. Amato was amazed at the mountains adorned with snow. The apartment was on the third floor of the condo. Once inside, each one used the bathroom, then stood on a terrace overlooking the lake and were surprised when they spotted a cow moose and her calf drinking at the edge of the lake.

"That's amazing," Amato said. "All these things."

"The cow is very protective of the calf," Peaky said. "Moose in general are aggressive."

"How she protects her little one from a bear?"

"You'd be surprised. They'll charge the bear and scare them off, but it doesn't always work. If a bear is aggressive from hunger, they'll kill the cow."

Peaky put up a fresh pot of coffee. He said they were waiting for a shipment of fentanyl laced pills called lollipops. They were on their second cup of coffee when someone knocked on the door. A Glock 9mm at his side, Peaky glanced through the peephole and then opened the door.

A middle-aged woman with dark hair and sunglasses nervously smiled and entered the apartment. She carried a small duffle bag.

Peaky opened the duffle bag, then closed it. He handed the woman a thick wad of fifty-dollar bills, then let her use the bathroom.

Peaky handed Amato a Beretta 9mm with a sound suppressor. "Shoot her when she comes out," he said.

Amato was surprised but knew he had to do it. The sound suppressor suggested it was the real thing. Amato didn't like the idea of shooting a woman.

When the woman stepped out of the bathroom, Amato pointed the Beretta at her and squeezed the trigger twice. The woman nearly fainted and had to be helped up by Peaky, who was laughing.

"No harm, no foul, dear," he said to her.

She asked for water and Peaky grabbed two bottles from the refrigerator. He gave them to the woman and laughed again as she guzzled half a bottle on the spot. He went back to the refrigerator and grabbed two more bottles for her.

"Might wanna use the bathroom again before you take off," he said.

"No thanks," she said.

Once she was gone, Amato said, "No mock, eh?"

"Worth a laugh," Peaky said. He pointed to the bag and said, "Take that down to the second-floor apartment. The door is unlocked. Leave the bag in the kitchen sink."

Amato did as he was told, still wondering about the stunt Peaky had just pulled. He knew the woman didn't think it was funny. When he entered the apartment, it was empty. He set the bag in the sink and left. Peaky met him on the second-floor landing. They went down the stairs and headed to Peaky's pickup.

"No questions?" Peaky said as they pulled out of the development.

"You tell me what I need to know, eh?"

"Good answer."

The drive back to Bozeman took under an hour. Peaky let the radio play and didn't talk. When he dropped Amato off, he said, "We'll pick you up when Curly's back in town."

"I'm be here," Amato said. Then Peaky drove off and Amato headed up to his room and Brenda Lee. He was surprised when she wasn't there.

Brenda Lee had gone for a walk shortly before 11 o'clock in the morning. It was a clear but cold day. She wore dungarees, a white pullover covered with a light blue sweater, a light blue ski jacket and brown leather boots. She walked through two parking lots to North 7th Avenue, then further south until she found a place where she might grab a light lunch. She was about to step inside the diner when she sensed someone had been following her. She looked over her shoulder but didn't see anyone.

She had a salad and iced tea and ordered a slice of apple pie to go. She began to worry about Reggie and where he might've gone as she walked back to the hotel-apartment. His car was still parked in the lot behind the hotel, but he hadn't called her since he left.

Again, she felt as if she was being followed. She stopped and quickly turned around. She noticed a woman wearing a heavy brown Anchorage parka with what appeared to be a frayed Native American designed skirt across the street. The woman stared at Brenda Lee before suddenly turning away.

Brenda Lee crossed the street and walked closer to the curb where she could use the side view mirrors of parked cars to see what was behind her. After a few steps she could see the woman was following her. Brenda Lee ducked into a clothing store and stood behind a rack of shirts as she watched the street. She stayed there a full minute before exiting the store and quickly turning right and bumping into the woman.

"What do you want?" Brenda Lee said.

"Excuse me?" the woman said.

"You're following me. Why?"

"I'm not following you."

"Yeah, you are. Why?"

The woman turned and walked away.

☐ ☐ ☐

Special Agent in Charge Thomas Wells and Special Agents William Ryan and Brian Fein met with Umberto Grasso, the underboss of the Cirelli crime family, in a warehouse under the Brooklyn-Queens Expressway. Grasso was upset. When his handler, Special Agent Ryan, offered him a coffee, Grasso rejected it with a wave of his hand.

"What's wrong with you?" Fein said. "You didn't know about Bruno?"

"Nobody told me," Grasso said. "I talked to my lawyer. He said it's one way you pricks get to overturn my proffer."

"You're a cooperating witness now," Ryan said.

Grasso pointed at Wells. "You their boss?"

"He is," Ryan said. "And I'm your boss as far as that goes."

"My lawyer also told me that in that capacity, you being my boss, my proffer is safe."

"At twelve hundred an hour, I'd tell you whatever you wanted to hear too," Wells said.

"Cute," Grasso said.

"Hey, nobody told your boy to try and sneak a quick fuck with that kid's wife," Fein said.

"Fact is," Ryan said, "Charlie Bruno was an extra big piece of shit. He hears from one of the kids he sent to South Dakota to kill Rapino that the Winkler kid's wife gives great head, and he must've jumped on it. Or what the hell was he doing there?"

"And why was the kid rejected when he tried to call you," Wells said. "He called and you wouldn't take his call."

"Maybe I was busy," Grasso said.

"Nothing should happen to that kid," Fein said.

"Why, you recruited him already?" Grasso said.

"Nothing should happen to him," Ryan said.

"Right," Grasso said. "First off, I didn't send anybody anywhere. That was Charlie Bruno's idea."

Wells said, "Because he had somebody inside the Federal Bureau of Prisons feeding him, or was that you being fed? Who is he? That's what we want to know."

"And you assume I know?"

All three agents waited.

"Charlie's the guy who knew the prison bureau guy," Grasso said.

Ryan said, "The tape we have of you and Charlie suggests you're the one who knows. Remember saying 'our guy?' Saying 'no paperwork?' An email about a game somebody was betting. You forget talking about name changes and so on?"

"Bluster," Grasso said. "Every wiseguy talks shit. He emailed something, action or whatever, that'd make it easy enough, no?"

"Unless it was code, or why the fugazi names?" Fein said. "Besides, three of them on that list of fake names have brothers and we assume they don't live in a bubble. Anybody could be calling in bets."

"So, you did check?" Grasso said, then rubbed his hands together. "I'm Pontius Pilate now."

The agents chuckled.

"What, you don't think wiseguys jerk each other off?" Grasso said. "Happens all the time, my friend."

"Somebody knew something about Rapino leaving Big Sandy," Fein said. "We find out who it is, you don't think he'll tell us which one of you was his contact?"

"I would think it'd be his word against somebody else's word," Grasso said.

"Unless he has evidence," Ryan said.

"And you best hope he doesn't," Wells said.

"You guys kill me," Grasso said. "You lost a rat and you wanna take it out on me now."

"Just remember," Ryan said. "You're exposed, there's no place to go."

"No WITSEC, no nothing," Wells said.

Grasso feigned a yawn, said, "Can I go home now?"

"She was following me yesterday," Brenda Lee told Amato. "Skanky looking thing she was."

She went through the feelings she'd had when being followed and then how she confronted the woman. Amato had tried to calm her, but then realized she was probably right.

"Maybe she does follow," he said. "These are serious people. Maybe they check you are a cop."

"Jesus, that's a little scary."

"They're scary people, *Bella.* The guy I'm with yesterday says he help get you work."

"Jesus, can't I have a few days off first?"

"Of course. Sorry. Come."

He held her tight against him. He kissed her neck and then her mouth, and then they were on the bed removing their clothes and making love. When they were finished and both had used the bathroom, Brenda Lee was still upset.

"What is wrong, *Bella*?" Amato said.

"I don't know," Brenda Lee said. "It doesn't feel right. Now that we're here, I'm afraid. That woman yesterday. You disappeared all day. What if they think the wrong thing? What if they see you with that FBI guy or something? What if they even think that?"

Amato shook his head. "No worry, *Bella*. Today I do something make them forget the law. I didn't disappear. Was business. Someone shows me around."

"You say that but how do you know? They're dangerous people. You say so yourself."

"I know what to do with dangerous people, eh. I tell you this already. The mafia in New York. I survive them, no?"

"I'm still worried."

He slid off the bed and headed into the kitchen. Brenda Lee followed him and was standing alongside him when he grabbed a bottle of water from the refrigerator.

"You also said the mafia is nothing compared to the cartels," she said.

"Sit," he said.

They both sat at the small table and Amato continued, "What I say is that the cartels have no fear like the mafia has. The American mafia, eh? They are brought up spoiled boys. They like to act tough, but they don't do time. The cartel people no fear jail. They come from nothing, so they don't care. Twenty years from now they have same problem as the mafia. Spoiled boys."

"But that's who you're dealing with now, right? The cartels?"

"The people they hire, *si*."

"That scares me."

"Don't be scared. I'm with you, eh? I take care of you."

"And if I'm being following again?"

"What I say, *Bella*? They are careful. They watch to make sure. Don't worry. I'm with you."

"And when you do what they want you to do, the government, I mean. What then?"

"Then we go away. Maybe Puerto Rico or Dominican Republic. Or

Italy maybe. We can go there, too."

"For real? Italy?"

"Why not, *Bella*?"

She went to him, sat on his lap, and then kissed him passionately.

They had dinner at a steakhouse in Bozeman. Amato explained more about the man nicknamed Peaky and how he seemed in charge of the operation in Bozeman. Then he told her about one of his nicknames, girlfriend fucker.

"Girlfriend fucker?" Brenda Lee said. "What's that about?"

"Dalton say this Peaky likes to fuck other men's girlfriends."

Brenda Lee's eyes opened wide. "Like me? Somebody thinks they can fuck me because I'm your girlfriend?"

Amato put both his hands up. "Easy, *Bella*," he said. "Take easy, okay? Is nickname. Who knows who he fucks, this guy."

"Not me! Nobody is fucking me but you, Reggie."

"I know this. You know this."

"Fuck that girlfriend fucker, whoever he is."

Amato laughed.

"I don't think it's funny," Brenda Lee said.

Amato said, "It doesn't happen with you."

"It better not. He better not try. I'll cut his dick off."

"Ouch, *Bella*, don't say this. Drink the mule."

Brenda Lee rolled her eyes. "Okay," said, "but it's a Montana Mule."

"Drink, *Bella*. Drink."

ELEVEN

It was after midnight when Robert Red Dalton picked up Luther Briggs. Dalton was heading back to Bozeman with a tied and gagged Curly in the back of the cab. Briggs was heading out for a fishing trip.

"I see you found him," Briggs said.

"Right where you said."

"And you're bringing him to Bozeman or losing him along the way?"

"Not sure yet. We'll see."

"Why ain't he whining?"

"Oxy."

Briggs turned to glance at Curly lying on the back of the cab floor. "That smell ain't him, I hope."

"Burger King," Dalton said. "I picked some up to save time."

"I don't eat that shit. I'll wait until we're in Deadwood. Get some real food."

"You have somebody there?"

"I do indeed. Drop dead gorgeous redhead. I got her for the weekend. I'd take her back home with me if she wanted."

Dalton smiled. "What's she costing you?"

"A grand. Five a night and worth every penny."

"That's some expensive strange."

"Ain't strange to me. Been with her a few times. Besides, man only live once. I watch my coin, but not when it come to my pleasures. Fly fishing, hunting, good food and pussy. I don't fuck with those things."

"It's a good philosophy."

"What's yours?"

"I married a couple years back. Developed some bad arthritis in my back and figured my playboy days were over. Married one of those good girls, the loyal and anxious to please type. Treat her with respect enough to keep her happy. She's all I need while I'm home."

"I ain't found one like that yet, although at this point in my life I'm not sure I'd want to change it up. Always did for myself, so I don't need more than pussy and I don't need to be married to it."

Dalton chuckled. "So, who's got it better than you?"

Curly was secured with rope and a gag in the back of the cab, but managed to pass wind. Dalton had given Curly a sedative when he was making too much noise crying. Now he had to open his window a crack to let the fetid odor escape.

"Fuckin' guy," he said.

Luther chuckled.

"You know, you could make some beaucoup bucks and live where you love it," Dalton said. "Think about it. An easy gig with all the benefits of living in prime fishing and hunting grounds."

"And I wouldn't have to live in Yankton," Briggs said.

"That too."

"Since when your people hire the law up to Bozeman?" Briggs wanted to know.

"Since the beginning of time," Dalton said. "Think about it, how crooked the police and government in Mexico is. Think about how crooked some police and most of the government here is."

"What you need there from me someone already there can't get you?"

"Fresh eyes," Dalton said. "Sharp fresh eyes."

"Meaning you don't trust nobody."

"You put too much faith in people doing illegal things, you deserve what happens to you. Kind of like Curly if you get my picture."

There was a moan from the back seat.

"Think he heard us?" Dalton said.

"Fuck what Curly heard. What's my guarantee I don't go down with the first big pinch?"

"No guarantees anywhere, Luther. You know that."

"How fuckin' safe is it? I can retire tomorrow, I want. Or I can wait 'til I'm home free and don't need to take chances."

"You like to fish, no?"

"Fly fish, yeah."

"You've been to Yellowstone?"

"Of course."

"How about along the highway, Gallatin River?"

"Once or twice."

"And?"

"It's prime. Your point?"

"You can do that all year. Every weekend, you want. It's the location, brother. You'll be an hour or less from prime fly fishing. Best in the world."

"That is appealing."

"And you'll have the time. It's not like you'll have to fit it in. We work in shifts there, same as your current job."

"The Gallatin, huh? I'll have to think about it."

"You know how to get in touch with me, right?"

"I do."

Dalton removed an envelope from his shirt pocket and handed it to Briggs. "That's for nailing Curly. There's also a bonus five hundred in there for coming to Bozeman."

"I have to give it back if I don't come?"

"No. It's yours either way. Consider it an enticement, like a signing bonus."

□ □ □

"My wife is driving me crazy," Fred Greco said. "She wants me to talk to this agent of yours."

"He's not my agent," Larry said. "He's the agent showed up at my front door because your sponsor was a fucking rat."

"Hey, I didn't know that about Charlie," Larry said. "I wouldn't've worked for him if I did."

"It's too late now, Fred. He was a rat."

Fred waved Larry's comment off. "What'd he have to say, this agent."

"Made it clear you're the bigger prize, for one thing," Larry said. "He wanted to talk to you, not me. He wanted to know if I knew why we were going to South Dakota. He said they already knew that you knew. I guess from the tapes with Charlie."

"Fuck me."

"He also said Charlie learned about Sharon because of you."

Fred was incredulous. "What?"

"That's what he said. He said you'd been with Sharon and told Charlie about her and that's why he was with her when Paulie walked in on them."

"That's bullshit."

"It's what he said."

"Fuck what he said. I told you those guys lie all the time. It's how they get people to turn on one another. Why, you believe that bullshit? You think I'd fuck around with Paulie's wife?"

"I don't know what to believe," Larry said. "Getting head from Sharon isn't the bigger picture here though, is it?"

"I didn't get head from Sharon. That's bullshit."

"Fine. Whatever. The point is they claim they have you on tape. Why they want to talk to you and not me or anybody else. He suggested more than once that I get a lawyer. He said he doubts they can do anything to protect me because there's no direct link to Charlie, but I need a lawyer to make a proffer, that it's in my interest to have a lawyer."

"You going to cut a deal?"

"I think he wants me to corroborate whatever they have on you."

"Of course they do. And?"

"And what? I didn't know about that trip until you told me, and I turned right around and came back. As for the other shit, I'll take my lumps if I have to. I'll admit to what I did, the jobs we did, if you do."

"And if I don't admit to them?"

"Then you're on your own."

"You're un-fucking believable, Larry. You know that? You really are."

"They already know how involved you were from the tapes, Fred. Charlie Bruno fucked you, not me. Now that he's dead, maybe you're okay. I have no idea, but I'm not looking to man-up for the mob. That's your thing."

"I'd have to confess to shit involves you too."

"I know that. I said I'll take my lumps."

"And then I'll have to go away. Not you."

"Hey, I've already been away, okay? And now I don't know if I'll have to go away again. Neither do you. Maybe you work something out with them, it has to be better than going to trial and losing."

"First I gotta know what they have, right?"

"They have you knowing what you were doing in South Dakota. That's conspiracy to commit murder. That's what he told me, the agent."

"Except nothing happened in South Dakota."

"Then get yourself a lawyer, Fred. Maybe a lawyer can protect you from this shit. If all they have are conversations between you and Charlie and Charlie's dead, maybe they're screwed."

"Why I don't wanna go see this agent. How do I know they don't arrest me soon's I'm in the building?"

Larry put up his hands. "Hey, whatever. It's your deal going forward. I'll wait and see until this shit is over. They come for me, I'll be here. Just remember, if you do have to go away, it's a lot better you go on a deal. You fight them at trial, they'll stick the time up your ass."

"Fuck that," Fred said. "I'll let a lawyer handle that shit. He tells me to deal, I'll have to consider it, but that'll cost a fortune. A fortune I don't have, but I'm not going to trial with a public defender. No fucking way."

Fred had been sitting on the edge of Larry's couch. He sat back and sighed.

"I cut a deal, I'll be branded a rat," Fred said.

"By future rats," Larry said. "Or rats still operating on the street. What do you care what they say? They're all full of shit, Fred. Charlie Bruno was full of shit."

"I tried to talk to Grasso. He wouldn't take my calls. That spooks me."

"I doubt anybody'll go near you now because of Bruno."

"He sends me to South Dakota to whack a rat and he's one all along. Un-fucking believable."

"It's a good thing that never happened," Larry said. "Imagine it did? We'd be going up for murder."

"You mean I would. You turned around and came home."

"You would've told me what we were going for in the first place, I never would've left Brooklyn."

Fred shook his head, then said, "This is so fucked up."

"Well, I didn't say shit."

"I didn't say shit."

Fred bit his lower lip. "Paulie really fucked us," he said.

"I think you need to thank him at this point."

"What?"

"Paulie, he doesn't turn around and come back, find Bruno with his wife and kill them, you kill that other guy, they'd have you for that. If it's on some wire, they'd have you dead to rights."

Fred glared at Larry a long moment, then frowned. "You're right."

"Maybe they let you off the hook for it," Larry said. "The conspiracy thing. Maybe we confess to the other shit we've done, they give us both a pass."

"They'll give you a pass," Fred said. "I'll have to do time. I got a kid, Larry."

"You also have parents," Larry said. "Maria has parents. They get by until you're out. It'd be a shorter sentence than if you're found guilty at trial. I'd plead guilty in a heartbeat. I will if that's the only other option."

"If I could only talk to Grasso," Fred said. "At least he could tell me what to do."

"Unless he's wired too," Larry said. "At this point, I wouldn't trust any of them not to be wired."

☐ ☐ ☐

Curly had been terrified. He'd wet himself shortly after being stunned with a taser. He wet himself again when Dalton dropped Luther Briggs off in Deadwood, thinking they were going to kill him.

A few miles from Bozeman, Curly's bowels released, and his diarrhea filled the cab with a smell that forced Dalton to pull to the side of the road and spew the cold hamburger he'd eaten a few minutes earlier. Furious that he'd have to drive the rest of the way with the smell inside the cab, he pulled Curly out and shot him in the head. He cursed as he dragged Curly's body to the side of the road behind a bush. Then Dalton cut Curly's stomach open and stepped back before the fat man's liquids splashed his boots.

When he returned to the pickup, Dalton realized he would have to drive with all the windows open in temperatures just above 20 . He did so, reaching 85 miles per hour for the last few miles before entering Bozeman.

He left the pickup in a parking lot behind a hotel and called an accomplice with instructions to bring the pickup to a car wash and get the cab cleaned until it smelled like new.

"I don't want to smell that shit again," he'd said. "I'll be staying across the street tonight. Make sure you get that thing cleaned in the morning."

Across the street from the hotel where Dalton and three others working for the same drug operation lived was another smaller hotel. Dalton went there and took his usual room.

He was disgusted at what he'd just gone through. He gagged thinking about Curly's diarrhea and how it had stunk up the cab of his pickup. He would shoot him again if he could.

If they couldn't get the stink out of the cab, he'd either trash the thing and put in an insurance claim or sell it to one of the Mexicans to bring back to Mexico. He'd have to get it to California first and he wasn't about to make that trip if the cab still stank.

Either way, if the cab retained Curly's smell, he'd have to buy a new pickup. He'd stop by the Chevy showroom if he had the chance the next day.

He called Peaky to let him know he was back and to ask if the new guy had shown up. He was surprised to learn they had already made the trip to Big Sky and was pleased to know Reggie Amato had passed the mock execution test. If he hadn't passed, Peaky would have known to leave his body in the woods somewhere and let the animals have it.

When Peaky asked about Curly, Dalton said, "Let's not bring him up ever again."

Then Dalton told Peaky that the cartel's man in charge of the operation, Enrico Sandoval Reyes, was due in town around midnight. Dalton was to meet him at Bozeman airport. He would also have to remind everyone in the hotel not to call Reyes by his middle or nicknames. Sandoval was his middle name. Sandy was his nickname. Enrico Sandoval Reyes was mister Reyes to anybody who knew anything about him.

□ □ □

Peaky was fresh off the phone when he learned the storm headed Montana's way was going to be a potential record setter. He'd had a local news station on in the background and had watched from across the room as the weather map on the television screen showed wide white arrows pointing across the northwest part of the state from Missoula down to Butte, Bozeman and then from Billings into North Dakota.

"Shit," Peaky said.

"What's that, hon?" his girlfriend, Jenna, said.

She was a petite, flat-chested woman with long blonde hair and wide hazel eyes. She'd been living in Bozeman, Montana long before she met Peaky, and long before the cartels had established operations there. She'd worked as a waitress and barmaid for several years, occasionally taking a john to her apartment for extra money. Until Peaky found her smoking weed outside the back of a bar she'd been working one night, she'd lived alone. Peaky befriended her that night and the next day moved her from her basement apartment into one of the rooms at the hotel the cartel had purchased under the name of a local Bozeman resident they had added to their payrolls.

She had been Peaky's steady woman ever since, although sometimes he brought home another woman or two, sometimes escorts, and sometimes women he found on the Internet swinger websites. Lately, he'd been using her to do some due diligence and basic surveillance for him.

When he asked her about the new guy's woman, Jenna told Peaky how she'd followed her but had been discovered doing so.

"Meaning?" Peaky said.

"She asked why I was following her. I told her I didn't know what she was talking about, something like that, but she insisted I was following her. Rather than get into it, I walked away."

"Good girl," Peaky said. "I'll assume she didn't meet anybody."

"Nobody. When I think about it, she was probably setting me up to confront. She must've spotted me early on and didn't let on."

"Some people are more observant than others. Not your fault. You did good."

Jenna smiled. "Anybody coming over tonight?"

"I didn't ask anyone. What this new one look like?"

"Okay, I guess," Jenna said. "Had some mileage on her. At least my age, maybe older."

"Shape?"

"Nice. Good size tits. Nice ass. Like I said, showing some age."

"Think we could get her to join us one night?"

"I don't know. She seemed scared when she spoke to me. Maybe. Maybe when her guy is out of town."

"Fair enough," Peaky said. "You can get her to have a drink, you know what to do after that."

"My good friend Molly," Jenna said. "You gonna send him someplace?"

"Not until I know he's not a plant. I don't trust anybody and especially anybody straight out of prison. We'll see. Befriend her, his girlfriend. Get close enough to go for drinks. Invite her up for a cocktail or two."

Jenna smiled. "Girlfriend fucker."

Peaky shot her a wink.

After Maria Greco received a third threatening phone call, she told her husband that she was taking their son to her mother's house on Long Island until he spoke to the FBI. She said she didn't feel safe and wanted some kind of protection. She had started to pack a suitcase when her husband said he'd think about it.

"If Larry is going to hire a lawyer, you need to also," Maria said.

"I told you Larry's got nothing to worry about. He said if they charged him, he'd cut a deal."

"And you still have to think about it? I'm not staying here while you think about it. Not with some asshole making threats. Not with Junior in the house."

"They won't touch you or Junior. You know that. Anybody makes threats over a phone is a jerkoff. We have to ignore that shit."

"You can ignore it, Fred. I'm not. Look at Charlie Bruno. How close you were with him and what happened? Larry is right. You're both lucky Paulie killed that asshole or you'd never know what he was. Thank God you learned about him before it was too late."

"Did you call your mother yet?"

"Of course I called her. I'm going there, Fred, and I don't think they'll want you there until you hire a lawyer and talk to that agent."

"A lawyer will cost us."

"I don't care what it costs."

"I'm talking about most of what we have."

"I don't care."

"And I still may go to jail."

"It's better than being killed. Or going to jail longer than necessary. I've stood by you through everything, Fred. You're my husband and I love you and I love the father you've been to Junior, but I'm not willing to risk our son's life for your desire to be a wiseguy. What does that even mean anymore? And if you don't get a lawyer and do whatever they want you to do, I won't be happy about it. Junior needs a father to help raise him, not a father he has to visit the next ten years in some prison."

Fred let her finish packing. When she was ready to go, he carried the suitcase down to their car ahead of Maria. She had their son in her arms when Fred was halfway down the stairs and shots rang out from a car parked at the curb. There were five shots in all, four going through the suitcase and striking the stairs before one pierced Fred's left shoulder. The car burned rubber pulling away. Maria began screaming from the porch.

TWELVE

Special Agent, Brian Fein, was waiting outside the recovery room for two hours before he was allowed to see Fred Greco. The surgery took 25 minutes. The bullet slug was removed from his left shoulder. It had cracked the clavicle in two. Fred's arm was immobilized with a figure-of-eight splint.

When Fein was finally allowed to visit Fred, it was in a private room arranged by the hospital for the time until the patient was released later in the day.

Fred was clearly on pain killers when Fein approached his bed. He saw the FBI identification and frowned. "You're the agent spoke with Larry?" he said.

"I am," Fein said.

"He agree to talk?"

"Larry?"

"It's okay if he didn't. This did it for me."

"Did you see who shot at you?"

Fred shook his head. "Ski masks. Driver and shooter. The shooter was in the back. My wife here?"

"She's with her parents on Long Island. We have an agent stationed there. It was just you they shot at."

"My wife was inside. I was taking the suitcase down for her. I heard her screaming after, but the shots came my way."

"How about the car? Recognize it?"

Fred shook his head again. "No. Probably stolen that day. Larry know about this?"

Fein frowned. "I forgot you were in surgery."

"What?"

"Larry Levy is dead."

"What?"

"He was killed about the same time they took a shot at you. Apparently, they were waiting for him to leave his apartment. His girlfriend escaped."

"Jesus. Are you serious?"

"Afraid so."

Fred's teeth clenched. "I can't believe this," he said. "Why the fuck Larry?"

"What they sent you to South Dakota for, apparently," Fein said. "Seems like getting rid of loose ends, and it had to come from Grasso, the order."

"Jesus fuck."

"I don't know if you figured it out yet, but you were set up. They weren't letting any of you survive whether you took care of Rapino or not. That kind of thing, a hit on someone in WITSEC, is too risky. Most guys in your line of work figured that out years ago when Sammy the Bull was walking around without fear of retribution. You weren't getting a button, kid."

Fred's jaw clenched.

"They're not family nor friends," Fein said. "All that bullshit about loyalty and family is just that, bullshit. These days, getting rid of anybody who could point back at them is their highest priority. The truth is, had you guys gone through with what you were doing in South Dakota, had you pulled it off and killed Giovanni Rapino, the same thing would've happened when you returned to New York. Charlie Bruno was already a CI for us. He had no intentions of you stepping up, whether you accomplished what he sent you there to do or not. You would've got clipped either way. You're lucky they missed this morning."

Fred smirked. "Aren't you supposed to warn people when their lives are in danger?"

"If we know for sure, we do. It never got that far, did it? You didn't kill Rapino and Bruno only hinted at what would happen. That tape came with somebody above Bruno."

"Grasso?"

"Maybe," Fein said.

"Maybe? So, what happens next? What do I do? If Bruno is dead and you had him wired, do you know who sent those shooters today?"

"Maybe Grasso, he was Charlie's boss. Maybe Grasso's boss."

"The boss? Falzone? Why would he give a fuck about somebody like me?"

"I said maybe," Fein said. "We don't know, but the word on the street is Falzone is keeping extra distance between himself and his captains, never mind his soldiers and associates. Somebody must've brought the situation to him, probably Grasso. Maybe Falzone okayed it. The old school Dons weren't big on delegating the power of life and death. If Vito Falzone is as old school as everyone seems to believe, he would've had to okay what happened to you and Larry. Technically, associates or not, and Larry and Paul couldn't be, not officially, you're civilians. That's a big no-no."

"What about Bruno? I mean before he was killed?"

"Look, there's no doubt Bruno would've handled it soon as you returned. Don't think because it might've come from above Bruno, he isn't the guy who would've done it. He probably would've handled it himself. At least with you."

"What about some other skipper. Maybe it was one of them. Bruno reported to Grasso. Maybe it was another captain."

"We don't know who took over Bruno's position, if it even happened yet. Once Grasso was bumped up to underboss he was still controlling the crew Bruno was part of. Bruno wanted his stripes. He would've done anything they told him, especially while he had us in his pocket to run to if it went to shit. His mistake was getting a blowjob from your friend's wife."

Fred took a moment, then said, "Larry told me you know about me and Sharon, Paul's wife."

"From your mouth in a conversation with Bruno before you left for South Dakota. There are other mentions about her on a few tapes."

"Is my wife going to learn about that?"

"Not if it's not necessary, but that's up to you, Fred. It's out of our hands if any of this goes to court."

"I don't want her to know."

Fein opened his hands.

"Motherfucker," Fred said. "I'll do whatever I need to do, but I don't want to wind up in prison. Not for those motherfuckers. Not anymore."

"I can't guarantee that. Depends on what you tell us and what we can corroborate and then use, and you'll have to tell us everything. One lie and whatever deal we come up with gets flushed. Whatever you were doing for Charlie Bruno, we need to know. Everything."

"Can it wait until I'm out of here?"

"Doctor claimed you can go home this afternoon."

"You sure my wife and kid are safe? If so, I can go to your office straight from here."

"Then I'll wait for you, and you can come to our office with me. We'll put you in a safe house after that, but again, I can't guarantee you a pass on any prison time. That'll be up to a federal prosecutor."

Fred gave it a moment, closed his eyes and said, "Okay. I'll talk. I'll tell you everything."

□ □ □

Amato left the hotel early to meet with Robert "Red" Dalton and Paul "Peaky" Warren. Brenda Lee had the day to herself and was eager to take a broader walking tour than the one she'd cut short when she realized she was being followed. When her cellphone rang, she knew it was Amato and answered with enthusiasm.

"Hey, babe!" she said.

"*Bella*, you're happy today."

"I am. What's going on?"

"You're getting a visitor in a few minutes."

"I am? Who?"

"Women who follows you. She's a friend."

"What?"

"Is okay, *Bella*. Her name is Jenna. I'm told she is good person."

Brenda Lee remained silent.

Amato said, "*Bella*, is okay. I'm telling you. I'm with her boyfriend now. Go with her. When you're ready to work, she helps you."

"You sure?"

"*Bella*, I am sure. Okay? I have to go now."

"Okay, if you say so."

Amato kissed the phone. "I'm sure," he said. "Have fun."

She still wasn't sure about the woman but had no choice. Fifteen minutes later, there was a knock on her door.

"Sorry about yesterday," the woman said, extending her right hand. "I'm Jenna. Did Reggie call?"

Brenda Lee took Jenna's hand. "He did. Just now."

"You ready to go? We can eat something first or just walk around and go shopping. It's best we do it today because they're talking about a big storm heading this way."

"Oh, okay. Let me use the bathroom and get my things."

"Sure," Jenna said. "By the way, Peaky, he's my boyfriend? He mentioned you were looking for a job. I can help out with that."

"Great," Brenda Lee said from the bathroom.

They spent the next few hours walking the streets of Bozeman, Jenna pointing out the good bars, clothing stores and restaurants. They stopped in a bar near the hotel and ordered lunch.

Brenda Lee was still leery of Jenna but did her best to play the role of a potential friend for Amato's sake. Jenna did most of the talking.

She asked where Brenda Lee was from and how she wound up with Reggie Amato. Brenda Lee kept her answers short but friendly.

Jenna picked up the tab for lunch and left a $5.00 tip for a $38.00 meal. Brenda Lee was tempted to leave another $5.00 but decided she shouldn't insult Jenna.

On their way back to the apartment, Jenna lit a joint and went to pass it to Brenda Lee.

"Oh, no thanks," Brenda Lee said. "I only smoke with Reggie."

"Really?" Jenna said.

"That's right," Brenda Lee said.

"Okay, but you ought to loosen up some about that. Peaky lets me smoke because I'll be more in the mood when he's home from work. He really gets into it when we're high."

Their conversation drifted off until they reached the apartment building. Then Jenna said, "Listen, if you two ever want to hang out with us, just let me know. That snowstorm, when that comes, you two might want to be around some company."

Brenda Lee waited for more.

"Sometimes we get it on with other couples," Jenna said. "You know, like trading partners. Swapping. Peaky is hung like a horse if you're into big cocks. Some people gave him this silly nickname, girlfriend fucker, but that's just jealousy. Women like him, but that isn't his fault."

"I'd never even consider it," Brenda Lee said, "but thanks for the offer."

Jenna lost her smile. "Oh," she said. "That's cool, I guess."

"Yeah, have a good night," Brenda Lee said.

"There's a big shot came in last night," Han told Amato. "Enrico Sandoval Reyes. Smarmy piece of shit but he's big in the cartel. Must be making the rounds. We tracked him from Mexico to California and now he's in Bozeman. Dalton picked him up last night. If we had the chance, we'd take him out, but he's got three bodyguards. It won't be easy. I'm getting some help in case we do get lucky."

Cautious about taking Han's calls in the apartment, Amato had gone to the stairway landing leading to the roof. His burner phone was new, one of several.

"How long he's here?" Amato said.

"No idea," Han said. "He was in San Diego and LA one night each, but he spent two nights in San Francisco. They move a lot once they go that far north."

"How we handle bodyguards?"

"Any number of ways. A simple traffic stop can do it."

"If he's driving. What if they stays in hotel?"

"We'll figure something out. I can't believe how lucky this is. He's a major player."

"What about Dalton, his people?"

"We don't know. Nor do we know of others guarding from the shadows. They won't come out or do anything while a police car stops them, but once the police are gone, they might. If he's here when this snowstorm hits, it'll be a lot easier to make something happen."

"Nobody stops Dalton's people?"

"No. We want it to look like something rogue. Nothing legal. If it's done right, the bodyguards'll go too."

"Rogue like another drug dealer?"

"Yes. Maybe if he hangs around another night."

"I don't know. Who lets me near this guy? Not Dalton."

"I guess we'll find out," Han said.

"You mean I find out."

Han paused a moment and then said, "Something like that."

Amato broke the phone before heading down to the fourth floor and tossing the pieces down the compactor.

Robert "Red" Dalton was having dinner in Enrico Sandoval Reyes' suite. One of Sandoval's bodyguards were stationed outside in the hallway and one inside the room at the door. Dalton sipped a vodka tonic.

"So," Sandoval said, his accent pronounced. "What goes on here?" He wiped his forehead with a wet hand towel.

"Things are fine," Dalton said. "Everything is running smooth."

"You're sure?" Sandoval said.

"I am."

"What happens in South Dakota?"

"Yankton? We had a problem. I fixed it."

"People were killed?"

"Two, yes. Two people."

"They are replaced?"

"Yes."

Sandoval stared at Dalton, making him nervous.

"We're okay," Dalton said. "I promise."

Sandoval continued staring.

"How's it going otherwise?" Dalton said, his voice was cracking.

"Depends on snowstorm," Sandoval said. "We hear this before we leave San Francisco. I don't like it, but I'm stuck here if storm is real, if vans can't come tomorrow?"

"From California is what I was told," Dalton said.

"Who tells you this?"

"Your people. Two vans."

"Change drivers when they leave."

"Huh?"

"Change drivers."

"Get rid of them?"

"No, just change. Different drivers. Change routes too. Switch. Different routes. Is safe after South Dakota."

"You mean for distribution."

"That's right," Sandoval said.

"Done."

"Okay, go now. Call when vans are out again."

"Sure. No problem."

Dalton could feel Sandoval's eyes on his back as he headed for the door. The bodyguard opened the door while dead-staring Dalton. Dalton was about to say something but nodded instead.

Outside the room, the bodyguard stared until Dalton forced a weak smile and headed for the elevators. He made it down to the street and made it to the corner before ducking around the hotel and using the front of his shirt to wipe the sweat from his forehead.

Last night had started for Peaky when some Mexican big shot from the cartel arrived at the Bozeman airport a few minutes after midnight. He remained in the background while Red Dalton played the subservient host at the Armory Hotel. He sat in his pickup listening to talk radio. Peaky often enjoyed the crazy back and forth between the radio host and liberal callers until the host cut them off with a wild rant about how Marxism was ruining the country. He didn't like the rudeness of the host cutting off callers.

Peaky used the hotel lobby's restroom. It was clean, for one thing, and he was able to splash cold water on his face to stay awake.

When Dalton finally returned, Peaky drove him home. Dalton remained quiet until he was dropped off with directions for the next day. "The storm may fuck everything up," he said.

This morning, after drinking coffee while watching the local weather, Peaky saw that Jenna was still asleep on the couch. He left her alone while he used the bathroom, and when he came out, Jenna was stretching her arms as she yawned. Then she stood, and Peaky stared at the landing strip of blonde hair between her legs. She was a petite woman, no more than 100 pounds, with tattoos up and down her arms.

Peaky liked her skanky look. It always made him horny when she wore one of his T-shirts, no panties.

"Hey," he said.

"Hey, babe," Jenna said through another yawn.

He made his way to the couch and sat alongside her.

"Blowjob?" she said.

"In a minute," he said. "What's up with Amato's woman."

Jenna told Peaky the new woman wasn't interested in partying with them. Jenna sounded angry about how Brenda Lee had spoken to her, more so than that she wasn't interested in swapping partners.

"Think you could get her up here?" Peaky said.

"She sounds constipated about partying."

"If you get her up here, we can slip her something."

"I thought about that, but not here."

"Then where?"

"Maybe at lunch. Maybe if you give her guy something to do and I go up to her room."

Peaky winked at Jenna, then motioned at his crotch. She winked back, then opened his pants and went down on him.

THIRTEEN

Wasfi Khalidi was a 52-year-old Palestinian-American lawyer, who had been practicing criminal law for 15 years in the United States, the first five of which as a public defender. Most of his clientele were poor men and women ensnared by poverty and a justice system that offered them plea deals with longer than average prison sentences. When the Levy couple retained him for $5,000 and their need of representation to a proffer agreement with a federal prosecutor, Khalidi promised them he'd do his best to keep Larry out of jail.

A day after the ruse the FBI was playing against other members of organized crime by spreading a rumor that Larry Levy had been murdered, Khalidi sat with a federal prosecutor and structured the proffer so that Larry, assuming his testimony was true and accurate, would serve a minimum amount of time, if any, in a minimum-security facility.

Khalidi brought the couple from the FBI office in Federal Plaza to his home for their protection. He spent the early morning explaining what the federal prosecutor was seeking. Maryanne wanted to know if they'd have to go into the Witness Protection Program. Khalidi assured her they likely wouldn't, and that since they weren't married, there could be a problem arranging security for them.

Larry was upset about Maryanne's exposure and insisted she be a part of any kind of protection.

"You're both getting ahead of yourselves," Khalidi said, smiling then. "There's a long way to go. First, they need to decide whether they're going to charge you, and then there's what happens with whomever else they're going to charge and how many cockroaches will come running out from under a table after that. The cockroaches can turn things upside down too. Look, they're clever, federal prosecutors are. Once they have your friend in to give his proffer, they'll compare it to yours. They'll want to see who might be lying, who might be holding something back, who is being honest and whether you both can provide information they can use against the mobsters they're looking to prosecute. Everything will depend on how things proceed, including whether you told them everything you needed to accurately. Until we know they're going to charge you, and there's a good chance they won't, I'm not saying that to celebrate, but I don't see what they have to charge you with. You committed crimes, but they probably don't need your testimony for the kinds of federal crimes they're pursuing. I can be wrong, because I don't know what they have regarding those tapes or others they might have. Until we know, you'll be fine. You're not a crucial witness. You're not somebody close to their organization. The other thing is this, if they decided to go to trial, it won't be for another year or two and you wouldn't have to spend it waiting in some prison."

"Finally, it pays to be Jewish," Larry said. "I was an associate to an associate. The street vernacular is a nobody. I was a nobody's nobody. I met Charlie Bruno once or twice, but we didn't talk. I was introduced is all. If Bruno has me on some tape, it's saying hello or goodbye. Not even that."

"That's good," Khalidi said.

"I worked with Fred and Paulie. Fred was the connected one."

"Consistencies. Inconsistencies. They'll look to corroborate what your friend says for or against you and whatever case they're looking to make. Like I said, they're clever. Charlie Bruno was already an informant, so I'm not sure what they'll need from you, especially if you're such an outlier to the organization they're looking to take down. What you gave them in the proffer, assuming it's true and accurate, is what they can work with. They may not even use it."

"Meaning I'm fucked?"

"No, not fucked," Khalidi said. "You may be instrumental. Some of the things you've listed in your proffer are quite serious. I counted three separate federal charges. Whether they want to waste their time with them is another story. Remember, they want made guys, not Jewish guys working for peanuts. They want soldiers and captains. They always want to land the bigger fish."

"I have to go to work, Mr. Khalidi," Maryanne said. "I don't have much money left and I can't quit my job."

"I understand," Khalidi said.

"No, I don't think you do," Larry said. "How long will it take to know what's going to happen? I'm not letting Maryanne go to work if those knuckleheads think the story about me getting clipped is real. Maybe some punk looking to score points thinks he's doing them a favor going after her. I dealt with some of these idiots. Trust me, the young ones can't stick their noses far enough up some wiseguy's ass to ingratiate themselves. They think they can prove themselves doing something to a woman, some of them will do just that."

Khalidi sighed. "You can stay here for now," he said. "Nobody is going to go after you or your wife. That ruse was to try and convince your friend to cooperate."

"Fred."

"Fred. We'll figure out some other living arrangement in the morning, but it'd be a lot easier if you two were married. Maybe you want to do that in the interim."

Maryanne held onto Larry's left arm.

"Okay, how do we do that?" Larry said.

"First we get you a license," Khalidi said. "There are plenty of ways once you have the license. We can do it here if you want. Or some church."

"Justice of the peace?" Maryanne said.

"Sure. Why not?"

Maryanne squeezed Larry's arm harder.

Maria Greco was waiting at her parents' front door in East Islip, Long Island. Her husband had called early in the morning and told her he'd be there before seven o'clock and was getting a ride by Special Agent Fein after spending the night in an FBI safehouse. Maria had argued with both her parents the night before. Neither her mother nor father wanted her husband in their house. Maria tried to explain that Fred had gone to the FBI and would be traveling with an FBI agent, but to no avail.

She woke up extra early, before her parents, and waited for him at the front door.

Then her father was in the kitchen, saw his daughter waiting at the front door, and approached her.

"He's not coming in this house," Thomas Pesci said.

"I told you, he went to the FBI," Maria said. "An agent is bringing him here."

"Which means they're still worried about him."

"He's my husband."

"That was your mistake. We told you that before you married him. He's a thug. A wannabe thug and now look what's happened?"

"Then I'll leave with him. We'll go someplace else."

"You'll put your son at that kind of risk?"

"He's Fred's son too."

"If Fred had any decency, he'd stay the hell away from his son."

"How can you say something like that?"

"How can you remain married to that man? He's a gangster. They already tried to kill him. With you and your son right there. What's wrong with you?"

"He's confessing to the FBI, Dad. And he still may have to go to jail."

"Where he belongs for dealing with those bastards. The mafia has been a disgrace to our people forever."

"He's done with them now."

"Because they tried to kill him, or he'd still be with them. How can you still love that man? He's no good, Maria. He's no fucking good."

"He's a good father and he loves me."

"Jesus Christ, where did we go wrong with you?"

Angela Pesci had heard the commotion and woke up. She grabbed the baby and made her way to the kitchen, where she stood alongside her husband with her grandson in her arms. "Your father is right," she said. "He's no good, your husband. And now if he goes to jail, how will you survive?"

Maria's eyes were wet, but she remained adamant and said, "If you won't let him stay here, I'm leaving and I'm taking our son with us."

When she turned toward the door again, she saw a black SUV with tinted windows parking at the curb. She ran out of the house as Fred and Special Agent Fein emerged from the back of the SUV. The couple embraced a long moment before Fein motioned toward the house with his head. Maria saw the front door had shut.

"This gonna be a problem?" Fein said.

"We have to go to a hotel," Maria said. "They won't let Fred stay and I'm not leaving my husband."

"And the kid?" Fein said.

"He's going with us," Maria said.

"Maybe it's better to let him stay here for a few days," Fred said. "Rather than fighting with your parents."

"No," Maria said. "I want Junior with us."

Fred put an arm around his wife. "It might not be worth it for now," he said. "It'll just make for more of a headache with them."

"You'll need the local police to make them give you the kid," Fein said. "I don't have the authority to make them give you your son."

"I'm not leaving here without Junior," Maria said.

"You sure?" Fred said.

"Yes," Maria said.

"Then I'll kick the fucking door open and take him."

□ □ □

Several Special Agents of the FBI arrived at Umberto Grasso's home late in the evening to arrest the underboss of the Cirelli Crime family. Grasso was wearing a New York Giants football jacket over a gray sweatshirt and sweatpants. He'd been on his way to visit his *cumare* while his wife was spending the night with their daughter on Long Island. He was halfway down his stoop when he saw that three FBI vehicles had blocked his driveway.

"The fuck is this?" Grasso said as continued down the steps of his stoop.

"You're under arrest," Special Agent Ryan said.

"You kidding me?"

"No."

Grasso looked at the five other agents standing behind Ryan. "I thought you guys did this shit in the morning," he said. "What's the big hurry, and why didn't my attorney let me know?"

"Exigencies," Ryan said.

"Ex-what?"

"Your life has been threatened."

"By who?"

Ryan turned to the other agents and nodded. Two proceeded to cuff Grasso's hands in front. They guided him to one of the SUV's and helped him inside the back. Ryan walked around to the other side of the SUV and sat alongside Grasso.

"The fuck is going on?" Grasso said.

"Somebody tipped your boss off," Ryan said. "We don't know who, but we have a tape with him giving the order."

"Yeah? You breaking his balls tonight?"

"Falzone has already been arrested. Half an hour ago. Him and one of his sons."

Grasso smiled. "He working with you guys too now?"

"I can see where you'd wonder about that."

"Motherfucker."

Ryan tapped the back of the front passenger seat to get the driver's attention. The driver turned to watch Ryan read Grasso his rights. When he was finished, he asked Grasso if he wanted a lawyer present when they booked him.

"You have to be kidding," Grasso said.

"I'm not," Ryan said. "Late last night Charlie Bruno's guy inside the Federal Bureau of Prison Affairs was arrested. He gave you up too."

"I don't know what you're talking about," Grasso said.

"Sure, you don't," Ryan said.

"Charlie's dead, for fuck sake."

"Probably why he's pointing at you."

"Whose pointing at me? I want my lawyer."

"And you shall have him soon as we're downtown."

Grasso knew enough to remain quiet, which was what he did during the drive to the Metropolitan Detention Center in Brooklyn. Special Agent in Charge Thomas Wells was waiting for them. He brought Grasso and Ryan to an administrative conference room, where Grasso's handcuffs were removed. He was given a can of soda and told that he could call his lawyer after he was briefed.

"I want my lawyer now," Grasso said.

Ryan said, "You might not need him."

"Excuse me?"

"You might not need him."

Wells said, "Does Vito Falzone know about Edward Johnson."

Grasso swallowed hard at the mention of Johnson. "Who?" he said once he gathered himself.

Both agents looked at one another and smiled.

"Edward Johnson," Wells said. "The guy we arrested works for the Federal Bureau of Prisons. The guy bets a ton of money with your office under the names Baby Powder and Orange. Does Falzone know about him?"

Grasso put both hands up.

"We're not going to waste a lot of time here, Umberto," Ryan said. "If you want to hear the tape with Falzone ordering your murder, we can do that."

"I'd like to hear that."

"Soon as you tell us what we need to know," Wells said, then produced a mini cassette. "I have it right here."

Ryan said, "You don't want to answer, we let you go and we ask around about this connection with Mr. Johnson."

"Ask around how?"

Ryan frowned.

Grasso said, "You motherfuckers would do that, wouldn't you?"

"Umberto, you already violated your proffer," Wells said. "Your lawyer will tell you that. We can lock you up or release you whenever we want.

Might not look good, you're being arrested in front of your house with a half dozen agents there, the neighbors and all, and then you're out the same night."

"You'll get me killed," Grasso said.

"Not if you can deliver Falzone," Wells said.

"You motherfuckers," Grasso said. "You dirty motherfuckers."

Maria, Fred, and Junior Greco were brought to an FBI safe house apartment in Queens immediately after they retrieved their son from Maria's father on Long Island. The plan was for Fred to retain a lawyer in the morning and present a proffer sometime in the afternoon. Special Agent Fein made sure the Greco family was secure and that their needs were satisfied before leaving for the night.

Once their son was asleep, Fred and Maria made love. Afterward, Maria was inconsolable as Fred listed the crimes he'd committed and their details on a notepad. They were sitting across from one another at the kitchen table.

"This isn't easy," Fred said. "There's a lot of shit I did for Charlie Bruno, that prick. They want everything, but I'm not sure I can remember it all."

"I don't like that you can still go to jail," Maria said.

"I think that's a guarantee. How long is the question."

"Can I see what you're writing?"

"Why not? You're gonna hear it in court if there's a trial."

Maria moved from her chair to standing behind her husband. Fred shifted to his right as he wrote the following: *"Push-in job in Whitestone, a jeweler Charlie Bruno said kept cash in his house. We got inside the house after ringing the doorbell. The wife answered the door and we were in. Charlie said we should threaten the young son. We did that with guns. The guy, Milken his name was, he gave up the cash. A little more than 40k. Paulie punched the guy and broke his nose before we left, and we brought the money to Charlie. Bruno gave me two grand. I kept one grand and divided the other grand for Paul and Larry. That was, like, eight, maybe ten years ago? Something like that."*

"Oh, Freddy," Maria said, upset then. "You did that?"

Fred swallowed hard as he covered the notepad.

"Tell me that was the worst of it," she said.

"Don't read it," he said. "I shouldn't have let you read it. There's worse.

That's all you need to know."

"You said you never was involved in a murder."

"I wasn't. Not directly. I knew when one was going to happen, but I wasn't there."

"Jesus, Freddy."

"I know, I know. I'm sorry, babe. Let me do this now. I need to get it all down."

Maria's eyes were tearing when she left him in the kitchen.

Freddy waited until she was out of the room before writing again.

FOURTEEN

The arctic front came on fast and furious. Six inches of snow were on the ground within the first two hours of the storm. It had started at six o'clock in the morning and was expected to last into the early evening. Enrico Sandoval Reyes used a burner phone to call Robert Dalton a few minutes after seven o'clock. Dalton had been sleeping soundly and was incoherent when he answered the call.

"What?" he said.

"What?" Enrico Sandoval said.

"Who is this?"

"Me."

"Huh?"

Sandoval ended the call. Five minutes later Dalton's phone rang again.

"Hello?" Dalton said.

"It's me," Sandoval said.

"Mr. Reyes?"

Sandoval killed the call again. Dalton's phone rang again a few minutes later. That time Dalton answered fully cognizant of who he was speaking to.

"Sorry," he said.

"Cancel today. The storm is too strong."

"I agree."

"Don't come here today."

"I won't, no—."

Sandoval ended the call one more time.

Dalton's wife could see the concern on her husband's face.

"What's wrong?"

"I fucked up."

"How?"

"I used his name on the phone."

"Sandoval?"

"Yeah, Sandoval."

"What did he say?"

"He hung up on me. He hung up on me twice. The first time I didn't know who it was. I was sleeping. His call woke me."

"You think you're in trouble?"

"I know I'm in trouble. Those people don't give many passes."

"You apologize?"

"Of course. People like him don't care. You're not allowed to make mistakes. I can't believe I said his name."

"Maybe he'll understand. I mean, you just woke up, right?"

Dalton didn't answer. He used the same burner phone to call Amato. It took several rings before Amato answered.

"Hello?"

"It's Red," Dalton said.

"*Buon Giorno.*"

"The storm is too strong. Everything is cancelled for the day."

"You don't need me all day?"

"I'll call if we do. I don't recommend going anywhere in this shit. It'll be a mess everywhere. You get stuck, you're on your own."

"Okay, boss. I'll be here if you need me."

When he ended the call, Dalton went to the window and looked out at the falling snow. It was coming down sideways from the wind. Drifts were already visible against the building across the street. His wife came up behind him and started to rub his shoulders.

"That feels good," he said.

"Come sit on the couch."

"You'll put me back to sleep."

"You can use the rest. I don't want you to worry about Sandoval."

Dalton frowned, then followed his wife to the couch.

Amato grabbed his jacket and headed down the hall to the stairway, then took the stairs to the top of the landing to call Han. It was cold at the top of the stairs. He made the call with his face to the corner where the door to the roof was located. Han answered after three rings.

"I wake you?" Amato said.

"What's up?"

"You look out the window?"

"Not yet, but I know there's a storm coming."

"Storm is here. They called everything off today."

"That could be a blessing."

"Big shot stuck?"

"I would think so. We have eyes on the hotel. If he moves, we'll know."

"And then you call?"

"I'll call."

"Sooner the better, eh?"

"Yeah, the sooner the better."

"I'll be here."

Amato headed down the stairs back to his apartment. When he walked in, Brenda Lee was already making coffee. She was wrapped in her robe and wearing light blue cotton pajamas.

"You went out in this?" she said.

"What? Oh, no, *Bella*."

He pointed up at the ceiling.

"Oh," Brenda Lee said.

Amato had told her how he used the stairway landing to the roof to call Han.

"It's crazy outside," she said. "Nothing is going to move in this."

"Vacation day."

"Really?"

He winked at her.

"That's great," she said. "We can drink coffee, eat peanut butter sandwiches, and then have sex."

"Just once the sex?"

"As many times as you can handle it," she said, then winked at him.

They had their peanut butter breakfast. Amato preferred his bread toasted. Brenda Lee ate the peanut butter with a spoon. Half an hour later, after watching the forecast on the local news station, they had sex and then napped.

Amato woke up first. He went to a window and looked out. The whiteout was over, but the snow continued to fall. He watched the news again and learned that nine inches of snow was on the ground in Bozeman. He couldn't believe people lived in this weather for 3-4 months a year. Yesterday he learned that it could snow as late as May.

Amato didn't mind the seasons, but what he saw out in the street was crazy. The thought that snowstorms could extend into May was too much.

Lately he'd been thinking about returning to Pizzoferrato, where the average snowfall was no more than 6.2 inches a year. He'd take Brenda Lee and maybe marry her where his mother and father had married, at *Chiesa di Santa Maria Del Girone*. The ocean city of Pescara was close enough to spend a few days during the summer. Pescara was no more than an hour and change drive from Pizzoferrato.

His assumption was that the government, whichever agency he was working for, the CIA or the FBI, wasn't going to honor their promise to end his prison sentence and all obligations attached to it. Whether they were counting on him getting killed or not was another story. Either way, he wouldn't allow them to renege on his deal without making a move to escape them. If he couldn't escape them and was still alive, he'd feed his story to some newspaper.

He'd learned that much from one of the books he'd read while in prison about the Watergate scandal some 50 years ago.

If the big shot was stuck in Bozeman, Amato felt the Mexican was vulnerable. The big shot had bodyguards Amato would have to account for, but if Han was so anxious to take the Mexican out of the drug dealing game, he'd keep up his end of the bargain and help. Amato remembered Han saying he was getting "some help."

He returned to the stairway and up to the roof landing and made the call. It felt colder than a few hours earlier, too fucking cold to stay in Bozeman longer than necessary. If he could take out the big shot, like Han had said, the sooner the better.

Han answered mid second ring. "What's up?" he said.

"Can you handle bodyguards at hotel?"

"Because Sandoval is stuck overnight?"

"Because I want to get the fuck out from this place."

"Works for me. Call me back in a few hours."

"Okay."

□ □ □

The snow finally stopped. Emergency snow removal services were clearing the main roads in Bozeman and other Montana cities. The snowfall total had reached 18 inches, and travel was severely limited.

Robert Red Dalton changed his mind in the afternoon and called to meet with both Amato and Peaky. They met in a hotel dining room for a late lunch.

Dalton yawned long and loud.

"Rough night?" Peaky said.

"Hardly slept," Dalton said. "I napped a few times. That's it. I was about passed out when he called, and I fucked up. Now I'm waiting on another call."

"Airport open?"

"I'm not sure. Probably not for another few hours."

"He leaving?"

"I wish, but I don't know."

Amato was hungry and eager to eat. He excused himself to head to the lunch buffet.

"How's he doing?" Dalton said, motioning toward Amato's back.

"He did fine up in Sky, but Curly would've been the real deal."

"Do another one. Make it a fake hit, but get it done while Sandoval is still around."

"Sandoval? Why?"

"Word travels fast with those people. Bring one of the Mexicans. I'd say take him to Big Sky, but you'll never get there with the roads now. Do it someplace in town."

Peaky said, "I'll cue Caesar in. He's done it before."

"Caesar's a good choice. Do it before the sun goes down. I'll call Caesar and fill him in. Get it done this afternoon sometime. Use rubber. Ceasar can pad himself. Do it after lunch. Earlier the better."

"No problem."

Dalton motioned toward the buffet. "I'll get something to eat when he comes back. You tell him the deal."

They waited for Amato to return to the table. His plate was loaded with fried chicken and potatoes, some bacon strips, and a toasted bagel.

"That looks good," Dalton said.

"I'm hungry," Amato said.

Dalton stood up. "Makes me hungry," he said. "I'm heading over before there's a line."

Amato set his plate on the table, sipped the coffee he'd left, and dug into the potatoes first. He refilled his cup with coffee and looked up at Peaky. "No hungry?"

Peaky held up his cup and said, "I need a few more of these before I can think about eating."

"I eat too much now, I'm lazy later," Amato said.

"Then don't eat too much," Peaky said. "We've got a job later."

Amato knew not to ask about the job. He shoveled another fork loaded with potato into his mouth.

"There's a big shot in town and Red wants to impress him," Peaky said.

Amato fed himself a piece of bacon with his fingers.

"I'll pick you up at three o'clock. We'll go straight there. Main streets will be clear by then."

"I need to bring anything?" Amato said.

"No."

"Okay."

"Jenna said she has a lead on a waitress job for your girlfriend. A couple jobs, I think she said. I'll drop her off when I pick you up."

"I let Brenda know."

"She's a hot one, that Brenda."

Amato glared at Peaky then.

"Down boy," Peaky said. "It's a compliment."

Amato held his stare a little longer before continuing to eat.

Peaky finished his coffee, smacked his stomach, then stood up. "Now I'm hungry," he said, "and then I'm gonna need to take my morning shit."

Amato stared at Peaky's back as he headed to the back of a small line at the lunch buffet. "*Strunz*," Amato said.

He took another few minutes to finish his meal, and then left without saying goodbye.

□ □ □

Brenda Lee wasn't happy when she learned Jenna was coming for a visit. She didn't need help finding a waitress job, and she didn't like Jenna. Amato told her it was best to go through motions for both their sakes, but if the woman brought up trading partners again, he'd tell her boyfriend to leave Brenda alone with that bullshit. Brenda Lee could tell that Amato wasn't happy with his decision to work for the government. She knew he didn't like the people he was dealing with. She wondered if it was taking orders in general. Amato didn't seem like the type to take orders.

She feared the government wouldn't honor its promises. She feared they might leave Amato on his own once he did whatever they wanted him to do. She also feared for his life because she didn't need a government briefing to know how dangerous drug dealers in general were, never mind some Mexican cartel.

She decided she'd allow Jenna into their apartment but wouldn't put up with any more talk about trading partners. Now that she had Amato's backing to end such talk, she felt she could handle Jenna and had a way to ask her to leave.

Amato had already left when Jenna showed up with a shoulder bag full of snacks and wine. After removing her jacket and the sweatshirt she wore underneath it, she removed her boots and took a seat on the couch. She asked if it was okay to smoke and Brenda Lee told her cigarettes only.

"That's what I meant," Jenna said with a smile.

Brenda Lee offered her a cup of coffee. Jenna said she'd prefer some of the wine she'd brought. Brenda Lee said she didn't have a corkscrew. Jenna produced one of her own.

Jenna said the storm was common, except for its strength. Brenda Lee said she was used to snowfall and storms from living in South Dakota.

"Sure you don't want some wine?" Jenna said.

"Positive," Brenda Lee said, "but I will refill my cup of coffee."

Jenna waited until Brenda Lee turned her back and headed to the kitchen before adding a crushed molly into the nearly empty coffee cup on the cocktail table. When she returned with the coffee pot, Brenda Lee poured while Jenna was looking at her cellphone.

"I can't get used to those things," Brenda Lee said as she set the pot on a napkin. "I only use mine when I have to. Half the time I forget to recharge it."

Jenna said, "I don't know how you do it. I can't live without mine. We never even use our landline anymore."

"We didn't bother getting one," Jenna said before sipping her coffee. Then she said, "Reggie mentioned you had some job prospects for me."

"Yeah, two actually. One is further out of town but a great gig money wise. You'd need to drive. The other is in town. Just a few blocks from here. They need a day person for breakfast and lunch. I know the owner there. Peaky has connections with the place."

Brenda Lee took another sip of her coffee.

The roads were still snow covered, but a big enough path had been cleared for Peaky to drive Amato to a warehouse on the outskirts of Bozeman. It was getting late in the afternoon and the sun had begun to sink in the sky.

"Reach under the seat," Peaky said once he parked in the warehouse lot.

Amato did so and felt the short barrel of a handgun. When he retrieved it up to his lap, he saw it was a Smith & Wesson .38 snub nose pistol. He checked the cylinder and saw it was loaded.

"Somebody dies today?" he said.

"Mexican named Caesar," Peaky said. "Little fuck was caught stealing a month or so ago. We waited until he was comfortable. He doesn't know he was caught, but he was. One of the hookers he uses gave him up."

"Here, inside or someplace else?"

"Huh?"

"I'm to kill him here or someplace else?"

"Oh, here is good. Warehouse is ours. He'll be alone."

"He's there now?"

"He better be."

"Let's go."

Amato stepped out of the SUV and started for the warehouse. Peaky caught up to him and said, "Slow down a second."

"Point him out," Amato said.

"He's the only guy in there."

"He know you're coming?"

"No."

"Point to him."

"Let me introduce you first."

"Why introduce? I'm to kill him, no?"

"Just let me introduce you first."

"Okay," Amato said.

Peaky led him to the door, opened it and let Amato in first. There was a short, stocky Hispanic man sitting on a plastic milk crate drinking a beer. He looked up at Amato, then Peaky.

"Caesar," Peaky said. "This is Reggie."

Amato took one step, leveled the .38 and pulled the trigger three times. The rubber bullets knocked Caesar off the milk crate. Amato saw that Caesar wasn't bleeding, and his brow furrowed. He turned to Peaky and said, "What the fuck?"

Peaky ran to Caesar and helped him up. Caesar was cursing in Spanish.

Jenna kept Brenda Lee involved in conversation while the Molly took effect. It took 10 minutes before Brenda Lee finished her coffee and another 20 minutes before she began to feel the drug. When it was obvious the drug was working, Jenna used the bathroom and crushed another Molly. When she returned to the living room, Brenda Lee looked sleepy. Jenna added some of the crushed Molly to the empty coffee cup and then poured more coffee. She mixed it with a pencil. She handed the cup to Brenda Lee and watched her sip it.

"Good?" Jenna said.

"Mmmm," Brenda Lee said.

Jenna waited a few minutes before taking the cup and putting it back on the coffee table.

Brenda Lee giggled.

"It is good, right?" Jenna said.

"You still following me?" Brenda Lee said.

"I am," Jenna said as she laughed.

Brenda Lee giggled again.

"Would you like a foot massage?" Jenna said as she removed a slipper from Brenda Lee's right foot.

"A what?" Brenda Lee said.

Jenna removed the other slipper and began massaging Brenda Lee's foot.

"That tickles," Brenda Lee said through another giggle.

"Relax," Jenna said. "It's all good."

She proceeded to massage both feet as Brenda Lee began to slump on the couch. After massaging Brenda Lee's other foot, she said, "Why don't I give you a full massage? I'm really good at it."

"A what?" Brenda Lee said.

"A massage, silly. Come, take your shirt off and lay down. I even have body oil I can use."

"Body what?"

Jenna grabbed her bag and removed a small jar of coconut body oil. "Body oil," she said. "Coconut body oil. Come, lay down."

Brenda Lee wasn't moving. Jenna guided her on the couch and eventually Brenda Lee was laying on her stomach on the couch. Jenna poured some of the oil into one hand and pulled Brenda Lee's blouse up with her free hand. She created enough space to apply the oil.

"It'll feel cold at first, but you're going to love this," Jenna said.

"It's cold," Brenda Lee said.

Jenna massaged with one hand as she pulled Brenda Lee's blouse up a little further. "Warmer now?" she said.

Brenda Lee moaned. "It's nice," she said.

Jenna continued to massage Brenda Lee's back until she convinced her to remove her blouse. She helped pull it off and massaged her shoulders and the back of her neck.

After a while, with Brenda Lee occasionally moaning with pleasure,

Jenna asked about Reggie and what he liked best in bed.

"What?" Brenda Lee said.

"You know, what's he like to do with you? Peaky, he likes blowjobs mostly, but he's good with his tongue."

Brenda Lee chuckled.

"What he really likes," Jenna said as she applied more pressure to Brenda Lee's shoulders and neck, "is a threesome. He likes the attention two women can give him. And he can last long enough to satisfy them both."

Brenda Lee moaned again.

"He only likes threesomes with women," Jenna said, "but one time he let me have two guys at once. That was awesome. Super awesome."

Brenda Lee folded her arms under her head as Jenna described a sex session with Peaky and two Mexican bodyguards. She wasn't sure if Brenda Lee was following the story Jenna was mostly making up.

More than an hour had passed since the Molly had taken effect.

Jenna said, "Wanna turn over now?"

"Huh?"

"Come, turn over and let me do your front."

Brenda Lee slowly turned. Jenna tickle-scratched Brenda Lee's stomach before moving up to her breasts. When Brenda Lee's eyes closed, Jenna caressed her face with both hands and leaned forward to kiss her.

FIFTEEN

The safe house was in Richmond Hill, Queens, in an apartment building on 102nd Street between 86th Avenue and 86th Road. It was inhabited by several window cleaners through a connection one of them had with the management company. When the address was leaked by one of the NYPD patrol officers stationed as surveillance in a patrol car parked outside the building, a captain with the Cirelli crime family sent one of his crew to the building carrying envelopes with $5,000 in each envelope. The associate slid the envelope under the door of a second-floor apartment with instructions to meet inside the stairwell within ten minutes.

Fred Greco wasn't apprehensive. The police were parked in the street in front of the building. He had an emergency number to call if there was a problem. His wife was napping with their son in the bedroom. He left the envelope with the money in the living room under a couch pillow, then stepped outside the apartment with a steak knife at his side. He went to the stairwell and looked through the window. Someone he didn't recognize nodded at him. Fred opened the door and stepped inside the stairwell.

"The money is from Falzone," the man said, then pointed at Fred's sling. "For that."

Fred waited for more.

"That was a mistake," the man said.

"Five shots," Fred said. "That's some mistake."

"That was Grasso. He ordered it."

"How do I know that?"

"Because I'm telling you, and there's another five dimes where that came from."

"Why?"

"Because we need your help."

"With what? I have a federal agent up my ass and a cop car outside."

"To protect you."

"Until I testify. If I testify."

"How'd that protection work so far?"

Fred bit his upper lip. "Okay, so?"

"If you don't testify and denounce the proffer, you're safe with us. Falzone's word."

"And then maybe I go away."

"Not if you help us."

"I don't understand."

"Grasso."

"What about him?"

"You know where his girlfriend lives, correct? Her home."

"I've been there a time or two, yeah, but that was months ago. I don't know if he changed things."

"I'm talking about his *cumare's* place. Where he goes to get laid."

"In Jersey? Yeah, I dropped him and Charlie off there. Picked them up, too."

"That's the help we need. Where is it? And anything else you might know about it."

"Sure, but how do I know this is legit?"

"Think about it."

"Think about what?"

"If we wanted you dead, I couldn't do that already, cops outside or not?"

Fred frowned. "And when do I get the other five thousand? We're broke, my wife and I, since this shit went down."

The man produced another envelope. "Soon's you tell us what we need to know about Grasso's girlfriend's place."

Fred said, "You got a piece of paper?"

After passing his test in the warehouse by shooting the Mexican, Amato complained about having to do it twice in a few days.

Peaky laughed. "I thought you might spot the dummies when you opened the cylinder."

"I don't think twice in one day. Stupid shit, eh?"

"Relax," Peaky said. "It's a show for Red. He's nervous about Sandoval being in town."

They were in one of the bars still open after the snowstorm. Amato had called Brenda Lee twice but didn't connect. Amato assumed she was still out with Peaky's girlfriend, Jenna, or had maybe called it an early night.

Peaky was having fun breaking Amato's balls about the look on his face when he realized Caesar wasn't bleeding.

"Shit, man, I thought you was gonna turn that gun on me," Peaky said.

"I already pass bullshit test," Amato said. "Who does this twice?"

"Now we know for sure," Peaky said. "And you better believe it'll make Red happy. Caesar will make sure he tells it a time or two dozen and that'll mean Sandoval eventually hears about it. That'll make Red even happier when that happens."

Amato was starting to feel his beers. He'd had a few since after dinner. He glanced at his watch and saw it was after ten o'clock. He'd last called Brenda Lee around two hours ago.

"I go home now," he told Peaky.

"Me too," Peaky said. "I'll drive you."

The snow had been cleared from the sidewalks and the middle of the street, but there were small mountains of it where the snowplows had pushed it near the corners. Peaky was parked alongside one and found a ticket on his windshield.

"Motherfucker," he said. He held it up for Amato to see. "You believe this?"

"In New York they tow."

"New York? I thought you're from California?"

Amato huffed, half embarrassed and half angry at himself. "I have friend there," he said. "His car is towed twice he says. Big expense. Why I never go to see him in winter."

Inside the cab of his pickup, Peaky lit a cigarette without offering one to Amato.

"I'll drop you out front," Peaky said. "Give me a call if you want to party into the morning."

"Party?" Amato said.

"Yeah, you know. A few more beers, some weed."

"No," Amato said. "I'm tired. I go in and sleep."

"Okay. Whatever you say, amigo."

Peaky pulled away from the snowbank he'd parked alongside. In a few minutes he stopped to let Amato out.

"Talk to you tomorrow," Peaky said.

"Okay," Amato said. "Tomorrow."

Then Peaky winked and said, "Let me know if you change your mind about tonight. I know Jenna will be up for it."

Amato shut the passenger door.

A few minutes later, when he entered their apartment, Brenda Lee was naked and asleep on the couch. Amato said her name loud enough to wake her.

Brenda Lee didn't move.

Amato had started to remove his coat, then stopped and went to Brenda Lee instead. He pushed on her shoulder and said, "*Bella*, wake up."

Brenda Lee slurred something he didn't understand.

"Wake up, *Bella*," he said, jostling her then. Her response was to moan and slur her words.

He realized something wasn't right. Brenda Lee wasn't responding except to mumble. He picked her up, then took her to the bathroom. He guided her into the tub and turned the shower on. He kept the water running cold until she opened her eyes, suddenly feeling the cold.

"Reggie," she said. "Turn it off."

He adjusted the temperature of the water as she struggled to get out of the tub. He stopped her from getting out twice before helping her out and then covering her with a towel and rubbing her dry. She was unstable on her feet. Amato had to guide her into the bedroom where he saw the bed was unmade. He helped her to sit on the bed, then kneeled in front of her, his face close to hers.

"*Bella*, are you with the drugs?"

"Jenna," Brenda Lee said.

"She drugs you?"

"She must have. I don't remember."

"Lay down, *Bella*," Amato said. "I take care."

He helped her under the sheet and blanket, then used his cellphone to call Agent Han first, then Peaky.

Umberto Grasso knew the FBI pulled stunts like claiming they had evidence they didn't have. Sometimes it worked and wiseguys panicked, taking whatever deal was offered. Sometimes the scam didn't work and wiseguys told them to fuck off. Grasso also knew there was a chance that what the agents had told him about Vito Falzone putting a contract out on him was too risky to ignore.

He had tried but couldn't think of who might've tipped Falzone off about his cooperating with the FBI, if what the FBI had told him was true. Charlie Bruno was dead, but it could've been him before he was killed. Then again, why would Falzone wait?

The agents had partnered with the NYPD organized crime task force and arranged for a police car to be outside his home until he was safely delivered back to FBI headquarters the next day. He'd asked them to use an unmarked car because the appearance of a squad car was akin to a government deal as far as the mob was concerned. He'd checked twice the night before and saw there was a car with two men inside his carport.

Grasso had agreed to testify against Falzone because he wasn't about to spend the rest of his life in jail, nor was he willing to give Falzone a shot at killing him. He was scheduled to be picked up by federal agents first thing in the morning. Today would be his last day in the $750,000 home he'd lived in the last 15 years. Tonight would be his last night with his wife of more than 30 years.

If he had to move somewhere to live out his life, Grasso was more than willing to do so rather than die in a federal prison. He hoped his wife would be allowed to keep most of their fortune. His attorney was sure he could work something out for them.

"Did you meet with other bosses and underbosses from other crime families?" his attorney had asked him.

"Of course," Grasso said. "They already know that."

"Then think of something they might not know and make it up if you have to."

"What are you talking about?"

"Think about it."

"What?" Grasso said, annoyed then.

"We'll work something out with them," his attorney said. "The federal prosecutor will want whomever you can give them."

Grasso had been around far too long to play the game anymore. It's why he'd made his first deal with the FBI more than six months ago, after getting caught in a drug distribution bust that would have been an automatic RICO charge and a likely prison death via violence or old age. The Feds had saved him back then and without either party to the drug deal knowing. Soon after Falzone was crowned the new boss, Grasso was bumped up from captain to underboss. In that case, to protect Grasso, the feds had allowed the drug dealers from Miami off the hook too. Grasso agreed to work with the feds and thought he could maneuver while skimming the cash tributes meant for Falzone.

Tomorrow he'd have to give the life up. He wasn't happy about it, but it was the only move he had left. In the meantime, he was going to get his last great blowjob with a woman who'd been his *cumare* for more ten years. It wasn't difficult ducking surveillance because of the water behind the house. East Mill Basin provided more than a few off-ramps to Whitman Drive and the streets. He could get to Hoboken and his girlfriend in 90 minutes with luck. He wasn't going to worry about Special Agent Ryan and his bullshit about staying safe, not if his last chance to be with Maritza Suarez was today. He brought $900 with him, some of it as a going away present Maritza would appreciate.

After breakfast his wife informed him that they'd run out of his favorite drink, Manhattan Special coffee soda.

"You kidding?" he said.

"No," Adelaide said, "but if you're going to go out for some, make sure you get the Diet. You're not watching your diabetes, Umberto. I hear how many times you're using the bathroom at night."

Grasso wasn't wearing his watch. "What time is it now?"

"Eight o'clock."

He stood up from the table. "We need anything else?"

"Milk."

"Anything else?"

"I don't think so. Don't worry, I can get it later on the way home from the kids. Just make sure you wear your scarf. It's cold out today."

He smiled at her then. They had met more than 31 years ago and were married after six months of dating. Umberto was five years older than his wife, and except for his longtime Cuban girlfriend, he'd been faithful to Adelaide. Last year she turned 50 and was still attractive. She was also loyal and devoted to her husband. She wished he'd chosen another life, but there was no denying the special lifestyle they'd lived because of his being a mobster. Adelaide also knew that sooner or later her husband would wind up dead or in prison.

They had two daughters, both out of the house, and two grandchildren from their eldest child. Adelaid spent a few hours a day watching their grandchildren, a six-year-old boy and a four-year-old girl. Umberto knew his wife was most happy when she was around their grandchildren, but she also enjoyed the time they spent together most weekends. Dinner out, a movie if they were in the mood, sometimes a Broadway show, and sometimes lovemaking back at the house in their bedroom.

He'd yet to tell his wife about either of the deals he'd made with the FBI. He couldn't do it until he was ready to surrender. He knew it would break her heart. It wasn't like he flaunted his ten-year affair with the Cuban.

He'd fallen for the Cuban at a beach party in Atlantic City when he spotted her on the boardwalk. She was with girlfriends for the weekend and Grasso couldn't resist approaching her. They'd been together, off and on, ever since, rarely spending more than a single night together.

If his wife suspected him of cheating, she never showed it. He, in turn, made sure to take care of business with Adelaide at home.

Now he chuckled at her overconcern and headed for the front door. He put on his heavy jacket, his scarf, and then his hat and gloves.

"Tie that scarf," Adelaide said.

"Okay, Mom."

"Never mind, Mom."

He tied his scarf, then walked back to her and kissed her cheek.

"Love you," he said.

"The Diet, Umberto. Your diabetes."

He kissed her again, then headed to the front door, stopped, and turned around.

"What?" his wife said.

"I forgot something out back," he said.

"What did you forget?"

"Something for one of the boys. I'll get it and go from there."

"Just be careful," she said, and then he walked through the house out to the back porch, down the stairs and used three backyards before using a burner phone to call a local car service.

Because of road construction, the trip to Hoboken, New Jersey took an hour and thirty-five minutes. Grasso was eager to see Maritza. He'd been thinking about how much he'd miss her and likely never see her again once he was moved into the Witness Protection Program, which could be as soon as the next day.

It had turned windy out, and as he stepped out of the cab in Hoboken, he shielded his face from a strong gust as he started for the front gate of Maritz's house. When a second gust nearly stopped him in his tracks, he never heard the footsteps behind him. As he opened the front gate, Grasso was shot in the right temple. A 9mm Parabellum entered his right temple. He never felt the next three shots that opened the back of his skull.

"How the fuck did that happen?" Special Agent in Charge, Thomas Wells said.

Special Agents Fein and Wells were in a black SUV at the scene of Umberto Grasso's murder. Umberto Grasso's body had just been removed from the scene.

Hoboken detectives were talking to Grasso's girlfriend inside the house along with a neighbor who had called the police after hearing the shots fired.

"How the fuck did he get out of Mill Basin?" Ryan said.

Wells said, "NYPD was guarding the house. Parked out front. His wife said he left the house through the back."

"To come here and get laid," Fein said. "Can't blame him for that, his last night of freedom."

"Unless it was a blowjob," Ryan said. "Remember what he said on those tapes about his Cuban girlfriend?"

"None of this is funny," Wells said to Ryan.

"Somebody gave up this address," Ryan said, "and since it wasn't one of us, it was somebody with the task force."

"Meaning NYPD," Wells said.

"Mafia cops," Fein said. "Wouldn't be the first time."

"What do we know about the girlfriend?" Wells said.

"She gives great head?" Fein said.

"The fuck is wrong with you?" Wells said. "It's not funny anymore. Not after this. This'll get me demoted."

"Sorry," Fein said.

"She have a job or was she funded by Grasso?"

"Secretary in Manhattan," Ryan said. "Some insurance company."

"She's no kid," Fein said. "Good body for her age, but she's not the typical *cumare* for wiseguys. They usually go for the ones can be their daughters."

Wells said, "I want the names of the NYPD guarding Grasso's home in Mill Basin. I want an internal affairs investigation over this one. Somebody leaked this address."

"Could be someone dropped him off here," Fein said. "Doesn't have to be a cop. Who was Grasso's second? Who drove him around."

"Before he went away, Tommy Zampa," Ryan said. "Zampa's younger brother John since."

"Maybe one of them had a beef with Grasso."

"Maybe."

"Check it out, because this fuckup is gonna be our asses," Wells said. "Mine specifically."

"I should've been here," Ryan said. "This is on me too."

"What about the Greco kid?" Wells said. "He give us anything?"

"He proffered through some bargain basement lawyer never handled anything this serious before," Fein said. "I could tell that much about the lawyer when I spoke to him on the phone. Prosecutor said there was enough if we had something else on Grasso."

"Which we did have until now," Ryan said. "Fuck me."

"He said Greco seemed willing to testify if there was a trial. We know he can corroborate what Bruno gave us, maybe something on Grasso through Bruno, but what good is it now they're both dead?"

"So, what we have is shit?" Wells said, then turned to Fein. "Still think it's funny?"

Fein shook his head. "No, sir."

"He's probably holding something back," Ryan said.

"And when he learns about this?" Wells said.

"He did want to hear those tapes," Fein said. "His lawyer was pressing me for that much. I told him that's up to a federal prosecutor, but he didn't seem to understand. Like I said, he was bargain basement, the lawyer."

"They took a shot at Greco, and he's still dicking around?" Ryan said.

"We can't protect him if we don't charge him with something," Wells said.

Ryan said, "He's an associate. He's not gonna have jack shit with those two dead now."

"Then we let the prosecutors cut him loose," Wells said. "Let it be on them, anybody cares. At this point, I couldn't care less."

"At least his secret'll be safe," Ryan said.

"I don't mind that," Fein said.

"Remind me," Wells said. "What secret."

"Banging Winkler's wife," Ryan said. "At least his wife never has to know about that."

"Any chance it was Greco killed Grasso?" Wells said.

"None," Fein said. "His shoulder, for one thing, and he was too nervous to leave the safe house in Queens. That plus his wife. I doubt she'd let him out of her sight."

"So, all in all, this was one gigantic cluster fuck," Ryan said. "Between the NYPD and ourselves, we accomplished nothing."

"Afraid you're right," Fein said. "And I'm afraid you're right too, boss. You're gonna catch it hardest over this."

"Don't I know it," Wells said. "Don't I fuckin' know it."

It was difficult enough for Fred Greco to explain the money to his wife, but when he told her he wasn't going to go through with cooperating because Umberto Grasso had been killed, she threatened to leave him.

"They tried to kill you!" Maria screamed. "What's wrong with you?"

"That was the guy was killed, Umberto Grasso," Fred said. "He's the guy tried to kill me."

Maria was furious. "What part of they tried to kill you don't you understand?" she said. "Look at your shoulder, for God's sake! What do you think is going to happen now? If you don't cooperate, you're the one who will go to prison, damn it! And maybe they kill you in there, in prison."

"Then why slip me ten grand?"

"Because you're stupid enough to think they're doing you a favor, that's why."

Fred pointed a threatening finger at her then. "Don't call me stupid, Maria. I mean it."

She stared at him; her teeth clenched.

"What?" he said. "You trying to intimidate me now? This is done now, it's over. Grasso is dead. Charlie Bruno is dead. What do they have without me agreeing to condemn myself? Why would they bother?"

Maria said, "Who gave you that money?"

"What's the difference who gave us the money. It's ours now. Ten grand. What'd we have before that?"

"You're so blind sometimes, Freddy. I love you but you're so fucking blind sometimes."

"Why pay me ten grand and then whack me? Think about that for a minute."

"Because ten thousand dollars to those people is nothing, that's why."

"Ten thousand bucks, even with the inflation, Maria, is not nothin'."

"Jesus Christ, this man."

"What man, Maria? Who?"

"You, damn it! You!"

"You're too emotional."

"Emotional, right. Okay, so what now? You want to go back with them? You want to return to a life that tried to kill you once already?"

"You don't understand. I'm sorry, but you don't."

"My father was right. You can't help yourself."

"Your father doesn't have a clue what he's talking about."

"I'm not going to live with this again, Fred. I'm not risking the safety of our son."

"Junior will be fine."

"Says the guy who they tried to kill once already."

"I know what I'm doing."

"No, you don't. You're going to leave us alone."

"I'll never leave you alone."

"If you get killed or go to prison you will."

"Jesus Christ, Maria."

"No, I'm not doing it. If you go back with those people, I'm leaving you."

"And you think I'd allow that? Seriously?"

"I'm going to leave you, Fred. I'm going to leave you and take our son with me."

Peaky and Jenna showed up 40 minutes after Amato called to tell them that he had changed his mind and was in the mood to party after all.

"I take shower and I'm awake," Amato had said to Peaky.

"Great," Peaky said. "I know it gets boring around here but maybe we can spice it up some, eh?"

"Bring something to smoke, eh?"

"Oh, I will, partner. You bet your ass, I will."

"Okay, see you."

"See you soon."

Jenna wasn't as convinced, but Peaky said he was eager to party with the dirty blonde, Brenda Lee.

They both showered and dressed before heading out to meet at Amato's apartment. Jenna said they should make him come down to the lobby in case it was a trap. Peaky told her she was being paranoid.

"Pro'bly from the weed," he said. "You just focus on Reggie, sugar. I'll take care of his woman."

"She may still be high. She had a lot of molly."

"Then maybe I'll get to back door her," Peaky said, and winked.

They went up in the elevator, then walked down the hallway to Amato's room. Peaky knocked twice before the door opened and he was staring at a Beretta 9mm with a silencer.

"What the fuck?" he said a moment before Amato put a bullet through Peaky's forehead.

Jenna had been walking behind Peaky and had gone up on her toes to better see at the same moment Amato fired the Beretta. Part of her boyfriend's skull and some of his brain matter splashed Jenna's face. Her hands went up in shock as she stumbled back onto her ass. She tried but couldn't scream. Amato stepped around Peaky's body and grabbed Jenny by the hair, then dragged her inside the apartment.

She was on her back then, holding onto Amato's hand, which still gripped her hair. He let go and she turned onto her right side.

"Don't fuckin' move," Amato told her, then called for Brenda Lee.

Brenda Lee stepped out of the bedroom holding a Smith & Wesson .380. She pointed it at Jenna without saying anything.

"I come right back," Amato said. He left the apartment to move Peaky's body to the stairwell. He removed the cash from his wallet and identification, then carried Peaky's body up to the stairwell landing to the roof. He dialed Han again, waited for the agent to answer, then turned his phone off and headed back downstairs.

Brenda Lee was almost feeling normal when she heard the commotion in the living room. When Amato called, she grabbed the .380 off the night table and stepped into the living area. When she saw Jenna on the floor with blood covering her face and chest, Brenda Lee said, "I should shoot you in the face, you skank."

"Please don't," Jenna said. "He makes me do it. Peaky makes me . . ."

Brenda Lee moved the .380 closer to Jenna's face. It shut Jenna up. When she relaxed again, Brenda Lee moved to the door and looked through the peephole. Amato was gone.

"Please don't kill me," Jenna said.

"I should for what you did."

"It was just molly."

"Just, huh? And what did you do to me while I was drugged out."

"Nothing, I swear. Peaky wasn't here so there was nothing I could do. I'm not a lesbian."

Brenda Lee moved to a few feet from Jenna and said, "Lie to me again, bitch, and I'll blow your fucking head off. Now, what did you do."

"Just some feels. Some cheap feels. I'm sorry. I swear I am."

"You piece of trash," Brenda Lee said. "Even if I could believe you, I wouldn't. You're a sick fuck, lady. A real sick fuck."

"It's not me. Not all the time. Mostly it's Peaky. He's like that, not me.

He made me like this."

"Oh, fuck yourself with that bullshit."

The door opened and Amato returned. He looked at the two women, then went to the telephone and ripped the cord from the wall and jack.

"Get the cord in the bedroom," he told Brenda Lee.

He told Jenna to stand up, then tied her ankles together. When Brenda Lee brought the telephone line from the bedroom, Amato tied Jenna's hands behind her back. He made the knot tight, then draped her over his shoulder and carried her to the bathroom. He set her in the tub and used a window shade cord to tie her feet to the tub's spout. He made the knot tight there too. Then he gagged her with a piece of towel he cut into a long strip.

When Amato was finished, he went through her purse, removed the $65.00 in her wallet, and then glared at her "You're still here when we come back, I let you live. I have to find you, I kill you, eh? Don't make sound, bitch."

Jenna nodded nervously.

"*Putana*," Amato said, then closed the bathroom door.

He went to Brenda Lee and said, "Get some things together. We go now."

"Go where?"

"We go away."

PART IV

SIXTEEN

Amato had taken Peaky's pickup keys and used them to let himself and Brenda Lee in the pickup to stay warm. He started the pickup, saw he had ¾ of a tank of gas and let the engine run. Brenda Lee was nervous.

"Okay, *Bella*, here's what we do now," Amato said. "When I go, you go. Take Peaky's car and drive back east. Drive careful, eh? Speed limit."

"What about you? I'm not leaving here without you."

"I join you later. I have money."

"How much? I took a thousand with me, remember? Take half at least."

"You're sure?"

"Positive."

Brenda Lee removed the cash from her wallet and counted out $500 in fifties and twenties. She handed it to Amato, and he kissed her again.

"Okay, now I do something with FBI guy, okay?" he said. "When he comes, I go with him. You give me address where you go. Maybe your cousin, eh?"

"In North Dakota?"

"You can go, no?"

"Of course, but that's a long drive."

"I call you when I'm free again."

"What do you mean free? You're scaring me, Reggie."

"Don't be scared. I do something with FBI. They get me to your cousin."

"And if they don't?"

"Don't worry. They have to do."

"I don't know. Can't I wait?"

"Where you wait, *Bella*? You can't go back to hotel. Where?"

"I can wait here in the pickup."

"No, when they find Peaky and his piece of shit girlfriend, they can find the pickup. You get away they don't start to look for another day. Maybe you stop somewhere and switch, take bus to cousin."

"Will you be okay? Tell me the truth."

"I will be fine, *Bella*. I know what I do."

"I don't trust the FBI."

"I don't trust them too. I have idea."

He could see headlights down the street and turned to Brenda Lee and kissed her forehead.

"I go now. You take off right away. Just go."

"You have your gun?"

"I have two gun. You have?"

Brenda Lee had tears in her eyes. "Yes," she said.

Amato kissed her once more and then stepped out of the pickup as a black SUV pulled up alongside him. He turned to throw a kiss to Brenda Lee before stepping inside the back of the SUV.

Brenda Lee started out of Bozeman at 1:15 in the morning. According to the GPS, allowing for a gas stop, she could make it to Minot and her cousin's house in ten hours. The state police might be alerted by then about Peaky's pickup, so she decided she'd try for a bus out of Miles City, which was 286 miles from Bozemen, another four hours and change of driving.

She had Cokes for caffeine, but she knew she'd need coffee to continue clearing her system of the molly that had rendered her unconscious five or six hours ago. The sun wouldn't rise for another few hours. She hoped to be in Miles City by then. She decided to hold off calling her cousin in North Dakota. There was no point in waking her up and scaring her.

Cecily had always been the one relative Brenda Lee could count on for support. Back when she fled the redneck she'd married too young and stupid to understand how some men were decent with a woman until they possessed her, it was Cecily who gave her shelter and convinced her to file for divorce.

Cecily aimed a shotgun at Brenda Lee's husband when he had come looking for her after he woke from his drunken stupor and couldn't find her. He'd gone straight to Cecily's place because it was where Brenda Lee often fled whenever they argued. He demanded Brenda Lee come home.

Cecily stepped out of the house with a shotgun and said, "Go home, and don't come back. You do and I'll blow a hole in your chest."

A week later, Brenda Lee was spared having to wait for a divorce when her husband was killed in a head-on with a tractor trailer.

It was still early when she pulled over for gas outside of Miles City.

She was still concerned about Amato. He hadn't called yet. She began to wonder if he was gone from her life and if he'd planned it that way.

After gassing up, she stopped at a diner for coffee and to use the restroom, where she broke down crying while sitting on the toilet. She was no longer sure she'd ever see Ruggiero Amato again.

When he was in the SUV with Han, Amato motioned toward the driver.

"He's with me," Han said.

Amato didn't like it. He was about to call Brenda Lee when Han adjusted his earpiece, then pointed toward the SUV's door. Both men slid out the same side and hustled behind the SUV and crouched. Han explained how two of his associates were already inside the hotel in a room on the floor beneath the one Sandoval and his bodyguards were on. His associates had been there minutes after Sandoval was checked in.

Now they were parked just out of view of the camera overseeing the loading dock. Both had black 3-hole face masks they pulled over their heads while waiting behind the SUV.

"What he say?" Amato half whispered to Han.

"One bodyguard outside the door," Han said. "Nobody near the elevators. We'll get off the floor below and use the stairs. There might be a guard inside the stairway, so he's checking that out now. We're waiting on him."

"And then?"

"In and out. We know he has three bodyguards, but they also have a separate room on the floor below where they sleep in shifts. The one on that floor is probably dead already."

"And me?"

"There's a guard outside the room. The freight elevator will leave us at the short end of a hallway. We take him out first."

"We?"

Han said, "I have another guy in the loading dock. He's going up with us. He'll go first, then me. You're behind me. I have the bodyguard inside the suite. You have Sandoval."

"If there's more than one guard inside?"

"We improvise."

"Impro-what?"

Han put a finger to his lips and cupped his ear. "Shush," he whispered.

A side door to the loading dock opened and Han said, "Let's go."

Amato didn't know what was going on except he was expected to kill the guy they called Sandoval. As they headed inside the loading dock, he noticed the mounted cameras were all blacked out with what looked like cardboard and tape. Even with the mask on, he kept his head down anyway.

They hustled through a set of doors and onto the freight elevator. Another of Han's men was already on the lift. He nodded at Han first, then Amato. Amato saw a small black duffle bag beside the man, then nodded back.

The freight elevator doors closed, and the elevator began moving.

Han spoke to his associate. "Suppressors?"

His associate nodded.

"Any trouble?"

"None."

"He's still up there?"

"As cleanup."

"Good."

"What is good?" Amato said.

Han put a finger to his lips, then motioned at his associate. The associate pulled two CCU Government .45 ACPs with the sound suppressors attached. He handed one to Han and the other to Amato.

Amato hefted the gun and thought it was too heavy. He said so to Han.

"You'll be fine," Han said.

The freight elevator stopped. All three waited for the doors to open.

Enrico Sandoval Reyes was in the living room on the phone with his wife back in Pedrego Hill, Mexico. She'd given birth two weeks ago while Sandoval was still at home, a week before he left for California and the roundabout traveling that was to end in Bozeman. A snowstorm had kept him from leaving. He was expecting to leave at noon, almost 12 hours away. Husband and wife were speaking Spanish to one another. One of his bodyguards sat in an armchair away from the couch. He held a cup of coffee in his right hand. Another bodyguard was seated outside his suite, and another one, already dead, was in a room one floor below the suite.

At 2:00 a.m. the bodyguards would change their shifts; one would go downstairs, the one in the living room would sit guard outside the room and the one from downstairs would replace the one in the living room. None of Sandoval's security had discovered the minicameras in the hallway clocking their shift changes since the day before.

Sandoval told his wife that he missed her and their son and that they would take a vacation without the baby in another week or two.

"Where do you want to go, my love?" he said.

"Hawaii, Enrico," she said. "I've never been."

"Me neither. Then that's where we'll go."

"I don't like being away from our son."

"He'll be fine with my sister."

"I know, but I'll miss him."

"So, we'll make another one."

"So soon?"

"When we get back."

"I'd like that."

"I love you."

"I love you, too."

They kissed one another on the phone and then there was a knock at the door. The bodyguard checked his watch and said, "He's early."

Salvador motioned with his head for his bodyguard to get the door.

The guard outside the door was standing up as Han, his associate, and Amato turned the corner of the short hallway. Han stepped to the side as his associate fired two shots at the bodyguard. Both shots struck dead center in the bodyguard's chest. He went down alongside the chair. His hand had let go of his weapon. Han kicked it away from the body, then knocked on the door.

A few seconds passed before he could see the light under the door darken from footsteps. Han fired two shots through the door, then stepped aside as his associate kicked the door open and headed inside. Han motioned at Amato to go inside. When he did, Sandoval was scrambling to protect himself. Amato frowned as he fired two shots into Sandoval's back, sending him sprawling face first onto the floor. Han motioned for Amato to continue. Amato huffed as he moved closer to Sandoval and shot him in the back of the head.

When Amato turned around, Han pointed at a briefcase on an

armchair.

"Take it," Han said.

Amato grabbed the briefcase and noticed it was heavy.

"Okay," Han said. "Let's go."

The three of them left the hotel room and returned to the freight elevator.

As the elevator descended, Han removed the sound suppressor from his gun and handed it to his associate. His associate put both Han's gun and the sound suppressor in the black bag. When Amato noticed the associate hadn't removed his sound suppressor, he didn't remove his.

"Remove the suppressor," Han said to Amato.

Amato noticed the associate was staring at him. He stared back until he saw the associate begin to raise his gun. Amato fired from the hip and hit the associate in the neck, knocking him back onto the floor and scrambling to cover his wound with his hands.

Amato quickly turned his gun on Han and shot him in the right thigh. Han collapsed onto one knee.

"The fuck are you doing!" Han yelled.

"Self-defense," Amato said, then turned to his right and fired another round into Han's associate, killing him with a head shot.

Then Amato kicked Han in the face, stunning him.

Amato had taken the briefcase with him but left the black bag with the guns behind. He tied Han's wrists and knees together, then gagged him. He fireman-carried Han off the loading dock elevator and through the loading dock while holding the briefcase. Amato left Han inside the side door and approached the SUV. The driver lowered the passenger window and started to say something when Amato shot him in the face. He pulled the driver's body out and dragged it between two parked cars across the street. Then he returned to the loading dock and helped Han stand, then draped him over his shoulder again, grabbed the briefcase, and carried him out to the SUV. He settled him in the passenger seat, then adjusted Han's seatbelt. He walked around the front of the SUV to the driver's side and stepped up into the driver's seat.

He started the engine and removed Han's gag.

"What the fuck do you think you're doing?"

"I tell you already. What you tell me, eh? Self-defense."

"What self-defense? You killed a CIA agent."

Amato chuckled. "No FBI?"

"Asshole, we'll execute you for this."

"*Si*, I figure this out."

"What?"

"Fuck you. We go for ride now."

"You think you'll get away with this?"

"I think you didn't get away with it."

"They'll kill you in the field, you dumb Wop."

"We see, eh? So far, not so good for you."

Then Amato slapped the briefcase. "I thank you for money."

"You stupid fuck."

Amato smiled. "I'm stupid, eh?"

"Where are we going?"

"Is surprise."

"Where!"

"Shush, no make noise."

Han started to scream. Amato slammed Han in the left temple with his handgun. Han was stunned but still conscious.

"I'll kill you myself," Han whispered. "I swear it."

"I don't think so," Amato said.

"I will."

"Okay, boss," Amato said. "You do that."

SEVENTEEN

The murders of high-ranking organized crime figures cost Thomas Wells his position as Special Agent in Charge of the Organized Crime Task Force. Special Agents Fein and Ryan each put in for early retirement. Both knew it was only a matter of time before they would also be reprimanded by an agency with egg on its face.

What had been a promising high-profile series of arrests turned into a disastrous waste of effort and money and a big win for organized crime. Vito Falzone remained untouched as head of the Cirelli crime family, and while a few of his captains were indicted, their indictments were useless without the men who had worn government wires.

The killings of both Charlie Bruno and Umberto Grasso before they could testify sent a message to those contemplating deals with a government that couldn't protect them, the exact opposite of what the government had managed to establish in the past.

In the entire fiasco only Fred Greco faced time, but federal prosecutors felt his attempt to cooperate was worth keeping him out of prison as a favor for potential future investigations. Although they didn't believe he'd be rewarded with the induction ceremony he craved, his value as a potential cooperating witness was too valuable to risk. It cost them nothing.

When he heard that all charges would be dropped, Fred Greco called his wife to give her the good news. "I have a table at Peter Lugar's," he said.

"I'm not going to have dinner with you," she said.

"It's over now. No charges and I'm back where I belong."

"You don't belong with those people," Maria said. "We don't."

"This could be a step up," he said. "It's gravy, baby. I'll earn big time like this."

"I can't believe what I'm hearing."

"Come with me to dinner. At least let's celebrate the money we have now."

"How long do you think ten thousand dollars is going to last, Fred?"

"It's just the start. Didn't we buy a house with what I was making before?"

"Oh, God, you're lost. You're really lost."

"Don't say that. I'm not lost, baby. This is good. Come and celebrate with me. Please, baby?"

"How's this for a celebration, Fred. I'm pregnant."

"What? Really? That's great, honey! That's fucking great!"

Maria sniffled.

"Oh, honey, now you gotta come and celebrate with me. Another boy, I bet. This is such great news, Maria. Thank you! Thank you so much. I love you, baby! I love you like crazy."

She was crying then and told him she had to go. He didn't hear her until just before the connection ended.

Maryanne and Larry Levy had been on edge after learning about the execution of Umberto Grasso, two days ago. They watched the news trying to guess whether or not Larry's proffer would commit him to prison. They had watched the overhead helicopter shots of the home in Hoboken, New Jersey, where the news reports claimed Grasso's longtime girlfriend lived. They'd watched the same reports at least 20 times.

The street level shots included the yellow crime scene tape that surrounded the sidewalk in front of the house. Now, two days later, their lawyer, Wasfi Khalidi, informed them it was over. There would be no prosecution and no need for what Larry had proffered.

"I already put in for a transfer," Maryanne said. "They don't think it'll be a problem, but I told them it's tentative, that I would know soon. Now we know, thank God."

"Which office?" Larry said.

"San Diego."

"Shit, I hate California."

"Why's that?"

"Bougie people. California is loaded with them."

Maryanne smiled. "Listen to you, bougie people."

"What else do you call them?" Larry said. "Fucking clowns. Last time I was in California, I lit up a cigarette in LA and some woman started waving her hand in front of her face like I was blowing the smoke up her ass. She was at least ten feet away from me."

Maryanne chuckled. "Maybe she was sensitive to smoke."

"Maybe she should'a got laid more often."

"Could be that too," Maryanne said. "You'll have to think about quitting smoking if we wind up in San Diego. What would the neighbors think?"

Larry was preoccupied. He said, "I wonder what happens for Fred now?"

"I'm going to tell them we're leaving for San Diego next week. Right after Thanksgiving. Now that you're out of trouble here, I want to leave New York as soon as possible. I'll use a week's vacation once we're there and find a place."

"Rents are crazy in California, Maryanne."

"The office said they'd will help me find something. We'll be okay."

"I hate running away like this."

"I'm not staying here after this. No way. We have to go."

Larry gave it a moment, then said, "I'm sorry about all this, babe. I really am."

"It's over now. We'll be fine."

"Thank you."

"You don't have to thank me, husband."

He smiled. "I have to admit it. I like the sound of that."

"It's a shame your parents don't know you're married now."

"They don't want to know. They haven't for a few years now."

"They're still your parents. They should know."

"Fuck them."

Larry's parents were conservative Zionist Jews and had rejected him after he was told he'd be going to prison. Neither he nor his parents had tried to repair their rift.

Maryanne still had the support of her family, although they weren't happy about her marrying Larry Levy. Her mother had more of a problem with his religion than the fact he'd gone to prison. Her father didn't care about any religion but was concerned about his son-in-law being a convicted felon and maybe going back to prison.

"Then what?" her father had asked Maryanne. "What if you get pregnant and your husband is in some prison?"

"Then we'll wait for him to get out and start over," she said. "Larry is finished with the street stuff. He saw what it was all about. The only reason he was involved was because of that drunken cop who hit him in that bar. Larry didn't know he was a cop, so he hit the guy back. Then he was arrested, and the cops and DA all lined up against him because that's what they all do, lie for each other. That conviction kept him from getting a decent job. You forget he was a college graduate and wanted to be a lawyer."

"Then let him go back to law school," her father said. "If he promises to do that, I'll help him with the cost."

"I don't know he can get in anymore."

"Bullshit. I looked it up already. There are only three states that won't allow convicted felons to become lawyers and neither New York nor California is one of them. I've heard about plenty of former convicts who became lawyers. It's not easy but it's doable. He does that and I'll treat him like a son."

Maryanne was still waiting to tell her husband about her father's offer.

□ □ □

Rather than risk waiting on a bus in Miles City, Brenda Lee decided to drive to Williston, North Dakota, where her cousin could pick her up.

Afraid she'd never see Amato again; Brenda Lee told her cousin everything as they drove back to Cecily's home in Minot. Once back in the house, Cecily fed her cousin two oxycodone and let her sleep.

Cecily sat on her living room couch and watched the news. It was close to noon when coverage of what was believed to be a series of drug related murders took place in Bozeman. The FBI and the Montana State and local police were investigating. Eight bodies in three different locations, all possibly connected, had been discovered. One other person, a female, was found tied and gagged in the bathtub of a hotel room by the hotel's maid service.

When Brenda Lee awoke, she showered while her cousin prepared a pot of strong coffee and cooked pancakes. She was still frantic about hearing from Amato and checked her phone for messages. There were none.

When she was dressed again, Brenda Lee sat in the living room with the television on. She ate while channel surfing for news about what one news station was calling the slaughter in Montana. Cecily told Brenda Lee about the news reports until one appeared on a local station. Brenda Lee stopped eating. She sipped her coffee as she watched and listened to the news report.

When it was over, with tears in her eyes she said, "They don't mention names. I don't know if he's alive or not."

"I'm nervous about the FBI being involved, honey," Cecily said. "If it was the FBI, they're gonna catch up with you. There's no way they won't."

"I don't care," Brenda Lee said. "I'm only worried about Reggie now. I don't trust the FBI or anybody involved in whatever they were trying to do with those cartels."

"What if that was a lie he was telling you," Cecily said. "What if Reggie was the one not to trust?"

"He wasn't lying. I know he wasn't. I know he loves me."

Cecily frowned, then said, "Okay, but what if something did happen to him? You can't try and find out. Not if the FBI is involved. They'll know you were with him when whatever happened in the hotel room."

"I don't care. I want to know he's okay. I want to know he's alive."

Cecily rubbed her cousin's back.

Then Brenda Lee's phone rang. She ran to the bedroom where she'd left it. She answered before a third ring.

"Reggie?"

"*Bella*," Amato said.

"Are you okay? Where are you?"

"I'm fine."

"Where are you?"

"Utah for now."

"Utah? Why? Did you see the news?"

"Relax, *Bella*. I'm okay. Why I call now, to let you know."

"When can I see you? Are you coming back?"

"No, *Bella*, first I send you something. Then you go someplace and we meet there. I give you plan now, eh?"

"Yes, of course. Yes. What do I do? What do you need?"

"First give me your cousin's address. I send package there for you."

Brenda Lee gave him his cousin's information.

Then Amato said, "Okay, now you write what I says."

Amato wouldn't have gone through with it if special agent Han, or whomever he worked for hadn't set him up, but whichever governmental agency Han was with, he was a killer himself and had had no qualms about using other people to kill.

Amato actually felt bad about shooting the big shot drug dealer in the back the way he did back in the Bozeman hotel, but at the time he was still hopeful that Han might surprise him, especially since Han and his associate had killed the big shot's bodyguards. What turned it around for him was back in the freight elevator when Han's associate had made the mistake of broadcasting his move by staring. When he saw the gun raising, Amato fired first.

And Han, that *pezzo di merda*, was the one who arranged the entire thing. He's the one who deserved whatever might happen back in Yellowstone, except there wouldn't be any cameras to film it.

Amato stopped in a shopping center parking lot on his way south and found an unlocked van with a key behind the driver's sun visor. He transferred Han from the SUV to the back of the van and left the SUV behind. He assumed he had a day, maybe less, to find another car before the van was reported missing. He drove south to Yellowstone and headed for the area he remembered driving with Brenda Lee best, the big lake.

Han was close to dead by the time Amato reached the Yellowstone River on U.S. Highway 191. He took a left before Grant Visitor Center, the restaurants and hotel, and drove along route 20 until he found a pullout parking area with trees on both sides of the road. He backed up on the lakeside of the road, cut the engine, and walked around to the back of the van. He pulled Han out, leaving a streak of blood on the floor of the van. Although the bullet hadn't struck the femoral artery, Han's wound had bled profusely. Amato dragged Han behind some trees and kneeled over him.

"I hope you die before animals find you, eh? But I don't care if they eat you first."

Amato then drove south, through Wyoming into Utah where he took a room in a small motel in Dutch John, Utah. He spotted a car for sale in an RV park and knocked on the door of a trailer where the car for sale was parked.

An elderly man with a thick beard answered the trailer door.

"Can I help you?" he said.

Amato pointed at the car with the for-sale sign in the trailer car port.

"How much for this car?" he said.

"Two thousand, but I won't lie. It needs some work."

"What kind of work?"

"It had an oil change last month, but it's got a bad taillight, and the tires are pushing it. Radio isn't too good either. It's a bit old for what's on the roads today. That's a 1999 Cutlass. Could probably use a paint job too."

"Sign says two thousand."

"Well, I don't get around much anymore anyhow. What do you think?"

"I have fifteen hundred. No, sixteen. Enough?"

"Sure, why not. It's been sitting there awhile now."

They made the transaction, with Amato giving a phony name and address for the title and telling the old man he'd have it registered during the week because he was on his way to visit someone. The old man wished Amato good luck.

Her cousin drove Brenda Lee to the Minot airport for a flight to San Juan, Puerto Rico. She had money and a few changes of clothes in a carry-on bag. The flight was scheduled to leave at 7:26 in the morning. The flight would take more than nine hours, with a single stop in Denver. Once she arrived in Puerto Rico, she was to take a cab to the coastal town of Quebradillas on the northern shore bordering the Atlantic Ocean.

Brenda Lee knew nothing about the town itself, except it was where Amato said he would meet her in a day or two. She used her cellphone and Google to read about the town and learned it featured six beaches that had once been known as hiding places for pirates. There were less than 25,000 inhabitants within the several barrios that made up Quebradillas. The central barrios called Quebradillas barrio-pueblo was where the administrative center was located.

Brenda Lee was nervous about Amato's plan. What would she do if he didn't show up? Brenda Lee neither spoke Spanish well enough nor had enough money to sustain herself for long. Her cousin had given her $1,000 for the trip, but even with Brenda Lee's money, it was just over $1,800 in total.

What if she was robbed? What if she couldn't get back to the states?

She continued reading about the American commonwealth of Puerto Rico and the suffering of its people from a sustained state of poverty and natural disasters. Four hurricanes had visited the island in one year alone. Brenda Lee had no idea where they would live or how they would live in such a place, but the year-round 80+ degree temperatures were something to look forward to.

The flight from Minot had taken off on time. After 40 minutes of reading about Puerto Rico on her cellphone, Brenda Lee closed her eyes wondering where Amato was and if he'd make it to join her.

Giovanni Rapino had learned about and visited the town of Quebradillas in Puerto Rico from a prior relationship with a woman he met while on vacation in San Juan. He'd gone there with a cousin, another soldier in the same crime family, and they were relaxing at the El San Juan pool when Rapino exchanged a few smiles with a brown skinned woman lounging nearby. The two were clearly flirting, so his cousin went upstairs to nap, and Rapino moved from his lounge chair to an empty one alongside the woman.

"Ciao," he said.

"Hola," she said.

"Are you here alone?"

"I am. And you?"

"Solo, *Si*."

"*Italiano?*"

"*Si. Puerto Ricano?*"

"Dominican."

Rapino had nodded. Both had blushed.

"Visiting?" Rapino said.

"Vacation," she said.

"Same. I am Giovanni."

"Graciela."

"Graciela. *Bella* name."

"Thank you."

"How long you are here?"

"A few more days."

"Same."

"And if I said two weeks?"

"I change return flight for two weeks."

Graciela smiled.

Rapino said, "Do you have dinner plans?"

"I don't, but I don't have plans for lunch either."

"Ah, I see. We can go now, eh?"

"Sure," Graciella said. "I'd like that."

The went into town for lunch and wound up in bed before and after dinner. The three-day fling included a trip to Quebradillas to visit and spend a night at Graciela's sister's home near the beach. Rapino and Graciela had spent the afternoon in the small beach town taking in the local sights. The sound of the ocean and the appeal of privacy had remained with him ever since.

His tryst with Graciela ended the day he drove her to the airport back in San Juan. When he suggested they see each other again, Graciella told Rapino that she was married and couldn't see him again. Rapino was stunned. He'd never met a woman as bold and confident before.

Now he was sure that he was in love with Brenda Lee, and although he didn't fully understand why, he wanted to spend the rest of his life with her.

On the assumption that the CIA would never want to be connected to the murders in Bozeman, Montana, Giovanni Rapino had used his fake identification as Ruggiero Amato to book a one-way flight from Phoenix, Arizona to San Juan, Puerto Rico. The flight would leave at 10:36 in the morning, making two stops, the first in Louisville, Kentucky, and the second later in Orlando, Florida. The thought of landing in Kentucky where they might grab him and take him back to Big Sandy momentarily unnerved him.

If it was the FBI who had plucked him from Big Sandy in Kentucky to assassinate a Mexican cartel big shot, they would find him and either throw him back in jail or kill him. Rapino was willing to take the risk.

If he and Brenda Lea could live out their lives together in peace, he'd do whatever was necessary to protect her.

He spent the night in a cheap motel in Tempe, a 10-minute drive to the Phoenix airport. He knew Brenda Lee was on her way to Puerto Rico. He had no connections there. Brenda Lee would be on her own. She'd be afraid being alone. He'd call her as soon as he was sure it was safe to do so.

EIGHTEEN

They were allowed to remain in the Queens' safe house another few days before Fred and Maria Greco would have to leave. Maria wanted to leave right away. Fred was adamantly against it.

A skipper from the Cirelli crime family had called him, and he felt he was back in and maybe with some clout. He was told to call a number when he was ready to meet. He still couldn't believe they'd turn over $10,000 if they wanted him dead.

Maria packed her bags. When she stepped out of the bedroom with their son in her arms, Fred said, "You're not leaving me."

"I am leaving you," Maria said. "If you try to stop me, I'll call the police."

"Like I'll let you do that."

"Then you'll have to beat me to stop me. Feel free. At this point, I wouldn't put it past you."

"What am I, some kind of animal now?"

"If you stop me from leaving, yes you are."

"Fine, go. Knock yourself out, but I'm going to see my son whenever I want, Maria. You can't stop me from that."

"I won't stop you from seeing our son, but you won't be taking him anywhere. You can see him at the house."

"The fuck you think you are telling me what I can and can't do? What is this?"

"This is the end, Fred. That isn't easy for me to say, but I have to, now. I won't put our son in danger. I have to start thinking about us, me, and him. My parents can watch him while I go to work again."

"You want a divorce?"

"Yes."

"You know how crazy you sound right now?"

Maria sighed.

"What?" he said. "What?"

"Please let us go. I'll call my father and have him pick us up."

"Won't he be happy to know about this."

Maria started to say something but stopped.

Fred smirked and said, "Fine, call your old man. Go ahead."

An hour later, they were standing outside. He kissed his son on the forehead and then tried to kiss Maria, but she turned her head. Her father took his daughter's bags to his car. Fred kicked over a garbage can. Both Maria and her father flinched from the noise. Once they were safe inside her father's car, Fred didn't stay to watch them leave.

He called the number he'd been told to instead.

"Fred Greco?" a man answered.

"Yeah."

"Somebody wants to meet with you."

"Who?"

"You'll see when you get here. Come to Brooklyn this afternoon."

"Where in Brooklyn?"

"Somewhere public, don't worry. I'll call back and give you the details later. Be ready to leave around two o'clock."

"Okay. Can I ask who I'm talking to now?"

"No."

"Why not?"

"Are you going to show or not?"

Fred gave it a moment, then said, "I'll be there."

Vito Falzone turned 61 two weeks ago. A short squat man with a full head of thick gray hair, Falzone had once worked on the Bayonne, New Jersey docks as a shipyard laborer. He was a union employee for more than ten years before leaving the position to buy a bar in the Canarsie section of Brooklyn. While the bar remained in his control, Falzone stepped up the ladder of organized crime. When he sold the bar to a cousin who was an associate of the Cirelli crime family, Falzone, then 38 years old, became a made member of the same crime family.

Eight years later, he was promoted to captain. He became consiglieri at age 60, and the boss six months before turning 61.

Falzone was considered an old school wiseguy who stressed a tight and violent hold onto the people under him. A close friend of the last boss, Aniello Fontana, another strict-minded mafia boss, Falzone quickly set about reorganizing his family.

When he was told his underboss Umberto Grasso was wearing a wire, Falzone had the man assassinated.

Now Falzone was waiting to learn how far back Charlie Bruno's cooperation with the FBI went. Fred Greco had been spoken for by Bruno and had provided the information for Falzone's assassins to take out Umberto Grasso. The problem was Greco was living in a safehouse. Had he already cooperated with the Feds, or would he be doing so as a paid informant on the street?

One of Falzone's captains brought Greco to a real estate office run by Falzone's eldest daughter. A floor-to-ceiling front window guaranteed it was a public space, although the office was empty except for Falzone.

He stood up from the desk he was sitting behind and shook Greco's hand and then pointed to the sling.

"How's that doing?" he said.

"It's fine," Greco said. "It's okay."

Falzone pointed to a chair across the desk. "Sit," he said. "I hope you know that was Grasso's doing?"

"I figured it was."

"We were slow getting to him. I apologize."

"No need to apologize."

"Grasso and Charlie Bruno. Who knew, right?"

"I sure didn't."

Falzone coughed into a fist, then excused himself. He took a sip of water, then held the glass up to Greco. "Want something?" he said. "Something to drink?"

"No, thank you," Greco said.

"Coffee?"

"I'm good."

"Water?"

"Thank you, no. I'm good."

"I have an office downstairs, but I thought you'd be more comfortable up here in the open."

Falzone poured himself a glass of water from a clear jug.

"My grandfather's jug," he told Greco. "He used to use it in the house for his homemade wine. I keep it downstairs."

Greco smiled.

"He was a bricklayer for more than forty years, but he loved his homemade wine."

"My father's father made his wine also," Greco said, "but my father didn't continue the tradition."

"It's a lost skill," Falzone said, then sipped his water.

Greco waited for more. Falzone made him wait before saying, "So, I hope the money helps."

"It does, thank you. We were pretty strapped."

"Charlie likely had you on tape."

"I'm sure he did," Greco said.

"Not to mention what he was doing with your friend's wife."

Greco swallowed hard.

"Not that it's so bad to get a piece on the side, but the woman was your friend's wife, if I heard right."

"She was," Greco said.

"There's a rumor he learned that from you."

"About Sharon, his wife, I'm afraid he did. We had a relationship before she married Paul."

"Before? Okay. I can see that."

Greco knew he'd been caught lying and immediately corrected himself. "We did get together once after that," he said. "It was a dumb mistake."

"And you were still just an associate, so it's not like you broke a rule," Falzone said. "Had you been a made guy, had your friend been a made guy, it would've been a problem. A big problem."

"I understand."

"It's good you do understand. Messing around with a made guy's wife is serious. Very serious."

Falzone stopped and sipped more water.

"I regret what I did," Greco said. "And I regret telling Charlie about it even more now."

"I'm sure you do," Falzone said. "On the other hand, it's how and why we learned about him wearing a wire."

"I'm afraid that was more an accident."

"A fortunate accident, make no mistake."

"I guess," Greco said.

Falzone said, "Anyway, what we're interested in, what I'm interested in, is what might have happened with you and the FBI. Don't be afraid to tell me. You're not on trial here, not after the information you provided for us."

Greco swallowed hard again, then said, "They wanted me to write up a list of the things I did under Charlie. A proffer, I guess they call it. I wrote up the list. They have it, but then they dropped my case. I guess once they heard Grasso was dead, they didn't see the point. I thought they'd charge me for whatever they had on Charlie's tapes, but they didn't. So far they haven't. One agent wanted to know everything I'd done. He wanted me to tie something to Grasso, I think. He also brought up the bit about Charlie and Paulie's wife, that he had me on tape talking to Bruno about that. At least that's what he said."

"Did you have contact with Grasso?"

"No, not really. I met him a time or two through Charlie, but he never discussed anything with me. Hello and goodbye. That's it. I dropped him off at his girlfriend's place in Jersey. Both of them, actually, Charlie and Grasso."

"That was fortunate for us you knew where she lived," Falzone said.

"If there's anything I can do to prove myself again, I'm here to do it," Greco said. "I would've done what they wanted to that guy Rapino, but I was alone by the time I got there. Paul went home because of his wife and my other friend shit his pants once I told him what we were doing."

Falzone said, "Imagine Grasso's poor wife in all this. She had to learn about his ten-year *cumare* from the news."

Greco was confused and remained quiet.

Falzone said, "In retrospect, it's a good thing nothing happened, or they would've had you for murder. It's good you came back, especially after what happened with Bruno and your friend."

"I think that was luck too," Greco said.

"Okay," Falzone said. "Give me a few days to do some inquiries. We can always use good people, men willing to do what you set out to do across the country, but I also have to be careful. The proffer thing. If everything turns out, we'll meet again."

"They dropped the case," Greco said.

"Good," Falzone said.

He stood up from the desk. Greco followed Falzone's lead and also stood up.

They shook hands, then Falzone allowed Greco to give him a cheek kiss. One of Falzone's men let him out where a car was waiting. Another of Falzone's men held the back door to the car open. Greco sat inside and the driver backed the car out of the parking space.

It was after midnight when Rapino landed in San Juan. He was nervous about what might be waiting for him. He used an airport men's room before heading out to find a taxi. A string of yellow and green Toyota vans and white Ford vans waited in line for fares. Rapino stepped inside the first one and told the driver where he was going. The driver was a gray-haired man somewhere in his 50s. He did a double take.

"You have someone there?" the driver said with a Hispanic accent.

"I meet someone," Rapino said.

"It's an hour drive. Maybe a little less."

"I know."

"You're there before?"

"A long time ago, *Si*."

"*Italiano?*"

"*Si*."

"*Hola*."

Rapino nodded at the driver.

"Now we go," the driver said.

Rapino smiled as the van pulled away from the curb.

They drove along Puerto Rico highway 22. Rapino consulted a paper map of the island in the back seat. After 40 minutes, he asked the driver to stop at Vega Baja where they could have a beer and relax for half an hour. The driver turned left off the highway where he could and found a small bar with tables outside. The place looked about to close when the driver beeped his horn. He spoke Spanish with the man sweeping up and then waved Rapino over.

Rapino was concerned the FBI or CIA, or whomever they were, might be looking for him and preferred it would happen before they reached Brenda Lee in Quebradillas. The driver seemed grateful for the break. They sat at a table alone and waited for their beer. When it came, Rapino considered ordering another and taking his time before seeing Brenda Lee.

They each had a Medalla Light Beer and drank from the bottle. When the driver left to use the bathroom, Rapino called Brenda Lee with a burner phone.

"Reggie?" she answered.

"*Bella*."

"Where are you? Are you here?"

"Close. Vega Baja. Forty minutes maybe."

"Oh, my God. I can't wait to see you."

"Another hour," Rapino said. "Maybe hour and a half. I'm having a beer."

"I can't wait."

"Where you are, *Bella?*"

She gave him the information and then told him that she loved him.

"I really love you, Reggie."

"Call me Giovanni now."

"Giovanni? Okay. I love you, Giovanni!"

Rapino ended the call with a kiss. He smiled thinking about Brenda Lee. He was looking across the highway straight ahead and wondering if they might find a place near the beach. Brenda Lee had once said she liked the ocean and missed it.

When his taxi driver returned from the bathroom, he was holding a Walther PPK .22 with a sound suppressor. Rapino was still looking straight ahead and thinking about Brenda Lee and a beach they might walk along. He was about to ask for another beer when his driver fired three consecutive shots into the left side of Rapino's head. Rapino fell out of his chair and rolled onto his back. His driver stood over the body and fired three more shots into Rapino's forehead.

Then the driver returned to his cab, headed out of the parking lot, and turned right heading back to San Juan.

□ □ □

After an hour had passed, Brenda Lee began to worry. Giovanni had told her he was close. When she looked up the town he said he had stopped at to have a beer, it was less than an hour away. It was too late for there to be traffic unless there was an accident.

Brenda Lee sat on the bed and tried to remain calm, but before another ten minutes passed, she began to panic. She had befriended one of the women in the motel office earlier and saw she was still working. Brenda Lee went to the office and asked if she knew anything about Vega Baja and if they were doing road construction there.

"Not at this hour," the woman said. "Why you're so worried?"

"A friend was coming here from the airport in San Juan and they're late."

"I can call a friend there and see if you like."

"It's so late."

The woman smiled. "Consuela is awake until dawn. I call her."

Brenda Lee waited nervously in the tiny motel office, constantly looking at her phone. The woman was smiling while speaking Spanish. Suddenly she lost her smile and looked upset. When she ended the call, she waived Brenda Lee over.

"What?" Brenda Lee said.

"Something happens there tonight," the woman said. "A car accident or something. Consuela says there is police and ambulance near the highway, a bar there."

Brenda Lee dropped to her knees.

The woman stepped out from behind the counter. She went to Brenda Lee and said, "Are you okay?"

"I need to go there," Brenda Lee said. "I need to go to Vega Baja."

"I can call you a cab if you want."

"Please, yes."

It took ten minutes for the cab to arrive, then another 40 minutes to get to Vega Baja. There was a small police presence outside a bar but that was it. When Brenda Lee stepped out of the cab and asked one of the police what happened, she was told there'd been a murder, a shooting, and the victim had already been taken to a morgue.

"Who was it?" Brenda Lee said, tears in her eyes.

"*No sé*," the officer said. "A man."

Brenda Lee knew then that Rapino was dead. She also knew that she shouldn't attempt to find where his body was taken. If the same people who had killed Rapino wanted her dead, she assumed they would have killed her already. It was best not to tempt them.

She didn't ask questions. She asked the cab driver to return her to Quebradillas and to wait until she was ready to return to the San Juan airport. She cried the entire trip back to Quebradillas and most of the way back to San Juan. Several hours had passed since the last time she spoke to Rapino. Someone had killed him. She assumed it was someone with the American government. She didn't know what to expect when she arrived at the airport. Would she be arrested? Would they take her someplace and kill her too?

She approached the departure board and looked for a flight out of Puerto Rico to the Dominican Republic, a place Rapino had once told her he enjoyed. He'd also told her about the good exchange rate and beaches. There was a flight to Santo Domingo at 1:30 p.m. Brenda Lee went to the Departure desk and paid for the 1:30 p.m. flight.

EPILOGUE

The last thing the organized crime task force under Special Agent in Charge, Thomas Wells, was able to accomplish was the flipping of Edward Johnson, an administrator within the Federal Bureau of Prisons arrested for selling inmate information to criminal organizations including the New York mafia, the Chicago outfit, the Philadelphia mafia, and members of MS-13.

A bureaucrat his entire career, Johnson was also found to have been an inveterate gambler, using a dead brother's identification to place Internet sports bets for more than five years, accumulating more than $400,000 in profits. There was no record of the illegal bets he'd placed with bookmakers in three different cities.

Johnson's direct ties to Charlie Bruno and Umberto Grasso and a few sloppy computer habits led to his arrest and subsequent cooperation with the federal government. Unable to prove a tie to the head of the Cirelli crime family, Vito Falzone, Johnson's plea deal cost him a 20-year prison sentence.

Promised that he would serve his time in minimum security Federal Prisons around the country, the deal was changed two days before he was to be transferred from the Metropolitan Correction Center to the Federal Correctional Institution in Fort Dix, New Jersey, also known as FCI Fort Dix. Johnson was notified that he would serve the first few years of his sentence at the United States Penitentiary, Lewisburg, in Pennsylvania, also known as USP Lewisburg.

Johnson, in despair over the change, hung himself in his FCI Fort Dix cell hours before his transfer was to take place.

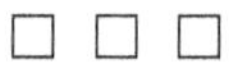

Two weeks after being tied and gagged after witnessing the murder of her live-in boyfriend, Jenna Olsen was found frozen to death outside a warehouse on the outskirts of Bozeman, Montana. Her autopsy revealed that Jenna had overdosed on fentanyl-laced heroin and had passed out during the night, exposing herself to sub-zero temperatures for more than eight hours before she was found by morning shift workers at the warehouse.

Notices were posted in city and state newspapers and on Internet sites. When nobody claimed the body, Jenna was cremated after three days.

□ □ □

Upon hearing of the bloodbath in Bozeman, Montana, and knowing some of the players, Luther Briggs put in for early retirement while sweating out the chance Robert Red Dalton turned state or federal evidence. Briggs only knew what he read or heard on local and national news stations about the slaughter that took place in a hotel in Bozeman, but he also knew that he'd been in a vehicle that transferred Dan Osborn, a.k.a., Curly, who was tied and gagged in the back of a pickup driven by Dalton.

Thus far there was no word about Curly, but Briggs knew it meant the fat kid was dead, disappeared by Dalton and his fellow operatives. Drug dealers, especially ones working under a Mexican cartel, were notorious for how they handled anyone dumb enough to steal from them. Briggs wasn't sure what Curly had done, but he knew Dalton had been looking for him. It didn't take Briggs long to find Curly, and rather than handle it himself, he let Dalton know where to look. The fact that Curly had been tied and gagged in the back of Dalton's pickup put an end to that story.

Dalton's job offer might've been attractive before the scene in Bozeman, but not anymore. Briggs was keeping a careful watch for any mention of Red Dalton on the news. Thus far, since the shootout in that Bozeman hotel, there hadn't been any. If Briggs was lucky, Dalton had escaped whatever had gone down and was maybe fleeing the country. Or he'd gone unscathed and was still in the drug business. Briggs wasn't about to try and find out. He certainly didn't want the job. He'd taken enough risks back in Yankton.

The night before he left Yankton, Briggs laid out a map and chose Wyoming to settle down for his retirement. Besides having Yellowstone Lake and others to choose from, he liked the idea of living as close to off the grid as possible. He'd already decided to start with a used SUV trailer, maybe a used SUV Winnebago to scout different locations in Wyoming. He'd live out of it until he decided on a place to buy or have a home built close enough to a river where he could enjoy his fishing and hunting activities.

He might even get married if the opportunity presented itself.

Briggs accepted the fact he'd been one lucky SOB escaping criminal charges for being a dirty cop the last several years. He didn't intend to make the same mistakes going forward. He intended to hunt and fish and spend the rest of his life in the kind of peace he'd always imagined.

He would also spend a few minutes every day going forward searching the Internet news for Red Dalton and whatever had happened to him.

□ □ □

Maryanne and Larry spent Thanksgiving with her family on Long Island. Immediately after a Thanksgiving toast, Larry learned that his father-in-law was going to help his son-in-law return to school. Larry was overwhelmed with appreciation and was emotional when he spoke.

"It's been a while," Larry said. "I'm not even sure I'll get admitted."

"So, you get a master's degree in the meantime, as a warm-up. At least with that you can teach if you want. Then apply for law school."

"That's a lot of money you're talking about," Larry said. "I'm not sure I can pay you back anytime soon."

"We have enough," Maryanne's father said. "What's the difference you two get it now or later?"

"Larry will do great in school," Maryanne said. "He was almost straight A's as an undergraduate."

"History, right?" her father said.

"American history," Larry said.

"What kind of law did you want to do?"

"Constitutional back then. Now it would have to be criminal law. As a defense attorney."

"Uh-oh."

"No, I've seen the crap the state can do, what it does sometimes. They're bullies with a big advantage. I rather fight them than join them."

"Okay, if you say so."

Maryanne rubbed Larry's back. "I'm so proud of him," she said.

"There's nothing to be proud of yet," Larry said. "Luck is what we've had for now. That's it."

"But I know you're smart and you'll get your degrees and be a great lawyer someday."

Her father raised his glass of soda. "Hear, hear," he said. "A second toast."

They all raised a glass.

"Buona fortuna," Maryanne's father said.
"L'chaim," Larry said.

It was messy and things were chaotic after the Bozeman murders, but once he learned that Enrico Sandoval Reyes and his bodyguards had been killed, Robert Red Dalton didn't panic. A state and federal investigation quickly ensued. The only questions the investigation teams had for Dalton involved his visiting the Sandoval suite a time or two. Dalton told the investigators he was there to discuss new hires for warehouse positions, which was legitimate cover for him and several others working for the cartel. The cartel also owned a hotel, two condo apartments and two homes in and around Bozeman.

"I had to pass everything by Sandoval," Dalton said, "especially new hires for a nine to five job. Sandoval was the boss, that's all I know, but I had nothing to do with anything outside of the warehouse, hotels and condos."

The investigators knew Dalton was lying, but until somebody collaborated in their investigation and could place him in the cartel's operation in Bozeman, there was nothing they could do. Thus far nobody in Bozeman was willing to talk to the law.

Two days before Thanksgiving, Sandoval's replacement from the cartel was in town and Dalton was promoted to oversee the entire Bozeman operation going forward, which included Billings and Miles City. Everything north was being run by a native Mexican a few rungs higher up on the cartel's Montana ladder.

Dalton was given a $10,000 bonus for holding his water and he promptly took his wife on a Hawaiian vacation. All things considered; Robert Red Dalton was still living the life.

Maria Greco knew in her heart Fred Greco was dead. He'd gone to Brooklyn a few nights ago and hadn't returned. Nor had he called. On Thanksgiving morning, her father was livid and could no longer remain quiet. Maria was holding her son and trying her best to remain calm, but the reality was her father had been right about her husband. Fred couldn't change. He'd put all his efforts into the wrong thing with the wrong people and now they had likely killed him.

"Tell me he kept up his life insurance," Thomas Pesci said. "Tell me he did at least that for you and his son."

"He did," Maria said. "I did."

"You did."

"Please, Dad."

"I told you he was no good."

"I know."

"We both told you, your mother and me."

"You were right, okay? Let it go now, please."

"What does an insurance company do when someone disappears?"

"I don't know."

"Well, you better find out or they'll cheat you."

"I will, Dad. Where's Mom?"

"Sleeping. She was up most the night worried about you because of that thug you married."

"I'm fine."

"No, you're not fine. You haven't heard from your husband in how many days now? Now it's Thanksgiving and he doesn't even call. If he took off, good riddance."

"And if he's dead?"

Her father couldn't hold his tongue. "If he's dead, it's because of the people he was so enamored with. If he's dead, it's because that's what happens to gangsters."

Maria gritted her teeth and closed her eyes.

"Now you're mad at me," he said.

"Because you won't stop," Maria said. "I need you to stop, okay? Fred is probably dead, Dad. That might make you happy, but we have a son and now his son doesn't have a father."

"If your husband is dead, it's the best thing in the world for that kid."

"That kid? That kid is my son. That kid is your grandson."

"I don't mean it like that."

"No? Then how do you mean it? You can't even hold him."

"You're taking this the wrong way."

"Jesus fucking Christ, you're impossible."

"Hey, don't curse in this house."

"Good God, you're a monster. A stupid fucking monster."

He stood up from the kitchen table and grabbed his coffee. "I don't have to listen to this from my own kid," he said. "I'm going to the den."

Maria watched her father storm off to the den with his coffee and realized there was no way she could live in the same house. She had to for the time being, at least until she found a job and could save enough money to move out.

Then Maria burst into tears and sobbed with her son in her arms at the kitchen table.

Brenda Lee, her cousin Cecily, and Cecily's lover, June, were taking in the sun on Playa Los Mino, a beach on the opposite side of the Dominican Republic capital, Santo Domingo. The white lounge chairs were facing the sun, no more than 20 feet from the water's edge. They had been there for 40 minutes, on their backs the first half hour, all of them covered with suntan lotion. The sound of the ocean's waves breaking in the distance, then rolling up on the sand was calming.

A small table with fruit on a plate and two bottles of water was set alongside Cecily's chair.

"Mango?" Cecily said.

"Not for me," June said.

Brenda Lee was staring ahead at the ocean and didn't hear her cousin.

"Bren?" Cecily said a little louder.

"Huh?" Brenda Lee said, then saw where her cousin was pointing at the fruit. "Oh, no thanks."

Cecily and June had joined Brenda Lee in the Dominican Republic a week ago, landing in Santo Domingo the day before Thanksgiving. They had brought the money sent to Cecily's house in an overnight FedEx delivery. The briefcase inside the FedEx package held $92,500 dollars and a burner phone. Cecily had broken down crying hysterically when she saw the money and had been inconsolable since.

The trip was to be a weeklong vacation to deliver the money and to make sure Brenda Lee was okay. After a few days in Santo Domingo, where Brenda Lee had been staying at a hotel for less than $60.00 a night, they decided on a road trip and wound up on the other side of the island at Playa Los Mino, where a hotel was costing them $43.00 a night.

Earlier in the morning, Cecily and June had talked about selling their home in North Dakota and moving to the island. Brenda Lee was ecstatic when they told her.

"That would be so great," Brenda Lee had said. "I don't think I could last here on my own. Between the language and being alone, I don't think I could do it. If you guys stay, we can work as waitresses when we need money. They're always looking for English speaking waitresses, and we can pick up Spanish in no time."

"Or we can find other work," June said. "I'd be a terrible waitress. I'm sure we can figure something out."

"And the profit from the house along with the money we brought will probably get us a dozen or more years before we have to think about working," Cecily said. "The exchange rate on this island is amazing."

"Jesus, what am I saying?" Brenda Lee said. "You two can relax. I'm ashamed. It's mostly your money. I don't mind waitressing. I already looked it up on the Internet. I can find work pretty easily. We might have to stay in Santo Domingo, at least for me to work. It's a three-hour drive between here and there. Or we can find a different place closer to Santo Domingo. It's an island. There are beaches everywhere."

June said, "We just brought you nearly a hundred grand, honey. I don't think you'll have to work again until you're sixty."

Cecily and June smiled. Brenda Lee began to weep.

Cecily said, "I'm sorry, honey."

Brenda Lee shook her head.

"I know you really loved him," Cecily said.

"And he obviously loved you," June said. "Or he doesn't send that package. He leave you a message or something on that phone?"

"I did love him," Brenda Lee said, ignoring June's question about the burner phone. "And I miss him so much. Before you guys got here, I was so depressed."

"We're here now."

"Thank you."

"And you'll have memories, Bren. At least you had some time with him."

"It was a crazy time."

"But there was love."

Brenda Lee started to chuckle as she cried. "Yeah, with bullets flying all over the place."

Cecily took her cousin's hand.

June said, "You two, I don't know."

All three laughed.

Brenda Lee raised her cousin's hand. "Take June's hand," she said.

Cecily and June joined hands.

"What are we now, the three musketeers?" June said.

"Why not?" Brenda Lee said. "Why the hell not?"

The newly appointed Director of the CIA, Hayden Settles, III, reclined with his feet on his desk while reading a report on operation Bear Food, a clandestine operation to assassinate a high-ranking Mexican cartel operative responsible for the distribution of fentanyl laced drugs in the South and northwest United States. Deputy Director of the National Clandestine Service, Robert Woods, sipped coffee in an armchair directly across the Director's desk.

"The girl went free?" Settles said.

"We know where she is if we want her," Woods said.

Settles set the report down and removed his legs from the desk. "Do we want her?"

"We don't need her."

"We're sure?"

Woods nodded.

Settles said, "I need to hear it."

"We're sure," Woods said.

Settled leaned both elbows on his desk. "What are we telling the families?"

"Plane crash. Black Ops, so there's nothing public."

"And when the wife or son or one of the brothers or sisters of one them goes crying to the press?"

"We show them a charred plane."

"And the bodies?"

"Incinerated."

"That gonna fly?"

"It has in the past."

Settles frowned. "The woman, she has the money?"

"She does."

"Do we want it back?"

"Up to you, but I don't think so. Maybe she stays quiet this way."

Settles frowned, then said, "What about—"

"Moved to a morgue in Ponce," Woods said. "Just in case."

"Phones, iPads? They cleaned up?"

"The iPads, yes. No phone."

"That makes me nervous?"

"We have Rapino's burners but not Han's phones."

"The iPad with the animals?"

"We have it."

"We did that, right?"

"We did," Woods said.

"One of theirs, I hope."

"Cartel guy, yes."

"There a chance Han's phone is still there in Bozeman?"

"I don't think so. The cleanup was intensive."

"Still doesn't feel right. Any chance the woman has it?"

"She was gone before anything went down. Probably scared for her life after that scene in their apartment. Page nine in the report, what we think went down there."

Settles huffed. "Last thing we need after that other bean eater, Genaro García Luna, is shit like this dropping on her heads. We have a string of fuckup operations I'd like to keep under wraps."

"I don't think it's worth going after the woman," Woods said. "Han still had the phone when she left."

"Long as we have deniability, Robert. Plausible deniability."

"I think we do, sir. This can't come back to us."

"The press looked into it, that little shit with the Federal Bureau of Prisons could've made trouble."

"Hung himself."

"Did us a favor."

"Yes, sir."

"Oh, well," Settles said. "I'm still not satisfied, but it's out of our hands now."

"I have a vacation coming up in two weeks, sir," Woods said. "That still okay?"

"Sure, why not?"

"Just checking."

Settles smiled. "Ever go down there, Puerto Rico?"

"Never," Woods said. "The wife prefers cruises. We've been on a few of those."

"This one coming up?"

"Alaska cruise. We're looking forward to it."

"You get the chance you should try Puerto Rico. The beaches are gorgeous. The women too."

"I'm sure, sir. The wife prefers the Keys. We've been there a few times."

"Passionate, the women in PR. *Muy apasionada.*"

"I'm sure."

"Trust me on this. I'm telling you. They can grind you into the floor the way they move their hips. I was twenty-six the first time I was down there. Couldn't believe how good it was."

"Navy, sir?"

"In PR? No, was a reunion a year after I served. Went down with a buddy was on the same ship when we were still serving. We took turns on some skinny *signorita* had the most beautiful cherry ass I'd ever seen. Made us pay per turn. Fifty from Max, fifty from me, and so on until we didn't have enough for one more each. I think she could've gone another ten, maybe twenty times."

Woods was repulsed by the story and had to force a smile.

"Anyway," Settles said, "Good work on the Reyes thing. President's party will be happy when MSNBC gets hold of it. This close to an election, with their numbers still in the toilet, they're gonna need all the fluff they can get, and him and the VP love MSNBC, especially those two morons in the morning, that husband and wife team."

Woods said, "Will you be handling the press once it's released?"

Settles sat back. "You bet your ass I am," he said. "My second fifteen minutes of fame? I'm not passing on that. Gonna spin it the way we intended. Unidentified assassins took out a cartel big shot and his money."

Woods said, "What time is it, the press conference?"

"Early afternoon," Settles said, then glanced at his watch. "You're gonna be there, I hope?"

"At your discretion, sure."

"Good."

"Anything else?"

Settles squinted a long moment, then smiled and said, "Check this out."

He used his phone intercom to ask for two bottles of water. Then he winked at Woods again and said, "Wait'll you see this kid."

Woods managed to hold a frozen smile.

"Twenty-two years old," Settles said. "She could be Playmate of the year with her rack. Chose to take her shot in the halls of power."

The office door opened and a short, very attractive redhead wearing a knee-length burgundy skirt and tight white blouse smiled as she brought two bottled waters on a small tray to the Director's desk.

"Just leave them there," Settles said. "And say hello to Deputy Director Woods, or have you met already?"

"No, we haven't," the woman said.

"Marsha, this is Deputy Director of the NCS, Robert Woods," Settles said.

Marsha held her hand out. "Nice to meet you," she said.

Woods smiled as he shook her hand. Then she turned to Settles. "Anything else?"

"No, thanks, hon," Settles said.

When Marsha was gone and the door was closed, Settles said, "I'd give ten years of my life for half an hour with that."

Woods forced one more smile.

THE END